Praise for Nick Sullivan and
ZOMBIE BIGFOOT

"*Zombie Bigfoot* is a super fun book that moves at a pace that will leave you breathless. The story is everything that I loved about the creature features that I used to watch on the late night horror shows of my youth."
- *Horror Maiden*

"From the ridiculous characters like the hunter to the multitudes of pulpy kills it aims to please the low-budget movie aficionado. The dialogue is good and the action is delivered in spades. If you like overly dramatic gory kills then *Zombie Bigfoot* will make you go all squishy inside."
- *Sci-Fi and Scary*

"No one can shift from gore to guffaws like Nick Sullivan!"
- Michael Reisig, author of the *Road to Key West* series.

"*Zombie Bigfoot* is one of those stories that will stick with me... I would put this up with the adventure greats Preston & Child and David Wood."
- Brian Krespan of *Brian's Book Blog*.

"Fantastic story telling from a very gifted writer."
- Wayne Stinnett, Down Island Press: author of the

"Sullivan was able to create his Bigfoot characters and make them so remarkable and almost believable. For a zombie story, it was incredibly dynamic. Sullivan put a lot of thought into every twist and turn."
- *AudioBook Reviewer.*

"Zombie Bigfoot is a thrill ride from beginning to end. It delivers laughs and shivers in equal measure. I predict that Nick Sullivan has begun a franchise that will have fans panting for more. Hollywood take note: this book screams to be a major motion picture."
- Tom Alan Robbins, playwright of *The Amish Girl's Guide to Armageddon.*

"I loved this story… plenty of surprises and action, with plenty of twists and turns. Five stars."
- *MP Book Reviews*

"Great fun and highly recommended...wonderfully wacky characters."
- Bill Pronzini, author of the *Nameless Detective* series.

"I love how the story is told from the perspective of the Bigfoot as well as the humans. The relationship Sullivan builds between the Bigfoot and Dr. Bishop, then later his daughter, is very touching."
- Todd Vogel: *AudaVoxx*

ZOMBIE BIGF👣👣T

-CREATURE QUEST SERIES-

BOOK 1

NICK SULLIVAN

Published by Wild Yonder Press

www.WildYonderPress.com

COVER DESIGN by Kristie Dale Sanders

COVER ILLUSTRATION by Kristie Dale Sanders

COPY EDITING by Eliza Dee of Clio Editing Services

BOOK DESIGN & TYPESETTING by Collen Sheehan of Write Dream Repeat Book Design

ISBN 978-0-9978132-0-3

For Dad.

Your ravenous reading always impressed me, occasionally intimidated me, and ultimately inspired me.

PROLOGUE

"You ready?"

"Almost…"

"Hurry up, would ya?" Billy grumbled as he stood and stretched. "I wanna get back to town."

You want to get back and bang a couple fangirls, Tony thought as he tightened the screws on the selfie stick mount for one of their many cameras. Satisfied, he powered up and scanned the clearing behind him. He was met with a familiar sight. "Clean up the beer cans, Billy… and the wrappers. And get that smoldering cigarette butt—unless you want to film a forest fire."

Billy waddled over to their little off-camera zone and grabbed a trash bag. As he picked up his leavings, he was pleased to find a forgotten bag of Gummy Fish. "There y'are… was wonderin' where you got to." He stuffed a technicolor handful into his mouth and finished tidying up their "workspace."

Tony watched his roly-poly partner stuff his bearded face. Billy wasn't the brightest bulb, but they'd needed at least one authentic backwoods hick for their reality show, and Billy was as 'good ol' boy' as they came. Tony, on the other hand, was from New Jersey. The show's speech coach had done wonders for Tony, helping him mask his pronounced Jersey accent with the twang of the South. Ironically, after he'd spent days working with the coach, the show's name, *Haunted Hillbillies*, had been deemed mildly offensive and the network execs had changed it to *Spook Stalkers*. Tony had decided he liked his newfound redneck accent better than his own and decided to keep it. Since it meant not having to reshoot the pilot, the network execs were perfectly happy to support his decision.

Billy wandered over, chomping busily on a rainbow of gelatinous goo. "Oh man, it is nice and spooky out here." He raised his camera. "Them pine trees are gonna look great… uh… hmm…"

"Lens cap."

"Oh, yeah… there we go." Billy panned across the tree line, the night vision filters making the closest trees stand out in stark relief to the blackness beyond. "Sweet. That's a creepy buncha trees! OK now, which one of us is the scared one in this shot?"

"Pretty sure it's you." Tony pulled out a folded shot sheet. "Yeah, you. I calm you down at the end of the scene."

Tony thought this was going to be a pretty good episode. They had planned to shoot at a Shoshone burial ground. Indian spirits, curses… maybe find a way to work some peyote hallucinations into the story. But then two things had happened. First, they couldn't *find* the burial ground, and second, one of the show runners heard a rumor that some other show was going to do a Bigfoot shoot nearby. Tony didn't believe in Bigfoot; he didn't believe in ghosts either. Ratings, though…

that was something you could see, right there in a graph. And ratings brought money, another thing Tony heartily believed in. No Indian burial ground? No problem. They would start the show as planned but before they could reach the nonexistent burial ground they would run into… a Sasquatch! Or rather, they'd hear noises in the woods and act scared, and then that drunk narrator with the deep voice would talk about all the Bigfoot sightings in the area. And not being able to find the burial ground would give them ample opportunities to get mad and yell at each other, which was what most viewers really wanted. It was brilliant.

"Let's get this show on the road!" Billy pointed the camera at his own face and hit the record button. "Action!" Billy put on what he called his "fraidy face" and looked fitfully from side to side. "Randy? You sure we're in the right place?"

As Billy lowered his camera, Tony raised his selfie stick camera for a two shot. They both assumed tense postures, looking like a pair of coiled springs. Had to keep the tension levels high or their viewers might flip channels to some other crap. Conjuring his speech training, Tony slid into a hick accent that would've been cut from *Deliverance* for being too over the top.

"Ah'm purty sure, Billy. That Injun boneyard oughta be up ahead through them thar trees." He dropped character and set the selfie stick camera on the ground, raising his smaller handheld. He scanned the trees ahead, then signaled Billy, who began looking for a rock or stick. "Boy, it's mighty spooky out there," Hick-Tony continued. "I don't know 'bout you, but I feel like we're being watched…"

Off-camera, Billy hurled a rock into the trees, aiming for a pine a few yards back. When he heard the thunk, Tony went into shaky cam mode, looking frantically from tree to tree. "What the fuck was that?" he hissed. Had to be sure to throw in a lot of curse words. If there wasn't a bleep every thirty seconds, they weren't doing their job. "Billy… you hear that?"

He pointed the lens at his own face as Billy did the same with his camera. The two of them ad-libbed a batch of frightened gibberish liberally sprinkled with expletives. Later the editors would pick the best bits. Critics complained it never made much sense that these shows spent more time with the camera pointed *away* from the phenomenon they were searching for, but Tony knew it made all the sense in the world. Since there *were* no ghosts or monsters, you had to fill your time with close-ups of frightened faces and lots of yelling and cursing.

Tony was just having this thought when he heard what sounded like a branch snapping. Lowering the camera, he peered into the gloom. "What the fuck was that?" said Jersey-Tony.

Putting his fraidy face on hold, Billy said, "You already said that bit. Thought it was a good take, too. Besides, ya lost yer accent on that one."

"No, I'm serious… I actually heard something." Another faint rustle. Tony raised the camera, using the night vision to try to see the source of the sound. Problem was, while the greenish image looked cool, it didn't have much range. More sounds now, this time from the left.

"I hear it now," Billy said softly. "Probably a couple deer."

"At night? Might be a bear… you got the spray?"

Billy dug in a cargo pocket and found the little canister. "Yep… but it don't sound too bearlike."

There! A shape moved into view amongst the trees. It was a man. Wearing a windbreaker and cap, he looked like a hiker and seemed to be having trouble keeping upright as he stumbled toward the clearing.

"Whoa, he don't look too good," Billy said softly. "Keep your camera rolling. A rescue in the woods'll make for good TV." He stepped forward to the tree line and raised his voice. "Hey, man… you OK? Come on over here, you're safe now."

At the sound of Billy's voice, the figure stopped suddenly, appearing to listen intently. After a moment he staggered forward again.

"What's yer name, fella?" Billy called out.

The man responded with a long, raspy intake of breath. Tony did not like that sound. A chill rolled up his spine. "Hey, Billy," he hissed, "back up a bit."

Billy remained where he was. "Sounds like the poor bastard's been without water for days… probably picked up a little pneumonia, too." He started forward. "Hey, man, lemme give you a hand."

Suddenly the lurching figure let out a hideous shriek and rushed at Billy. Acting on instinct, he raised the bear spray and let loose an acrid stream at the oncoming hiker, hitting him squarely in the face. The twisted, rotting, slavering face kept advancing, and Billy had no time to react as the oncoming thing crashed into him and drove him backward onto the ground, its jaws gaping at him. He reached up to push its head back and was rewarded with a searing pain as its teeth clamped onto his fingers, tearing through the skin. The pepper spray coating its mouth didn't help the sensation. "Tony! Jeezus, Tony, get it offa meeeeee!"

Tony had been staring into his camera's viewscreen this entire time, momentarily captivated by some of the best footage he'd ever seen. Billy's terrified screams snapped him back to reality, and he was about to toss the camera and come to his aid when another ruined voice snarled behind him. He spun the camera and another face, perhaps female at one time, filled the viewscreen. Though his mind quickly boiled over with fear and an urge to flee, his first thought, lasting only a microsecond, was: *Too close... out of focus.* Then it bit his face.

The man and woman didn't smell right. First, there was the death-smell. He was very familiar with that odor. Animals died all the time in the forest, but usually they didn't continue to walk around once they acquired that scent. They just lay there and rotted. These two were walking. Not walking *well*… but walking. There was another scent, though… under the death-smell. It was a new odor to this young Bigfoot. It seemed *other*. Wrong. Dangerous. A human without a boom-stick was of little threat to a Bigfoot, but there was something about these two.

He watched the lurching figures intently with his brilliant blue eyes. He had always been an observer… a watcher. His mother had named him for his beautiful, shining eyes, and he had known how right she was the first time he'd looked into the glassy surface of a mountain pond. Later in life, he'd encountered a human who had named him Brighteyes. The man had laughed when he'd first said it, and though the Sasquatch didn't understand human speech, the man had pointed at his eyes and pointed at a bright flashlight, repeating the name each time, until the meaning of those sounds had become clear. Brighteyes had liked that human, had been comfortable with him. These two were different.

These strange humans had come from a nearby camp, and he had followed them at a discreet distance. He knew he should return to the troop and warn them, but the patriarch was likely to ignore anything coming from him. Ever since Brighteyes had entered adulthood, the alpha male, known to the troop as Silverback, tended to respond to his concerns with either dismissal or a swift backhand.

It was quite dark now, and Brighteyes noticed that the other denizens of the forest had gone very still. The two human (not-human?) shapes generated an area of *wrongness* around them that the animals knew to avoid. He began to make out voices ahead. It was likely those two loud men he had watched the night before. They had been holding up small objects and pretending to be frightened of them. Although they had looked and sounded afraid, Brighteyes knew they really weren't; there was no fear-smell. After a while, they would stop and laugh and drink from the little metal containers they had brought before doing it all over again. It was actually quite funny. Humans and their rituals! At least these weren't the ones with boom-sticks. Brighteyes shuddered at a distant memory that tried to rear its ugly head.

The two not-humans (he was sure of that now) heard the voices as well. They stopped and listened, croaks and rasps emanating from their throats. The female one staggered off to one side, unsure of where to go. Brighteyes heard a bit of human speech from the nearby clearing: "Let's get this show on the road! Action!" With a low growl, the two things moved toward the voices. Brighteyes silently crept after them.

The events that followed were horrifying. Brighteyes watched as the not-humans threw themselves on the loud men, tearing into their flesh. He should help the men. Humans were not all bad. Something told him that the Alive-Dead things should not be touched, so he looked for a branch or rock. His nostrils burned with a sudden peppery sting. One of the humans must have one of those sprays they used on bears. The screaming from the clearing raised the hairs on his body, and a low moan escaped him as he fought down a wave of fear. By the time he found a stout piece of oak, the noises had changed. Tearing. Ripping. Chewing. Slurping. It was too late. Quietly setting the makeshift club aside, he backed away into the forest. He had to warn the troop! That *wrongness* that he smelled was something worse than death. They had to go far, far away from here.

2

The dawn chorus began. There was only a hint of sunrise on the horizon, but there were always a few feathered forest dwellers eager to get things started. Silverback burrowed deeper into the bed of needles and pine boughs his female had prepared. This nest was pretty good, and he would reward her for it. Well… her reward would be *his* reward, too. *Ahhhh, it's good to be the king.* True, the actual term *king* was not really what Silverback thought, but in their little troop, the alpha male was, for all intents and purposes, the king.

He started to slip back into a particularly enticing dream, but a nearby bird unleashed a piercing *hoo HEE hoohoohoo*, and just like that, sleep time was over. One of these days, he was going to get up early… pick up a rock… wait patiently, watch and listen intently… and when that feathered fuck started up, he'd pulp it against a tree trunk.

Rising from his bedding, Silverback yawned and looked around. The troop was already beginning their morning. There was Littlefoot, the youngest member, testing his climbing skills on a small cedar tree. His elder brother, Scratch, was adjusting his sleeping area, looking a little disgruntled. Silverback had taken a couple of Scratch's best boughs for his own nest, a ritual he'd begun as Scratch neared adulthood. The males of the troop needed to be kept in line, particularly when there was only one female left. And there she was. Silk was laying out some berries on a stump, preparing a pre-foraging snack. Her unusually fine hair caught the early-morning light, giving the appearance of an aura. That only left one Sasquatch unaccounted for. Brighteyes.

Silverback drew his lips back in a soundless snarl. That willful fool had wandered off on one of his adventures the night before. He would need to be reminded of his place when he returned. True, Brighteyes had never shown any interest in challenging Silverback's position in the troop, but you could never be too careful. One burst of hormones and the young explorer might make a play for Silk.

A distant snap drew his attention, and Silverback whuffed, scenting the air. Brighteyes was returning and he stank of fear. Probably stumbled into a bear. Or maybe some boom-stick humans. The troop's territory had been quite secluded for many years, but lately there had been more and more humans showing up in the west, and Silverback had been debating a move to the north. Brighteyes displayed a fascination with their hairless cousins that could put the troop in jeopardy one day. It had happened before.

Silverback rose and stretched his powerfully muscled body. Time for another lesson in discipline. As he debated what form this alpha male beatdown would take, Brighteyes burst into the clearing. He looked frantic and immediately began signing wildly with his hands toward Scratch and Littlefoot. That willful male had picked up a small language of gestures from some foolish human many years ago and had secretly taught it to the two youngest members of the troop. Silverback beat them every time he caught them doing it, and he was surprised Brighteyes would dare use the human hand-speak so openly.

'Brighteyes!' Silverback roared. 'Stop human hand-talk!' He pounded a fist on the ground to punctuate his displeasure.

Brighteyes blinked in momentary confusion before utilizing the purely Sasquatch communication that Silverback insisted upon. 'Humans! Not-humans! Wrongness! Death! We go!' Brighteyes quickly grunted out these concepts, then sagged, gasping for breath.

At first Silverback was uncertain… the fear coming off the young Bigfoot was very real. But then the alpha male remembered how often Brighteyes had wasted his time in the past. The fool had probably stumbled too close to a human camp and been startled. He flared his nostrils and could detect a whiff of that peppery spray the humans used to ward away bears. Snarling, he shoved Brighteyes to the needle-strewn forest floor.

'You play with humans again. One day they kill you. Like your mother.' Silverback stood over the young Sasquatch, watching his brilliant blue eyes for any sign of defiance. And there it was… a flash of rage. Good. Time for the lesson.

Brighteyes slowly stood, the anger turning to a different emotion. Resolve. 'No fight. Listen.' He pointed back the way he'd come. 'Humans dead. *Others* kill. Others… eat.'

Something in Brighteyes' tone gave Silverback pause. He remained tense, ready to bludgeon the brazen youth if necessary. 'What *others*?'

Brighteyes seemed to look inward, working his mouth, searching for an explanation. Then he calmed and held Silverback's fiery gaze. 'Alive-Dead.'

Only two things kept Silverback from pummeling the fool into the dirt. First, the cool certainty in his eyes, shining through the earlier fear. And second... an odor clinging to Brighteyes' fur. He hadn't noticed it before. It was very faint, buried beneath the peppery tang of the bear spray. It was something Silverback had never scented in his time in this world, and for a fleeting moment, he felt the hairs on his back rise.

The chilling sensation infuriated the alpha male. He hated the feeling of weakness, so naturally he lashed out at its cause. His powerful arm whipped across and backhanded Brighteyes. The blow staggered him, and he stumbled back several steps but did not fall. Silverback was aware of the troop watching. Time to show them that their leader was without fear.

"These *others*. You show me."

3

"**H**ey, Sarah… look at this!"

Liz Torres had been about ten yards ahead, and now the young intern was squatting by the side of the trail, masticating a wad of chewing gum while peering intently at something. Sarah trotted up the path to join her and looked down.

Sarah's young graduate assistant looked up, her wide eyes shining with excitement. "It's a Bigfoot print, isn't it?"

Sarah squatted beside her and looked at the nearly perfect print, smushed into the moss and mud. About eighteen inches long, deep toe and heel divots… you couldn't ask for a better print. She stood and looked around, her fists clenching.

"Real cute, Russ." She scanned the trees. Their survivalist guide had offered to "scout ahead," and now she knew why. "Russ! Come out, you idiot!" Nothing but the breeze through the needles of the trees. "*Russ!*"

Bud Sorenson came trudging up the trail, puffing and wheezing. The group's sound expert had a walking stick in one hand and a parabolic dish microphone in the other. While he caught his breath, Bud slowly swept the mic from left to right. Abruptly, he stopped his sweep and listened intently in his headphones. "He's behind that tree."

Sarah strode off the trail and up to the thick spruce Bud had been aiming at. Crossing her arms, she planted her hiking boots and waited. A snicker. "Come out, you ass clown."

Russ's doo-ragged head peeked from behind the tree, the paragon of innocence. "Why, hello, Sarah! I was just checking the back of this tree for moss…"

"Give it."

Barely suppressing a grin, Russ guiltily retrieved a short pole which was capped with a large foot-shaped stamp, molded in foam. He held it up to her. "Back scratch?" he offered.

Sarah gave him a taut little smile and then snatched the prank stick out of his hand, giving it a cursory examination. "Wow, Russ… it looks like you put a lot of time into this little prank. Hid the pieces in your pack and carried it all this way?" She walked purposefully back toward the trail and then beyond, to where the hillside fell off into a beautiful vista. Cocking back a well-toned arm, she flung the foot-stomper into empty space. It arced down into the treetops below.

Russ held his arms out in mock horror as he reached the trail. "Footsy! Nooooo! You heartless woman, he had just three weeks 'til retirement."

Sarah glared at him, shaking her head. "Russ… I know you don't believe in the Sasquatch. You've made that abundantly clear. But my father believed. I believe. And many of the people who tune into your show will believe… so at least have some respect for your own viewers!" She stormed away up the trail, ponytail swaying angrily.

"Aw, c'mon, you gotta admit that was pretty good." Russ watched her go. The beautiful young scientist took this way too seriously, and Russ had hoped to lighten her mood a little. Bud chuckled as he passed Russ, muttering, "Good one," and Liz gave him a shy smile. *Well, at least* they *thought it was funny.* Russ turned and stooped by the fake print to admire his handiwork.

Not bad. He'd modeled his little toy on a Patterson-Gimlin cast and used his tracking skills to find a perfect spot to plant it. Nevertheless, Sarah had instantly known the print was a fake. He prodded the edges of the impression, looking for any flaws that might have given it away. He didn't notice anything, but then it came to him: she must have recognized the shape of the specific cast he'd modeled it on.

Her father had been one of the foremost Bigfoot research-ers in the country and Dr. Sarah Bishop had followed in his footsteps. Russ recalled an article in the expedition orientation packet he'd been sent. In it, Dr. Anthony Bishop had firmly declared his belief that the loping figure in the famous Patter-son-Gimlin film was authentic; the twist was he'd also declared that the Bigfoot tracks at the site were fakes. Sarah's father was convinced that Patterson and Gimlin had indeed captured a Bigfoot on film but realized that the footage was shaky and brief. Not confident of the film's quality, they had decided to gin up some additional physical evidence to support it. The ends justify the means. If a little extra evidence helped support the truth, then why not provide it?

The ends justify the means. Russ sighed. That phrase could have been uttered by his agent. Russ Cloud had had a perfectly respectable television career going. *Survivor Guy* had been groundbreaking when it first hit cable television. He brought his viewers out into the wilderness with him, shooting each episode completely by himself. With just a couple cameras and his extensive outdoor survival skills Russ would spend each show in a different location, sharing his knowledge with the television audience.

Unfortunately, the very simplicity that initially made his show so successful soon became a liability. Russ just wasn't as flashy as that Wolf Wallace douchebag. That handsome newcomer knew a few tricks, but his army of support staff and cameramen killed the realism. Russ heard the guy actually had a masseuse travel to the shoot locations. They'd shoot three or four angles of Wolf doing some stupid stunt before taking a break and hitting the craft services table.

And then had come all the other garbage shows: a veritable torrent of manufactured "reality." Soon cable television was full of hirsute, foul-mouthed truckers and fishermen and prospectors and lumberjacks and moonshiners and blacksmiths. Even the Weather Channel was getting in on it. Russ had tuned in to see what the weather was going to be like for an upcoming shoot and instead found himself watching some toothless wonder hitting a rock with a pick and cackling like a lunatic. *Hey, Weather Channel, here's a reality show idea for you: "The Weather Forecasters".* Well… he was the Survivor Guy. And he would do what he needed to do to survive.

The ends justify the means. "Russ, my friend," his agent Murray had said. "Your show is beautiful… it's pure… still got a lotta fans… but you're hemorrhaging market share. Your ratings are falling off. Ya gotta shake things up, Russ. What do people like? Ghosts! Aliens! Monsters! Now, stay with me here… you run around in the woods… guess what *else* runs around in the woods? No, wait! Sit back down and hear me out…"

Russ heard him out. The first ten minutes had been harder to sit through than when that Maori chieftain had hammered a tattoo into his arm, but after his initial discomfort, he began to gain interest. Although he didn't believe in the Sasquatch, there were many tribes of Native Americans that did; tribes that he had learned valuable skills from. While Russ didn't have much respect for monster hunting shows, he had a wealth of respect for indigenous lore.

When Russ hinted he might be open to the idea of a Bigfoot-themed edition of *Survivor Guy*, his agent had plunged ahead with a detailed plan. Clearly Murray had counted on Russ caving, because much of it was already lined up. First, he would be teamed with a top Bigfoot researcher. Russ had sighed as he imagined the fat, bald nerd he was likely to be saddled with... until his agent slid a photo across the desk and raised his eyebrows knowingly. Smiling up at Russ from the glossy confines of the photo was a stunningly beautiful blonde. Sure, it was a carefully staged promotional shot, but still... wow. But Murray wasn't done.

"Russ, my boy... if you like that, try this on for size: the show is going to be fully funded by none other than that eccentric billionaire, Cameron Carson."

No wonder Murray was so gung ho for this project. Carson had parlayed an already substantial ancestral fortune into an astonishingly successful business empire. From high-tech ventures to his own record label, his own news network, and his own airline, Carson seemed to dominate the news cycle at least once a month. His brilliant smile and feathery locks of hair had graced the covers of *Time*, *Forbes*, and *Wired*.

In the last few years, however, he had been making the news for all the wrong reasons. He had begun to use his vast wealth to fund several high-profile stunts that had all ended in epic failures. An attempt to raise the *Lusitania* had resulted in the loss of the research vessel with all hands. An effort to wipe out malaria by genetically sterilizing a population of mosquitoes had yielded a new mutated, pesticide-resistant super mosquito (dubbed *Anopheles Carsonius* by furious entomologists). And late last year, Carson's space division, Maiden Galactic, had launched a private-sector space flight to the moon. There had been a few miscalculations, and as of last month the two-man craft was halfway to Venus. It was a small mercy that the crew's oxygen had run out long before their sanity as they hurtled into the void.

Carson's representative had told Murray—off the record—that the billionaire was desperate for a spectacular success, and the capture of a live Bigfoot would fit the bill nicely. And if they didn't find one, then *Survivor Guy* would simply have an entertaining batch of episodes, all expenses paid. Carson would only attach his name to the project if it succeeded. A week later, the contracts were signed, the Faustian bargain made. The man who had brought real-life survival skills to the masses while avoiding flashy production values and phony reality show conventions was going to hunt for Sasquatch. Murray estimated the ratings would quadruple. *The ends justify the means.*

So here he was on a mountain trail in Idaho, heading to a noon rendezvous at a billionaire's base camp. *Enough woolgathering*, Russ thought. Sarah and the others were almost out of sight. Russ went to the tree he'd been hiding behind and grabbed his pack. Shouldering it, he powered on his GoCam to get some hiking footage as he jogged after the group.

Brighteyes easily retraced his route, with Silverback following close behind. Every so often, the huge alpha male would instinctively shoulder past Brighteyes to take the lead before realizing he had no idea where they were going. He'd give Brighteyes an impatient grunt and gesture at him to hurry up. The young male found Silverback's constant obsession with the pecking order tedious. Brighteyes had no desire to lead the troop but had no way of convincing his elder of that. The world was so vast and wonderful, and such petty squabbles were simply insignificant in the grand scheme of things.

As they neared the clearing, Brighteyes noted that the birds were completely silent. Soon that odd deathlike scent was in the air, and he signaled Silverback for caution. Moving with surprising stealth given their size, the two Sasquatch edged close enough to view the clearing and the carnage it contained. The two not-humans were feasting on one of the funny loud men. The other lay mostly devoured a few yards beyond, his empty rib cage buzzing with flies.

Silverback looked to Brighteyes and grudgingly touched the back of his wrist to the young male's shoulder. An apology, of sorts... a rare display from the troop leader.

Brighteyes anxiously gestured back the way they'd come. Very softly, he vocalized, 'Must go back. Must move family.'

Silverback's momentary softening vanished in an instant. He snorted and curled his lip in disgust at what he saw as weakness. 'You fear? *You* run. Silverback protect family his way.' Rising from his crouch, he strode into the clearing, planted his huge feet, filled his mighty chest, and bellowed an ear-splitting roar!

Brighteyes knew the big male expected this display to make the not-humans flee, since that was almost always the result when man met Sasquatch in the forest. But he was certain these... these Alive-Dead things would not flee. Would not feel fear. Spotting the stout branch he had dropped the night before, Brighteyes grabbed it and moved to help his leader.

Silverback finished his mighty roar but was taken aback when the man and woman didn't even appear to flinch. Instead they snarled and clumsily rose to their feet. They had no boom-sticks, no knives... nothing at all. Foolish humans. With a feral gleam in their eyes, they rushed the huge Bigfoot. This was going to be easy. Silverback stooped and twisted slightly as they drew near. With blinding speed, he unleashed a massive backhanded swing that crashed into the man's face, snapping his neck, crushing one side of the jaw, and sending the figure hurtling backward. Instantly, his other hairy arm shot forward and grabbed the female by the throat before lifting her high in the air. She kicked and flailed her arms, frothing at the mouth. Silverback held her in his iron grip, noting the strong deathlike stench and the rotten-looking flesh of her face. What was wrong with these humans?

Brighteyes had watched as Silverback swiftly batted one of the not-humans away and effortlessly grabbed the other. The alpha male's speed and strength were unmatched and Brighteyes relaxed; the situation was under control. Silverback was still holding the female-looking creature aloft when Brighteyes watched the other one raise its ruined face and slowly get to its feet. Impossible! He had heard the bones snap, and it was quite clear by the angle of the head that its neck was broken. Brighteyes had been on the receiving end of Silverback's blows before, and he still had a rib that ached when the weather turned cold. And the leader always held back when meting out discipline to the troop; this blow had been unrestrained.

The thing staggered toward the alpha's back, but the big male was too engrossed with his squirming prey to notice. Brighteyes leapt into action, swinging the heavy branch in a downward arc as he charged forward. The branch crashed into the top of the not-human's skull and completely pulped its head. All animation left its body and it crumpled straight to the ground. Brighteyes looked wildly at the other flailing thing. '*Kill it!*' he vocalized.

Silverback snorted, disgusted at the panicky note in the young Bigfoot's voice. Calmly, he gripped the top of the female's snarling head with his free hand and ripped the head cleanly from the body. The body instantly stopped squirming, and he tossed it aside. Holding the head aloft, he pounded his chest with his other fist, reveling in his show of strength. 'Silverback strong! See me! See my strength! You fear too much. You follow me and I protect.' Silverback held up his grisly trophy and chortled. Playfully he took hold of its jaw and mimed human speech. 'Brighteyes afraid of humans, blah blah blah…'

Suddenly the head's eyes popped open, and its ravening mouth chomped down on the webbing at the base of Silverback's thumb. He roared in pain and disbelief, shaking his hand. The thing's jaws remained clamped shut and Brighteyes rushed to help. Prying it off, he quickly hurled the head to the ground. Enraged, Silverback raised a massive foot and brought its heavily calloused underside crashing down on the head, reducing it to a flattened mass of blood and brain matter. Brighteyes looked at the leader's bleeding hand.

'You hurt.'

'*NO!*' Silverback roared at Brighteyes, his wild-eyed face filled with rage and pain. 'Not hurt! Little bite not hurt Silverback!' Slowly he calmed. 'We go home now. You tell others how Silverback kill enemy. Protect family.' He looked around the clearing and grunted with satisfaction, his massive chest swelling with pride and importance. 'Family always safe with Silverback.'

Russ turned off his GoCam and glanced at his GPS, confirming they were right on schedule. He could've looked at the little compass he always carried and matched the bearing to the topography he'd memorized. Hell, he could check their position with a tiny needle on a piece of hair if he needed to, but you just couldn't deny the game-changing utility of a portable GPS.

Sarah and Liz were up the trail ahead of him, and Russ couldn't stop himself from admiring the view. Liz's raven hair shone in the morning sunlight. She was stunning, but she wasn't really his type—far too young and shy. Sarah, on the other hand—that was his kinda woman. Dressed in khaki shorts and hiking boots that showed off her calves, she looked right at home trudging along a forest trail. She'd tied her shirt around her waist, revealing the tank she wore beneath, and Russ admired her toned arms. He had little doubt she could kick his ass if she set her mind to it. This was a scientist who didn't spend all her time in a lab swirling liquids in a beaker; she got down in the dirt with her fieldwork. He'd read some of her research and knew she'd undertaken several deep woods expeditions solo. Watching her blond ponytail swaying with each step, Russ was reminded of Lara Croft from those *Tomb Raider* video games. Did he have a thing for that look because he was the outdoors adventuring type?

A few yards ahead of him, Bud tripped on a root and stumbled. He instinctively held his precious parabolic mic high as he fought to regain his footing, his oversized backpack tugging at his center of gravity. Bud's doughy frame wasn't at home in the wilderness, and he'd had some real difficulty on some of the steeper inclines, but when it was suggested he travel to the site with Carson's entourage, Bud had refused and insisted on coming with Russ and Sarah. Just as Russ had wanted to shoot some initial footage as they headed to the base camp, Bud had wanted to get a baseline of localized sounds from the area so he could set up filters to tamp down some of the background noise. Selectively masking some of the insects, birds, and even the breeze moving through the trees would make it easier to detect any distant unidentified vocalizations. Russ went to give Bud a hand, but the tubby sound engineer had already recovered. Still, his bearded face shined with sweat and he was breathing hard.

"You need a hand with any of your gear?" Russ asked. Most of their equipment would be waiting for them at the camp, but Bud was carrying more than the rest of them, insisting on bringing a collection of personal gizmos.

"I wouldn't say no." Bud chuckled and rotated his backpack toward Russ. "If you could shoulder my pack for a little while you'd give my spine a chance to fuse back together." As Russ removed the pack and transferred its bulk to his own back, Bud twisted and stretched. "I guess I should've let Mr. Carson's group bring some of that equipment for me, but I've got some sensitive little toys in there."

"No worries. I've climbed up sheer cliff sides with three cameras and survival gear, so this is heaven." Russ headed up the trail and Bud followed. "Pick up anything on that microphone?"

Bud hesitated. "Yeah... I mean, I think so. A few hours after dawn, I heard something that sounded like a loud roar, but I had the dish pointed away from the sound at the time. When I tried to establish the correct bearing, I caught a couple more roars but nothing after that."

Russ stopped. "Why didn't you say anything?"

Bud gestured with his parabolic gun. "This is the little brother of what they'll have for me at base camp. I'll have a much better chance to pinpoint and isolate a sound once I'm set up there. It was so brief, and I'm pretty sure it was miles away. Pitch was too low for a cougar. Probably a bear. I've been recording everything so we can check it once I've got the rest of my gear."

Russ remembered spotting some bear scat early in the hike, and this was certainly brown bear country. He'd shot a Pacific Northwest episode early in his career and had come across a big female swatting salmon from a stream. Russ's stomach rumbled as he remembered the fresh salmon he'd managed to salvage from the bear's feast. He'd cooked the hunks over a campfire and it had been delicious. *Maybe we can work a salmon- or trout-eating scene into this shoot. I'll have to remember to ask Sarah if her Sasquatch eat fish...*

Russ suddenly stopped in his tracks. He stood in the trail, thinking. *I saw something. What did I see?* He retraced his steps and there it was: a print. Not a bear print... or a fake Bigfoot

print. A human print. Hiking boot. And there was another…
and a third. Nothing odd about finding boot prints on a trail,
and Sarah and Liz were up ahead. But these were several hours
old; more importantly, they went *across* the trail. Someone
had been traveling perpendicular to the well-worn track. He
crouched, scanning the area. There… another line of tracks,
also traveling from east to west across the northbound path.

"Russ!" Sarah called out. She and Liz had stopped, looking
back at him. Liz was chomping on a fresh piece of gum and
Sarah had her hands on her hips. "Hurry up! The meeting's
at noon."

Russ gestured for them to come back. "Sarah. Come take
a look at this."

Bud came over and looked down. "What are you looking
at?"

"Tracks," Russ said as Sarah strode up.

"We don't have time for any more shenanigans, Russ…" she
began but stopped when she saw what Russ was pointing at.
"A boot print. So? A hiker was on the trail and left a print…"

"Two hikers. And they weren't on the trail, they went across
it." He went to the east and pointed up an incline. "They came
down that hill. Looks like one of them took a spill—see that
area of upturned dirt and needles?" He followed the tracks
back across the trail to the west. "A man and a woman… or
maybe a man and a teenager. And see that scuff at the edge of
the man's left boot print? Looks like he was dragging the foot."

Liz had paused in her gum chewing, her mouth agape in
awe. "Wow… you can tell all that?"

Russ didn't respond, deep in thought. "I thought this area
was remote. Wasn't expecting to run across anyone else."

"It *was* remote when my father was here," Sarah said. "Other than a little ghost town and some campsites to the east, it was all wilderness. I did hear something about the Park Service planning on opening up some new trails in the area."

Russ straightened and looked off to the west, where the terrain sloped gradually downward. They didn't have time to follow tracks that were hours old, and it was nearly time for their noon rendezvous.

Sarah echoed that very thought. "This is all very interesting, but we've got a billionaire to meet. Once we get settled, maybe we can look for a couple lost hikers… who might not be lost at all. Maybe a couple hunters tracking a deer?"

Russ shook his head. "I don't think so. But you're right, we need to get going." As the group resumed their trek, Russ turned to Bud. "Hey, Bud. That loud roar you thought you heard? If it was a couple hours ago, we would've been…" He thought for just a second before his extraordinary directional sense kicked in and he gestured southeast. "About two miles that way. You said you weren't sure exactly where the sound came from, but if you had to make a ballpark guess…?"

Bud stopped and raised the parabolic dish, going through the motions of his earlier audio scan. Russ could sense him factoring in the distance back to where they'd been. He raised a finger and weather-vaned it to and fro before stopping and pointing down the incline where the tracks had gone.

"That way. Roughly. But it could've been miles to the left or right of that line. In this kind of hilly terrain, the sound could bounce quite a bit. Still, if I had to lay down some money, I'd bet it came from down that way."

Russ had had a gut feeling, so he wasn't surprised. "Thanks, Bud. No worries. Once we get set up at camp, I'll go take a look-see. Let's catch up to the gals." A final glance at the boot prints and Russ started after Sarah and Liz. It was then that he noticed something else. He didn't hear any birds.

Fifteen minutes later, they reached the tree line at the edge of a vast mountain meadow. The meadow was filled with… grass. No base camp. Not a soul in sight.

Sarah looked at her GPS. "These are the coordinates, and it's just past noon. Where the hell is Carson?"

Russ looked over her shoulder at the device. "Well, he *is* a narcissistic billionaire. Noon for him might be half past two. Or, if he's an idiot, maybe he meant Eastern Standard Time." He powered up his GoCam and swept it across the empty meadow. "Day One. Our expedition begins. The hunt for the elusive Cameron Carson!" He pointed the camera at Sarah. "Dr. Bishop, you're our scientific expert. Do billionaires have a distinctive mating call we could imitate to draw him out of hiding?"

Suddenly, Liz called out in a high-pitched bird call. "Publicity! Publicity!"

After an instant of surprised silence, Russ burst out laughing. Liz was always so quiet and reserved; this unexpected display of goofy humor seemed to surprise even her, and she giggled bashfully.

Sarah gave her a playful nudge and smiled. "Good one, Liz. Though I think it might be easier to just call the man." She shrugged her little backpack off her shoulder and dug in an outer pocket. "Won't be able to get a cell signal out here, but he set me up with a satellite phone."

"I don't think you'll need it," Bud said. He had his microphone pointed off to the northeast, his free hand pressing his headphones to an ear.

Soon they could all hear it. "A helicopter," Sarah said, shading her eyes and looking toward the treetops on the far side of the meadow.

"Helicopters," Bud corrected, stressing the *s*. "There are at least three distinct rotary engines heading our way."

Minutes later, a trio of helicopters roared into view, fanning out over the wide meadow. The sleek chopper in the center sported the gaudy red-and-gold logo of Maiden Air, Cameron Carson's airline. The other two were enormous twin-bladed Chinooks. As the helicopters began to descend to their respective landing zones, Sarah threw her pack down, muttering obscenities.

Russ powered on his GoCam. "The man certainly knows how to make an entrance." He panned from the helicopters to himself. "Hey there, *Survivor Guy* fans! For those of you who wanted me to ratchet up my production values, check it out!" He reframed the view on the helicopters and started singing "Ride of the Valkyries." "Suck it, Wolf Wallace. You may have a masseuse, but I've got a billionaire!"

The red-and-gold helicopter touched down first, and a tidy little man hopped to the ground, ducking as he walked under the whirling blades. His coffee-colored skin was complemented by an expensively tailored tan suit, and his bright green silk tie fluttered like a banner in the rotor-driven gale. He scurried up to the group.

"Good afternoon, ladies and gentlemen," the man shouted in a clipped British accent, pitching his voice to cut through the roar of the helicopter engines.

"You're not Cameron Carson," Sarah stated.

The little man laughed. "Oh, no, ma'am. I'm Bill Singleton, Mr. Carson's assistant. Mr. Carson should be along shortly. We dropped him off a couple minutes ago."

Russ lowered his GoCam. "Dropped him off?"

A high-pitched sound grew, barely detectable over the sound of the helicopters: a primal scream of exhilaration coming from the treetops. An instant later, a red-and-gold wingsuit zipped into view. Shaped like a flying squirrel, the figure banked away from the choppers and their whirling blades. The man arced toward the edge of the clearing before pulling up abruptly and deploying a small square parachute. They all gaped as the man steered with precision and came to a landing ten yards away. Not even breaking stride, he detached the chute and walked right up to the group, removing his helmet and handing it to Singleton as he reached them. Shaking back a bushy lock of hair and flashing his pearly white teeth through a well-groomed beard, he offered a tanned hand to Sarah.

"Doctor Bishop, I presume? I'm Cameron Carson. Welcome to Home Base. If there's anything I can do to—"

"There is, actually," Sarah said abruptly. She pointed at the helicopters. "You can tell the pilots to kill the damn engines! You were supposed to hike in. I thought you wanted to *find* a Bigfoot, not scare them all away!"

6

The matriarch of the troop looked up at the treetops as she heard a deep *thup thup thup* in the distance. Silk yawned. The folk of the forest were quite used to human machines. This sound belonged to the flying one with the spinning wings. They always reminded Silk of maple tree seedpods that spiraled to the ground when the wind picked up. Littlefoot jumped up, stretched out his long arms, and spun in a series of swift circles before stumbling and collapsing into the leaf litter in a fit of dizziness.

Silk chortled. 'Yes, Littlefoot. Maple seed machine.' The youngest member of the troop was fascinated with human contraptions.

Scratch sat on the ground behind her, plucking pine needles from his mother's thick fur. He paused in his grooming. 'It is High-Sun. Where are Silverback and Brighteyes?'

Silk shifted and gave a short grunt of uncertainty. Silverback rarely left the troop for long. He preferred to remain close in order to protect the family from predators, humans, and any roving bachelor males eager to usurp his position. If it had just been Brighteyes out there, Silk wouldn't have given it a second thought. The young male was always traipsing off on adventures, exploring for miles in every direction. Silk suspected he spent some of his time lingering near the distant camps of humans. Staying hidden from their hairless cousins was second nature to most Sasquatch, but Brighteyes seemed drawn to them. And lately, there seemed to be more of their hairless cousins in the area, enough that Silverback had hinted that the troop might need to move soon. Brighteyes' fascination with humans had led to tragic consequences on one occasion, and a later, more extended encounter with a human had been brutally punished by Silverback.

Silk's reminiscence was interrupted by a short vocalization from downslope. Brighteyes was giving the gentle warning that all Sasquatch gave when approaching camp. That was odd. Given the hierarchy in the troop, the alpha should have given that grunt. It wasn't like Silverback to allow another to undertake one of his duties, particularly a young adult male.

Soon, Brighteyes entered their little glade, his brilliant blue eyes filled with worry. He looked back over his shoulder as Silverback approached. The huge alpha trudged right by Brighteyes, giving him an unnecessary shove as he passed. He was holding his right hand and Silk could see dried blood between his fingers. Silverback's facial features twitched as he came to a stop in the center of their camp. She suspected he was fighting to control his pain, not wanting to show any weakness to his family, but underneath the pain there was something else he was fighting to suppress. *Rage?* Silk rose and Littlefoot clamped onto her leg, trembling.

Silverback didn't look at them as he vocalized, seeming to focus inward. 'Family safe. I protect. I *kill.*'

With this last word, the corner of Silverback's lip curled up in a gleeful smile. His eyes shone and looked wildly from side to side for a moment before his massive frame shuddered and he shook himself as if he were warding off an unexpected chill. Without another word, he turned and trudged straight to a large fallen tree on the edge of their camp and sat heavily upon it, the dead wood creaking with the sudden addition of weight. He merely sat, breathing heavily for a few moments before raising his right hand and turning it front to back, examining the caked blood.

Suddenly he stopped and slowly looked up at the others, who were all watching tensely. He expelled a disgusted *whuff* and pivoted on the log, facing away from the family. He hunched over, breathing slowly and deeply.

Silk peeled Littlefoot off of her leg and started forward cautiously. Brighteyes grabbed her arm. He held her eyes and shook his head slowly. She shrugged his hand off and moved to comfort her mate. The shaggy, silvery pelt rose and fell, an occasional hitch in the deep breaths. She could detect an odd odor rising from him, but that might have come from the humans he'd encountered. Slowly, tentatively, Silk extended her hand. She hesitated, her fingers hovering over his powerful shoulder. Touch was an essential component of the family bond. She would groom her mate, calm him. Then he would set aside his wounded pride and allow her to clean his hand. She gently lowered her fingertips to his shoulder.

Silverback's head whipped around with astonishing speed, his face bearing a rictus of rage. His eyes glowed with madness and his lips were drawn back, trembling over bared canines. Silk leapt back in shock. A weird strangled sound burbled in his throat as he stared at her. Then, just as suddenly, the madness fled his face and the mate she loved was looking at her, a mix of bewilderment and sadness in his eyes. A tear ran down his cheek and again she reached for him.

He stiffened. '*NO!*' Silk froze and Silverback vocalized again, softer now. 'No touch. You go. Silverback… rest.'

The base camp was bustling with activity, and a small village of tents had sprung up. Russ stood with Bud outside Sarah's tent, which was the size of a small cottage. Many of the temporary structures looked like military barracks, high-ceilinged and quite long.

Russ sipped at the coffee he'd just gotten from the mess tent. The rich aroma filled his nostrils. "Wow. Where has this been all my life?"

"I know, right?" Bud tapped his coffee cup against Russ's in a cardboard toast. "The chef said it was from some small Costa Rican farm. Best coffee I've ever tasted."

A slight man of East Indian descent approached them. He sported a tee shirt emblazoned with the iconic '70s image of "Keep On Truckin'"; but instead of Crumb's long-striding man in the logo, it had a long-striding Bigfoot. He spotted Russ and smiled.

"Russ Cloud! Big fan of your work... especially when you upgraded from the EX-3 to the EX-70. The colors really popped." He offered a handshake and continued, "I'm Dhir

Patel. I'll be handling any and all of your tech needs. And on that note, I'm looking for our audio expert, Bud Sorenson."

"You found 'im," said Bud.

Dhir shook his hand, practically vibrating with kid-like excitement. "I read your specs and you are going to *love* what we've got for you. Please, follow me. Mr. Carson wants you up and running right away."

As Dhir scurried off, Bud shrugged and started after him. "Catch ya later, Russ," he tossed back over his shoulder.

Russ raised his coffee cup to him, then turned and went into the tent. The interior was tidy and filled with assorted camp furniture that Carson's organization had brought in. Sarah was leaning on a sturdy camp table, a well-worn topographical map spread out before her. Her laptop was positioned to one side, the screen displaying satellite views of the area. A couple stray locks of blond hair had escaped her ponytail, hanging down over her face as she stared intently at the map. One again, Russ was struck by her beauty. Her rugged hiking clothes fit her form well. Russ looked over her shoulder.

"I love a gal who can read a paper map. Very sexy. If you can navigate by the stars, I may have to propose."

"I *propose* you dial back the charming lothario shtick and hand me that journal," Sarah said as she pointed to a pile of books in the corner.

Russ picked up the topmost book, a small Moleskine notebook conveniently labeled "BFJournal." He held it up and grinned. "Does this stand for—"

"Big Fucking Journal? Never heard that one before." She snatched the little book from him, but there was a playful smirk at the corner of her mouth.

Aha… methinks the humorless hard-ass facade might be cracking. He came over to her side and sipped his coffee as she opened the journal to a later page and scanned the entries. Russ noted the densely packed, hyper-neat handwriting. "Wow… that is some exceptionally tidy writing. You know, a handwriting analyst would have a field day with that."

Sarah tilted her head slightly and raised her eyes toward him, giving him a look that was equal parts flirtation and disdain. "Really?" She turned her body toward him and rotated the book to face him, holding it up in front of herself, her green eyes hovering over the top of the pages. "So, Professor Cloud, what do you see?"

It took a supreme effort to lower his gaze from those beautiful eyes, but Russ glanced down at the pages, pleased she was playing along with his habitual flirtation. "Well, let's see what my powers of observation can divine. The tiny lettering tells me you are focused and intelligent. The exceptionally neat script indicates an obsessive attention to detail and an organized mind." He flicked his eyes up to hers. "And you have some amazing curves." Her eyebrows knitted ever so slightly and he quickly arched his own. "What?" he said innocently as he pointed at the pages. "The curves on these final consonants are quite exceptional. They tell me the writer has passion." He placed a finger on the top of the journal and nudged the book down so they were face-to-face. "What do I see? Intelligence, focus, passion… and really great curves."

Sarah continued to look at him, the ghost of a smile more prominent now. "That's a very… flattering analysis, Russ." As she spoke, she gently closed the journal and reopened it to the inside flap, holding it open in front of his face. "And if my father were still alive, I'm sure he would be flattered." She tapped a signature on the flap with a fingertip. "This is my father's journal." She snapped the book closed in his face, a little victory smirk on her lips. "That *was* some pretty good material, though."

Russ shrugged. "I was trying to seduce a playwright in a bar. Googled 'handwriting analysis' while she was off powdering her nose." He finished off his coffee. He wanted to continue their playful banter, but he knew there was a topic that needed to be discussed. "I…I'm sorry your father passed. I heard a little about what happened."

Sarah's father, Dr. Anthony Bishop, had been a highly respected anthropologist and an ardent outdoorsman. He had spent much of his career researching the early history of several Native American tribes, focusing in particular on the period prior to European settlement. Russ had actually spoken with the man shortly after the first season of *Survivor Guy* aired. Amidst the fan mail, there had been a hefty letter from Idaho State University marked Return Receipt Requested. Dr. Bishop had taken issue with Russ's assertion that a particular deadfall trap had originated with the Paiutes and had gone on to offer detailed descriptions of various ancient Native American traps and snares. Russ had thought himself an expert on the subject, but as he'd flipped through the sketches, he'd felt like a babe in the woods.

It turned out that Dr. Anthony Bishop, the then-chair of the Anthropology Department at Idaho State, was a huge fan of the show and respected Russ's attempts to implement survival skills from local indigenous groups. Russ had looked up his bio on the university's web page; there was a handsome photo of a distinguished older man sporting a full beard streaked with gray. His bio was impressive, and Russ had contacted him while shooting the second season, asking for additional advice on a few of the more complicated examples of ancient woodcraft.

After the final episode of the second season was in the can, the studio decided to throw a big wrap party. The finale had been a double episode shot on the Alaskan island of Sitka, and Russ was particularly proud of it. He decided he would invite Dr. Bishop to the wrap party and pay for his plane ticket to Los Angeles. When he called, he was greeted with a voice mail that Dr. Bishop was on a camping trip and would be out of the office for the weekend. It was a Tuesday, but Russ figured the professor had neglected to change his outgoing message. He left a message detailing his invitation and hung up.

Later that day, Dr. Bishop's secretary called him back, her voice tinged with concern. She explained that the professor had not returned from his trip to the mountains. Dr. Bishop had once told Russ that he always preferred to hike or camp alone, finding the solitude conducive to organizing his thoughts. It was Russ's own "solo trekking" that had attracted the professor to his show. The secretary said he always brought a cell phone, but no one had been able to reach him. His mobile provider thought it might be powered off, as the last signal they'd had from it was on Saturday. A search effort was being mounted, but Dr. Bishop was known to pick his hiking destination at the last second and had never called in with his location. Russ had done his best to reassure her and made her promise to keep him in the loop.

Several days later, the secretary called again. The professor had turned up in a hospital in Grangeville, Idaho, claiming to have seen a Bigfoot. The doctors had been quite certain it had been a hallucination brought on by dehydration and a fever.

It was what had happened next that Russ needed to talk to Sarah about.

He searched her face, and after a moment she looked away, gazing down at the journal in her hand. "How much do you know?" she asked softly.

Just then Liz popped her head into the tent. "Sarah? There's someone here to see y—hey!"

She was shouldered aside by a mountain of a man. Once he was inside, the whole tent seemed smaller. Dressed in a tank top and camo pants and sporting a sidearm in a shoulder holster, the man had a military bearing. Under a spikey salt-and-pepper haircut was a chiseled face that was a study in scar tissue. The face spoke. "Mr. Carson wants to see you."

Whattaya bet he's got some scarring in his throat, too, Russ thought when the man's voice rumbled out. *Sounds like he gargles with gravel.* Russ stepped forward. "And we'd love to see Mr. Carson." He stuck out his hand. "Russ Cloud. And you are?"

The man looked at Russ's hand as if he was unfamiliar with that particular part of human anatomy. Looking back up at Russ, he said, "Follow me, please," before ducking back out of the tent.

Russ glanced at Sarah. "Was that a Bigfoot?" he whispered loudly.

Sarah sighed and shook her head. She rolled up the map she'd been looking at and slid it into a tube. "Liz, please finish up that analysis of edible flora in the area. We'll be back in a bit." Gathering up the map tube and pocketing her father's journal, she walked past Russ. "Let's go, Cloud."

They left the tent and followed the shambling mound through the camp. Russ looked at the man's heavily muscled arms. *Guy's arm veins are bigger than my biceps*, he mused. *Definitely enjoys some steroids with his morning Wheaties.*

"Hey! Sarah! Russ! Check it out!" Bud's familiar voice rang out from off to their left. Sarah headed that way, and Russ watched the incredible bulk stop and turn, looking after her with a less-than-pleased expression. Russ trotted after Sarah. Bud stood just inside a large three-sided tent surrounded by tables topped with electronic equipment. With a look on his face like a kid in a candy store, he waved them inside. "You guys won't believe the gear they've got!" He disappeared inside.

As Sarah followed him into the tent, Russ saw the walking slab moving in. "Mr. Carson doesn't like to be kept waiting. Wait here while I get Bishop."

Russ stepped into his path. "Easy there, big fella. Bud is part of our crew. If *Doctor* Bishop needs to examine Bud's research equipment, she's gonna go ahead and do that." The man moved deep into Russ's personal space, looking down at him. Their faces were inches apart.

"You don't wanna piss me off, Boy Scout."

The man's nostrils flared and his massive chest rose and fell with his breathing. Waves of testosterone emanated from his muscular frame. Russ didn't have the most refined sense of self-preservation; he held the man's gaze and smiled nonchalantly.

"You should consider a nose ring," he said lightly. "Take that whole 'snorting bull' vibe to the next level." A forehead vein pulsed, but Russ soldiered on. "You still haven't told me your name. Let's see… is it Moose? Chunk? Gorgar? No… you don't have horns." He knew he was going to die shortly, but Russ couldn't stop himself. "How 'bout Big Bertha? Kong? Brick?"

Suddenly the man's eyes wobbled, a look of surprise poking through the 'roid rage.

Russ was equally surprised. "Really? Brick is your *actual* name?" Suddenly Russ had an epiphany. He looked at the man more closely. "Holy shit, you're that wrestler, Brick Broadway! I remember you. I used to watch you after class in college. You were fantastic! Loved the sparkly outfits."

The flattery followed so swiftly on the heels of mockery that Brick was thrown. Torn between acknowledging a former fan and visiting violence upon said fan, he settled for something in between. He poked Russ in the shoulder with a finger the width of a broom handle. His voice, shredded from years of screaming scripted threats in a wrestling ring, rasped out, "Keep your voice down. I'm retired. Glad you liked my work, but I got a new job now. And that job is doing what Carson tells me." The finger-pole left his shoulder, and Russ watched Brick's brain decide to give peace a chance. "I'll go to his tent and tell him you're on your way. Go look at your friend's toys, but hurry it up."

Russ tipped him a two-fingered salute. "You got it, BB." Whistling "On Broadway," he turned and entered the tent. Sarah and Bud were huddled over a laptop alongside a tall bank of audio equipment. Sarah was holding a set of headphones to her ears, her eyes wide.

"Russ! Listen to this! Bud, cue up the Sierra Sounds."

Russ joined her and she pivoted one earphone away from her ear, pressing it over his. Though briefly distracted by the scent of her hair, he quickly focused on the sounds emanating from the headphones. What he heard brought an involuntary chill to his spine. An otherworldly chorus of grunts, howls, and growls filled his ears. It was unquestionably eerie, but the skeptic in him thought it might be a mix of human and monkey sounds. On the other hand, given what he knew of what the Bigfoot was supposed to be, that analysis made sense.

"What is this?" he asked.

"That right there is one of the most well-known audio samples of Bigfoot vocalizations. Al Berry and a friend recorded that in the Sierra Madre Mountains in 1972," Bud said. He leaned over his laptop and tapped a couple keys. "Now... take a listen to this."

At first Russ heard nothing but an occasional bird and general background noise. "I don't hear anyth—" The serene soundscape was suddenly shattered by a deep, guttural roar. Russ jumped. He looked at Bud. "Is that from this morning?"

"Yep. Got a couple more that followed after, but that one is the best sample."

Sarah took the headphones they were sharing and set them down. "*That* is a Bigfoot."

"You sure that wasn't a bear?" Russ asked.

Bud shook his head. "I don't think so. I pulled up a couple samples of bears and cougars and there was no match. I'll try some more bears once I get settled. Maybe a Kodiak? I doubt it, though."

Russ turned to Sarah. "It sounded a bit different than the Sierra sample. And I didn't really hear anything quite so... well... *angry*-sounding in that seventies clip."

"Sasquatch are thought to live in different groups. They may have different dialects." Sarah was quite animated now, her eyes shining. "Furthermore, what we just heard might be an exceptionally large individual that was angry at the moment of recording. They have emotions, just like us." When Russ gave her a raised eyebrow she continued, "They *do*, Russ. My father—"

Suddenly they were interrupted by a loud buzzing at the open side of the tent. A small quadcopter drone hovered there, a piece of paper dangling from a clip. It tilted slightly and edged through the air, coming right up to Bud. On the paper was printed, "It's ready." Bud laughed and gave a thumbs-up to the camera lens on the front of the drone. As it backed out of the tent, Bud followed, gesturing to Sarah and Russ.

"This way, folks. There's more."

The drone buzzed around the side of the tent to a patch of clear ground. Dhir brought the drone to a landing at his feet using a simple double-joystick controller. Behind him was a huge parabolic dish mounted on a tripod. Dhir grinned as Bud walked over to the pole under the dish. "I present to you… the Dhir Ear!" He flipped a switch and the pole telescoped up, sending the dish nearly twenty feet into the air.

"Oh, baby…" Bud whistled and walked slowly around, looking up at the microphone assembly. "Is that an EML-900 booster?"

Dhir crossed his arms and smiled like a proud parent. "Good eye. This beauty can pick up sixty decibels at a range of a half mile. Every half mile after that, add ten decibels to the detection threshold. A loud call, like that sample you played me, Bud? You could pick that up out to about five miles, maybe more depending on pitch and ambient interference."

"Fantastic!" Bud grinned at Dhir. "I want to start building a gate for the local ambient levels. I take it the controls are all in the tent?"

Dhir nodded. "The workstation for the Ear is in the back. There's a set of joysticks for raising, lowering, and rotating the dish, and I've set up a laptop with the software you requested."

As the two techies chatted, Russ noticed a large object under a tarp about twenty yards away. "Hey, Dhir. What's that over there?"

Dhir practically vibrated with excitement. "*That* is my favorite toy!" He jogged over to it and started gathering up one end of the tarp as the others approached. He held their eyes before whipping the tarp off like a magician. Beneath was a very large tricopter drone. Though the rotary blades weren't installed yet, it was clear what it was. Russ noted various lenses on a pod underneath the drone's nose. Dhir cleared his throat. "This is TED. Tricopter Extra-large Drone."

"Wouldn't that be TELD?" Bud interjected.

"The 'extra-large' is hyphenated. Shut up. TED here has a primary UHD camera as well as high-grade night vision and infrared sensors. She's also capable of carrying up to two hundred pounds. We can use her to deliver specialized equipment to the field or transport specimens from out in the field to base camp. She's a beauty, ain't she?"

"TED is a 'she'?" Bud teased.

Sarah punched him in the bicep before crouching between two of the drone's arms. "What's the resolution on the infrared?"

"So-so," Dhir responded. "We'll be able to tell a Bigfoot from a deer, if that's what you mean, but the features will be indistinct."

Something was nagging at Russ and he realized what it was. "Sarah, I think we oughta get going. Carson's troll was pretty insistent we not take too long, and I'm kinda partial to not being pounded into goo."

She looked up at him with an impish smile. "What, you don't think you can charm your way into his good graces?" She rose and looked him in the eye. "Maybe you can offer to analyze his handwriting… I'm sure he'd be impressed."

"I suspect he's one of those guys who signs his name with an *X*," Russ bantered back. "Either that or he just inks his knuckles and punches the paper."

Dhir and Bud were already halfway back to the tech tent, chattering excitedly. Sarah pointed to a tent top that was quite a bit higher than the rest of the camp. A flag on a pennant rose next to it, the red and gold of the Maiden company on it. "I'm guessing that's Carson's tent."

"What gave it away? The 'royal pavilion' vibe? I'm having Renaissance Faire flashbacks; if he's wearing a crown and eating a giant turkey leg I may not be able to contain myself." They headed toward the huge tent in the center of the camp. "How well do you know this Cameron Carson fella?"

"Not well. I only met with him once. Apparently he had staff looking into all areas of cryptozoology and took an interest in my father's detailed account. And unlike so many others… he believed him."

"About your father's Bigfoot sighting…" Russ began.

Sarah stopped walking and sighed. "Russ, let's table your skepticism for now and meet with Carson. We can talk about what happened to my father later."

"Sarah, I didn't…" But she was already gone, disappearing around a corner in the tents.

Cameron Carson signed the last of his assistant's pile of documents. "Thank you, Bill. See to the particulars if you would." Bill bustled off and Cameron turned his attention to Brick. His massive bodyguard was fidgeting, his jaw tense and twitching. "Brick, I sense a certain amount of tension… do you think you could dial it back a tick?"

"I'm sorry, Mr. Carson," he rumbled. "Those two shoulda been here by now. I told them to hurry up. It's disrespectful. Pisses me off."

Carson reached up and laid a hand on Brick's shoulder. He flashed a megawatt smile from his flawless set of white teeth. "I don't feel disrespected, Brick. There is so much to do, a little tardiness is simply not something to get worked up over." Carson spoke with a patrician Southern drawl that seemed to have a calming effect on the seething bodyguard. "I appreciate your dedication to duty, but your aggressive vibe is a bit harsh for this meeting. Why not take a stroll? Check in with your men, see that they are situated."

Brick opened his mouth to say something but thought better of it. He turned and ducked out of the tent. One of the two remaining men chuckled. "Where did you find that one?" he asked. "Wouldn't want to see *him* angry. The man is *kranksinnig*." He spoke in a soft, easy voice, a clipped Afrikaner accent giving his words a crispness. His gaunt face and thin nose gave him a somewhat malnourished appearance, but the man's thin frame was all wiry muscle. Sporting a wide-brimmed safari hat, he was dressed in a khaki outfit topped with a tactical vest full of wide pockets.

"Now, now, Willem," Cameron chided. "Brick is more than just muscle and rage. He's completely loyal and determined to prove himself in all things. If I asked him, to… let's say…

wrestle a partially sedated Sasquatch to the ground while we waited for the drug to take effect…" He gave Willem a meaningful look. "He'd do it."

Willem Jaeger snorted as he flopped into a chair and plunked his boots up on the table. Cameron had been curious how the famed hunter would react to that suggestion. The man had hunted large mammals and reptiles across seven continents, even traveling to Antarctica to bag a bull leopard seal—an underwater speargun kill, no less. And Carson knew that Jaeger had illegally hunted lowland gorillas, which might have some bearing on the conversation.

Willem shook his head. "Not wise. Assuming the Sasquatch is a form of great ape—*Gigantopithecus*, or whatever—an adult male gorilla is at least six times as strong as a human. Even if it's partly tranquilized, I 'spect an adult would rip his arms off."

Cameron grinned at Jaeger. "Well, good thing we have *you*, then, eh, Jaeger?" He sauntered over to the wet bar and removed the lid from an ice bucket. "Pappy with ice, right?"

"Wouldn't say no."

The other man had been silent all the while, looking down at the ground. About five and a half feet tall and deeply tanned, he exuded a calm stillness. Joseph Washakie was a full-blooded Shoshone and was considered the foremost tracker in North America. Well versed in the tribal lore of the area, he claimed to have tracked a Bigfoot before.

Joseph raised his head. "They're here."

Russ and Sarah entered the enormous tent. The main entrance led to a large central room. Hanging screens sectioned off smaller rooms along the sides and at the rear. A large table sat in the center of the main space, surrounded by chairs and several smaller tables. Cameron Carson was at a small wet bar plinking a couple ice cubes into a crystal highball. A thin man with a chiseled face who looked like he was dressed for an African safari sat at the table. A large canine tooth was strung on a length of rawhide around his neck. He rubbed it between his fingers and gave a little nod of greeting as they entered. A third man, short and tan with long black hair in a braid, stood apart from the others near the back of the tent.

Carson looked up from the little bar and smiled his megawatt smile. "Dr. Bishop. Mr. Cloud. Welcome!" He turned to the others. "Gentlemen, this is Dr. Sarah Bishop, one of the foremost Bigfoot researchers in the country. Her father, Dr. Anthony Bishop, is the reason why we are here in this particular area. And this is Russ Cloud, survivalist expert and the creator and star of the popular television show *Survivor Guy*. I can assure you, his skills are far more than Hollywood fluffery."

"I've watched your show," said the man seated at the table. He spoke in an unusual accent that Russ couldn't place. "Not bad. Actually picked up a trick or two from you."

"High praise," said Carson. "Russ, this is Willem Jaeger. A phenomenal marksman and one of the greatest big game hunters in the world."

"*Hunters?*" Sarah stepped toward the table. "This is a nonlethal capture attempt. This expedition doesn't need someone who blows away rhinos for fun."

Jaeger remained seated, but Russ saw his eyes take on a steely edge. Russ put his hand on Sarah's shoulder as Carson held up a placating hand. "Dr. Bishop, I assure you... Mr. Jaeger is here to deliver a tranquilizer dart to the target, not a bullet. He is an expert stalker and should be able to get close enough to dart a Sasquatch safely."

Sarah didn't seem completely convinced, but she relaxed a bit and looked toward the Native American–looking man at the rear of the tent. "Have we met? You look familiar."

The man came around the table. "I knew your father. I live in the Fort Hall Reservation a few miles from the university in Pocatello. I helped him with a study on ancient Shoshone lore." He extended his arm and offered a hand. Sarah took a chance and grasped his forearm, emulating a greeting her father had told her was traditional in some Native American tribes. He smiled approvingly and returned the grip. "Your father was a good man. I am Joseph Washakie. I will be your tracker."

Russ spoke up. "I thought I was going handle the tracking."

Carson poured a generous dollop of Pappy Van Winkle into the glass. "Russ, you're our jack-of-all-trades. Your skills will be useful across the board, but as for tracking..." He chuckled. "Joseph here is the real deal."

Joseph released Sarah's arm and stepped toward Russ. "That's not entirely fair, Mr. Carson. I too have watched this man's show. His tracking skills are quite good. But," he hedged, considering what to say before simply shrugging, "I'm better."

Joseph's boast actually came across as quite humble and Russ had to laugh. "OK, then. Well, I'm looking forward to learning a thing or two from you." He extended his hand, and the two of them grasped forearms.

Carson came to the table and slid a highball of whiskey toward Jaeger, who arrested the slide with a quick hand. Other than the hand, he scarcely moved, his feet still propped on the table. "Thanks, boss."

Clapping his hands together and giving them a vigorous rub, Carson began the meeting. "All right, boys and girls, introductions over, let's get down to brass tacks. Sarah, your father's map, if you please. Willem, love the boots but let's put them on the floor, shall we?"

Willem Jaeger swung his feet off the table and rose as Sarah extracted the map from its tube and spread it out on the table. One corner insisted on curling, and Jaeger set his glass aside and pulled a large survival knife from its sheath. Holding the corner down, he raised the blade, clearly intending to pin it to the table.

Just as Sarah cried out, "No!" Joseph's hand whipped up, catching the knife hand by the wrist. She hadn't even noticed him crossing to that side of the table. "This map was one of the last things my father gave me so let's not do the old macho 'pinning things to the table with a knife' shit, OK?"

Russ saw a flash of surprise in Jaeger's eyes at the speed with which Joseph had moved. The Shoshone released his wrist and placed a palm down on the curly corner. "You are right to protect this map, Dr. Bishop. Your father's spirit is strong in it." Reaching into a jeans pocket, he retrieved a smooth, pale stone the size of a chicken's egg and placed it on the corner of the map to hold it down.

"Thank you, Joseph," Sarah said as she looked at the stone. She had thought it was white, but now that she looked more closely, the stone seemed to have a hint of pale blue in it. "That's very beautiful. What is it?"

"White turquoise. Some call it white buffalo turquoise because it is as rare as a white buffalo. I've never seen a white buffalo, so I don't call it that. My father gave it to me. It is said to absorb danger." He shrugged. "It also makes a nifty paper-weight." He winked at her and stepped back from the table.

Russ was chuckling at this exchange when his eye was drawn to a spot on the map. Near the bottom of the map next to the map title and legend was a crude crayon drawing. The kind of drawing a child might do before a proud mom and dad stuck it onto the fridge with a magnet. A fuzzy brown crayon body with big pink crayon feet. The drawing was of a Bigfoot. And near the center of the map, another one: this one in pen, clearly emulating the childish figure. If he was reading the topography correctly, the ink drawing was by a creek at the base of a sheer drop-off.

"What're these?" he asked as he pointed to them. He looked to Sarah for an answer and immediately knew. "Wait. *You* drew them. Didn't you?"

Sarah indicated the one in brown crayon. "I drew that one," she said before looking to the pen drawing. "My father drew the other."

Carson leaned over the table, tilting his head to examine the topography under the pen-drawn figure. "This is where your father had the accident?"

"Wait. Accident?" Russ asked.

Sarah looked at him. "I thought you knew what happened. Didn't you know him?"

"Not very well. We corresponded a bit but I only spoke to him directly once, and that was before…" He hesitated, then gestured to the map. "Before he claimed to have seen a Bigfoot." *And before his career and life unraveled*, he thought.

Carson came around the table to stand face-to-face with Russ. "Sarah's father did far more than simply *see* a Bigfoot, Mr. Cloud." He turned to Sarah. "Did you bring the journal?"

She nodded and slipped it from a pocket, handing it to him. "The ribbon is bookmarking the day he went missing."

Carson held it out to Russ. "I think you should read this. Now. Just so we're all on the same page."

Russ took the book and sat in a camp chair off to the side. While the others began to discuss expedition logistics and scheduling, Russ began to read.

8

6 A.M. FRIDAY
SEPTEMBER 14, 2012

Got an early start and am eager to head into the wilderness, but I want to jot this down. Last-minute change of plans. Was planning on hiking into the White Moose Forest, but now have a better idea. While packing my gear, I came across an old topographical map of the Nez Perce–Clearwater National Forest, where I took my daughter camping when she was six. In 1994, it would have been. Time flies. This was the trip where we heard weird screeching on our last night in the forest. I told my daughter it was probably Bigfoot.

Stupid thing to say. She didn't sleep a wink, and when we got home, she wanted to go straight to the library to look for anything she could find on Bigfoot or Sasquatch or Yeti. She also drew this adorable crayon Bigfoot on the map from our trip, to remind me that we had to go back there one day. Just like any kid her age, her interests quickly changed to other obsessions and the map ended up tucked away with all the others. I had forgotten all about that outing until I saw the drawing. I'm going back. Impulsive, and it'll mean a longer drive, but I'm off to Orogrande.

4 P.M. FRIDAY
SEPTEMBER 14, 2012

Drove through Orogrande. Remains of an old hotel in the middle of town. Might check that out on my return. I've taken Buffalo Hump Road all the way to the end and will leave the car and hike west from here. Too late in the day to head out, so I'll sleep in the car tonight. There's a creek right here. Fish sounds good. Will try my luck.

6 A.M. SATURDAY
SEPTEMBER 15, 2012

A little trout left for breakfast. I'll head northwest and by noon should reach the spot where I took Sarah camping.

NIGHT
hurt   stupid   fell   leg broken   head hurts   strange noises   sleep

9 A.M. SUNDAY
SEPTEMBER 16, 2012

Head is clearer. I'm such a fool. I was on a ridge when I heard something moving downslope. I set down my pack and looked over the side. There was something moving in the trees. I could tell it was covered in fur, and at first I thought it was a bear, but as it reached a gap in the foliage, I could see it was man-shaped. I took out my cell phone to quickly take a photo.

Not having the best vantage, I found a small tree I could grip to allow me to lean out for a better shot. Stupid. The tree gave way and I fell. I must have hit my head. When I woke, it was night. My leg is badly broken. Compound fracture. I can hardly look at it. I am at the bottom of a steep drop-off. No way I can climb back up. I called for help, but no answer.

I can hear a creek nearby. I will need to drag myself to it if I want to avoid dehydration. Pain is too much right now. Will try later. I have some water left in the bottle I carry in a belt pouch. Strange thing. There was a pile of berries next to me when I came to this morning. Huckleberries, I think. There sure as hell aren't any berry bushes in sight. Maybe I landed next to some animal's stash. Either way, I've got some fresh food to supplement the PowerBar I have in my pocket. Hope they aren't poisonous, but beggars can't be choosers.

2 P.M.

There's something out there. I can hear it moving through the brush. I've managed to drag myself back under a little outcrop at the base of the drop-off. Got a few rocks together just in case. I'll need to build a fire. Not just for protection; it was quite cold last night. Not much wood within crawling distance, but enough for a small fire I think.

6 P.M.

Something threw a pinecone at me. I had gathered some kindling, pine needles, and a smallish log and was working on fashioning a spindle with my multitool when it hit the rock wall I was leaning against. I called out but heard nothing. Just as I was thinking it might have fallen from above, another pinecone hit the wall. *This* one I saw arcing through the air. I may have taken a blow to the head during my fall, but I know what I saw. And I'm pretty sure I know what's going on here.

The figure I saw before was a Sasquatch and it was out there now, curious about me. I retrieved one of the cones and tossed it in the direction the last one had come from. About a minute later, a chunk of branch thunked into the outcropping and landed right next to my pile of kindling. I laughed and raised it in the air, waving it back and forth.

"Thank you!" I called out and then added it to my pile of kindling. There was no further contact, so I went back to work on my spindle. Using a bootlace, I got a simple firebow going and the dry pine needles caught fairly easily. Leg is still in agony, but at least I'll be warm tonight.

8 A.M. MONDAY

I had a visitor in the night. I woke to another batch of berries, a few small branches, and a rotten log. Either I'm sleeping deeply due to my injuries, or my mystery friend is incredibly stealthy. This morning's project is to splint my leg or I'll never be able to drag myself to that creek.

11 A.M.

Contact. I had just finished my rough splint job when I heard a sharp knock, almost like a rock or stick striking a tree. I'd once read something about Sasquatch signaling by knocking on trees, so I crawled—more like "ass-hopped"—back to the rock wall and picked up one of the rocks I'd gathered there. I gave the rock a single sharp rap and waited. I was greeted with another knock, this time much closer. I admit a tiny part of me felt fear, but that sensation was overwhelmed by a feeling of exhilaration. I struck the rock wall two strikes this time. I waited a moment, expecting to hear two knocks in return. There were none.

Instead, my mystery friend stepped fully into view from behind a copse of trees. The figure was about fifty yards away, and I could see him quite clearly. I say *him* because, as I stated, I could see him *quite* clearly. He was about the height of a tall man, his fur or hair quite long and auburn in color. His face was certainly apelike in appearance, particularly around the brow and mouth. The center of his face, though, was surprisingly human. What stood out most were the eyes. They were a brilliant blue. Even at this distance, I could see that they shone with intelligence. I immediately understood why so much of the lore of Native American tribes referred to the Sasquatch as "the wild *man* of the woods."

He was holding something in his left hand. It was dark and wet and I could see an occasional drip of water fall from his fingers. He watched me for a moment, then gave a gentle sort of grunt or snort from his nostrils, remaining where he was and continuing to watch. It felt like he was giving me a tentative greeting. I was about to say hello, but opted instead to try to emulate his vocalization. He shifted his weight, and I decided to make the sound again and then lifted my hand, palm facing him. He watched attentively. I turned my hand and gently patted my chest. He grunted again and moved a little closer. This huffing grunt sounded the same both times. How to describe it? Think of the human noise *hmm*. Except the *h* is blown sharply through the nose and the *m* is short and sounded in your chest.

I butt-scooted toward my remaining huckleberries, and my movement caused him to stop in his tracks. I held my palm up and gave a quick *hm*, then reached down and scooped up some berries. I held them out to him and risked some human speech. "Thank you." He seemed to understand, in principle, what I was saying (or he might have thought I was just asking for more berries, I don't know). He bobbed his head with a softer little grunt and then continued to move closer, though the closer he got the more skittish he seemed. He stopped about thirty feet away and raised the wet object, which I could now see was a balled-up wad of dense moss.

The Bigfoot lifted the dripping moss above his face and opened his mouth. I couldn't help but notice the huge canines, but I kept my mind on what he was doing. He squeezed a trickle of water into his mouth before looking at me with what appeared to be a smile. Next he extended his index finger and made a very human gesture. He pointed. First at the moss, then at me. Then he made as if to throw the moss, but with a couple gentle swings, like he was waiting for me to be ready to catch it. I was put in mind of a master and his dog: "See the ball, boy? See it?"

I set down the berries and held out both hands. With a gentle underhand toss, he landed the bunch of wet moss right on my palms. I said "thank you" again, then raised the moss and squeezed a trickle into my mouth. I expected a dirty, grassy taste, but the water was quite fresh. When I lowered the moss, the Bigfoot was already striding away. "Thank you," I repeated, louder this time.

He looked back and grunted but kept walking and was soon out of sight, disappearing down a slope toward where I figured the creek to be. I will end this entry now and try to find my phone. I believe I rolled or tumbled quite a bit during my fall, but the phone might have landed somewhere nearby. I doubt I'll have a signal, but it's not the cell service I'm thinking of. It's the camera.

3 P.M.

No sign of my phone, which was unfortunate because my friend returned. I was dragging myself back to my 'campsite' after searching along the base of the drop, and the Bigfoot was near the ashes of last night's fire. He was dropping another batch of wood as I scooted toward him. He seemed less skittish now and only retreated a couple steps as I neared. I raised a hand and grunted a short *hm* and he responded in kind, this time raising his own hand to me. He picked up a stick and poked at the ashes and made a different open-mouthed sound while raising his brow.

I took up my bow drill and spindle, positioning some of the tinder material I had gathered near the fire. Since my friend understood pointing and had used the gesture with the moss this morning, I tried it with him. I picked up a stick I could reach and placed it on the dead campfire. Then I pointed at the pile of wood he had brought and then at the ashes. He gave a double pant from an open mouth and nodded. A bit of a deliberate and clumsy nod, but a nod nevertheless.

He picked up several logs and branches and placed them on the ashes. Curiously, he arranged them in a leaning teepee manner, the way a human might. With the pointing, the nodding, the campfire building, and the general lack of fear around me, I was beginning to think this Bigfoot had spent a fair amount of time observing humans. I focused on his bright blue eyes and held up the bow drill and spindle.

"Watch," I said, and proceeded to work the bow; after several minutes, a thread of white smoke curled up from my tinder bundle. I cupped it in my hands and blew. As a tiny flame sprung to life, my friend uttered some excited pants and didn't look fearful at all. I placed the bundle under his stack of wood and soon we had a small fire going. He stared at the fire in wonder and I realized he was probably quite young, probably a teenager. It was hard to judge, given his size, but something about his face made me sure of this.

He uttered another happy pant, then straightened and lumbered over to a dead tree. Grabbing hold of a thick branch, he wrenched it off of the trunk with ease. Snapping it into three pieces, he brought them over and laid them beside the fire. I looked him in the eyes and said, "Thank you." He nodded again, then went over to where I had placed the bundle of moss. He held it up, gave a quick grunt and pointed downslope. As he headed toward the creek, I had a sudden inspiration.

"Wait!" I called, then scooted myself over to where I'd set the water bottle from my belt pouch. There was a little water left in it, and as the Bigfoot returned I held it up to my face, opened my mouth and looked at him. Mimicking what he had done with the moss, I poured a trickle into my mouth. I then held it up again and pointed to its top. Making each motion slowly and deliberately I unscrewed the top and held the bottle up, mimed scooping it through imaginary water, then replaced the top. Finally I pointed at the bottle, then toward the sound of the creek, then back to the bottle.

He looked at me a moment, then gave me three happy pants and a vigorous series of nods. I held the bottle out, and he approached and reached for it. Suddenly he seemed to realize how close he'd gotten to me and pulled his hand back. Instinctively I tapped the palm of my free hand to my chest twice and said, softly, "Friend." He probably picked up on the feeling behind my word if not the meaning, because he reached out and gently took the water bottle. He then tapped a palm twice to his own chest and grunted a soft *hm* before heading off to the creek.

6 P.M.

My friend has just left, and I suspect he won't return until tomorrow. After he left with the water bottle, he took quite some time to return. I soon realized why. He had the water bottle in one massive hand and in the other he held a large trout. I thanked him and proceeded to clean and fillet the fish with my multitool. He watched my actions with intense interest, and for the first time he sat down on the ground. Selecting two sticks, I sharpened one end on each and threaded the fillets onto them before positioning the fish over the flames. I took up the water bottle and popped open the spout, taking a long drink.

The water was delicious and I said, "Good." I looked to the Bigfoot and raised the bottle. "Drink?" I asked, tipping the bottle and letting another stream fall into my mouth before extending the bottle to him. "Drink?" I repeated. He panted once and gently took the bottle, upending it over his mouth. Only a tiny trickle fell from the nozzle and he lowered it, looking at it quizzically. He shook his head side to side, as if he were saying "no water." Had he learned that head shake from humans too?

I gave a little grunt to catch his attention, then held up a hand and made a gentle squeezing motion with my fingers. He looked at the nozzle and squeezed. Not surprisingly, his powerful fingers applied quite a bit more pressure than mine would have and he was rewarded with a spout of water straight into his face. He yelped in surprise and dropped the bottle, then looked at me, his face dripping. I was frozen in place, unsure what he might do. Seconds later he burst into laughter. Not the way we humans do, of course, but a series of open-mouthed pants. It was clear from his eyes and tone that he had found the sudden drenching hilarious. I erupted into laughter as well, and we both laughed even harder when he lifted the bottle and gave me a blast in the face.

Then, in the midst of our shared hilarity, a sudden sound. It was a distant whoop, and it cut right through our laughter. My companion instantly stopped laughing and I followed suit. We listened and another whoop, rising in pitch, cut through the stillness. The Bigfoot rose and started to leave.

"Wait!" I called, and he spun around and pointed at me and then held a hand over his mouth. The whoop sounded a third time. Holding my gaze, he pointed at himself and patted his palm against his chest. Then he pointed off into the woods and very slowly, very deliberately, shook his head. As he turned again and headed off in the direction of the calls, I thought about what he was saying to me: "Quiet. I am a friend. But that… that is *not* a friend." A chill runs up my spine as I write this. My Bigfoot is not alone. This is going to be a long night.

7 A.M. TUESDAY

Full of fish and warmed by the fire, I actually slept quite well. When I awoke just before daybreak, I found my furry companion had returned. He was sitting across the fire from me, the flames reflected in his bright, intelligent eyes.

"Brighteyes." I said, still half-asleep. He looked at me and I realized the name was perfect. I repeated the name and laughed. "What does that make me? Dr. Zaius?" *Planet of the Apes* had been a favorite movie in my youth, and the irony was too good to pass up. Besides, I needed a way to refer to him, and he had seemed to recognize repeated speech patterns even if he didn't always understand them.

I sat up, my leg screaming at me with the change of position. I pointed at myself and said slowly, "An...tho...ny. Anthony." I pointed at him. "Bright...eyes. Brighteyes." He cocked his head and furrowed his brow. I thought a moment, then pointed at my eyes, naming them first. He understood. Next, I took out my multi-tool; it had a tiny LED penlight built into it. Shining it at his eyes, I said, "Bright." I pointed it at my own eyes and mimed squinting at its glare. "Ooh! Bright!" He chuckled at my performance. I flicked the light at him, pointed at my eyes, and repeated, "Bright. Eyes." Finally, I patted my chest, "Anthony..." and pointed at him. "Brighteyes."

I saw understanding bloom in his brilliant blue eyes. He nodded energetically and pointed at himself, raising his brows expectantly. "Brighteyes," I said, smiling. He panted happily, nodding all the while. He seemed to be saying, "OK, good, I like it." He then looked intently at me, and after a moment, he reached out and gently took hold of my beard between two fingertips. I'd grown tired of shaving long ago and had quite an impressive set of whiskers. He gave it a little tug, then took hold of the hair on his own face and tugged it.

"Beard," I said. Then, very slowly and deliberately, he pointed at me. A moment later he tugged his facial hair again and repeated the deliberate pointing gesture. He was naming me! I laughed. "OK, fair enough. Forget

Anthony." I pointed at myself and tugged my beard. "You can call me Beardface."

He whuffed and nodded sagely before breaking into an enormous yawn. I was surprised by the size of his canines. He tugged his facial hair, waved, then lay down and closed his eyes. I translated this as "Goodnight, Beardface." I noticed that the fire was burning brightly. It occurred to me that he must have come earlier in the night to put more wood on the fire; it should have been nothing but embers by now. I looked up at the predawn sky and decided to get a little more sleep myself.

Later, I awoke to find Brighteyes laying another batch of wood on the fire. I sat up, and when he looked at me I gave him a simple wave. "Hello, Brighteyes." He thought for a moment, then raised a hand and returned my wave before pointing at me and tugging his chin hair. In the light I could now see there was something wrong with his face. There was some dried blood at one corner of his mouth, and the cheek on that side seemed swollen. "Brighteyes, what happened to you?"

He continued to look at me without understanding. I turned my face to the side, tapped a finger to my cheek and the corner of my mouth and mimed a wince; then I pointed at his face. He understood, nodded, drew back his lips from his teeth and gave a throaty sound that was the first aggressive noise I'd heard him make. He pointed toward where we'd heard the whoops the evening before, jabbing his finger once, twice, thrice. Then he sat, his tense posture sagging. He sighed and gingerly touched the side of his face, tensing a little and letting out a soft whimper of pain.

I thought of my daughter and what I could do for her when she was hurt. Obviously I couldn't kiss the booboo and make it better; I might end up with some lethal booboos of my own. But another strategy occurred to me: candy, cookies, ice cream. I dug in my pocket and found the partially smushed PowerBar. Chocolate chip. I unwrapped it and tore off a hunk. Scooting myself closer to Brighteyes, I offered it to him on my palm.

"For you," I said softly. He looked at the morsel, then at me. He chuffed once, then gently took the piece of food and sniffed it before popping it into his mouth. After a couple chews, something in his face changed. He nodded vigorously and grunted with pleasure. As he finished swallowing his portion, I unwrapped the rest, offering it to him. He reached for it, hesitated, then took it and carefully tore it in two, offering half back to me. I smiled broadly and took it, then opened my mouth and held the piece of food near my lips as I looked at Brighteyes expectantly.

A mischievous look came into his eyes and he held his piece up as well, mouth open in anticipation. We mirrored each other, slowly moving the chocolaty pieces closer to our open mouths. Suddenly Brighteyes twitched his head, and I gobbled my chunk of PowerBar. Brighteyes gave a hearty panting laugh, still holding his own piece. That cheeky bastard had "head faked" me! I laughed as I chewed, giving little nods of appreciation. I threw in a shrug too, since he understood that motion. Still "chuckle panting," he popped the remainder into his mouth.

We enjoyed our sweet treats, and when he finished, he gently placed a massive hand on my shoulder. Looking into my eyes, he actually made an attempt at speech. "A… oo…" The first syllable sounded like the vowel in *cat*, the second a round-lipped *oo*. I knew immediately.

"Thank you?" I asked. He nodded vigorously and gave a couple vocal chuffs.

Since he clearly understood my words but couldn't recreate them, I decided I should attach a gesture to it. I remembered a particular hand motion the Arab characters used in *Lawrence of Arabia*, an elegant touch of the forehead prior to a bow, and decided it would do nicely if I paired it with the open palm I had offered the food upon. While our exchange was fresh in Brighteyes' mind, I dragged myself a couple feet over to the wood he had brought. I held up a piece with one hand, then raised the fingertips of my other hand to my forehead, touching it once before lowering it to a point in front of my chest, palm up.

"Thank you," I said as I made the gesture. I set the branch down and pointed at the little pile of wood and repeated the gesture and the words. Brighteyes didn't even hesitate. He nodded, then reached down to pluck the empty PowerBar wrapper from the pine-needle-strewn ground. Holding it up, he raised his other hand

and copied my gesture exactly. I smiled and nodded deliberately, saying "yes" as I nodded. I resolved then and there to try to teach him some other words and gestures.

5 P.M.

It was a productive day. Brighteyes picked up quite a few gestures, and I've adopted a couple of his. I will note these on the back pages of this journal. I was able to communicate my desire for my pack, which was up at the top of the drop-off, and he retrieved it for me. The tent, flashlight, extra layers of clothing, and packaged food gave me quite a morale boost. I also took a look at the little first aid kit I always bring. I have done my best to keep my injury clean, and the spot where the bone pushed through isn't very large, but I am increasingly concerned about infection.

Brighteyes watched me examining it. He approached and crouched beside me, sniffing the air above the wound. He straightened and signed, 'Bad.' He pointed at it, then mimed pressing something to his leg a couple times. He signed, 'I go. I get,' and headed off into the forest.

I boiled some water while I waited. Brighteyes had brought me an empty can he had found, and it would work well to purify enough to rinse the wound. A few more days and I might be strong enough to make my way out of here with the help of some sort of crutch. My head still hurt, but not as badly as it had after the fall, and the dizziness I had felt was mostly gone. Brighteyes would probably help me part of the way, at least until we came near people.

He soon returned, carrying a bunch of white flowers in one hand and what looked like a small chunk of honeycomb in the other. He set them down on a rain poncho I'd pulled out of my pack and signed, 'Good.' He looked around, spotted something, signed, 'I get,' and went to a very large rock, on the cusp of being what I'd call a boulder. He pulled it loose from the ground and lifted it with little difficulty, bringing it near the fire and setting it down so a flat surface was on top. He pointed at the water bottle and made the squeezing motion with his fingers. I handed it to him and he went down to the creek.

While he was away, I looked at what he'd brought: the bunch of white flowers, leaves, and stems looked like wild yarrow, and the other object was indeed a chunk of honeycomb containing a good amount of honey. From my studies of early Native American woodcraft, I knew yarrow to be a widely used medicinal herb possessing many useful qualities: anti-inflammatory, styptic, astringent, and antiseptic. The honey would provide antibacterial properties.

Brighteyes returned with a full water bottle and a smoothly rounded stone, probably from the creek bed. He sat next to the small boulder and pointed to the yarrow and honeycomb I was sitting next to, signing, 'Give.' I could see he was planning on making a poultice, using the boulder and creek rock as a mortar and pestle. I set the yarrow on the rock and pointed at the honeycomb, giving a questioning grunt. I held it over the yarrow so the honey dripped down on the flowers, and Brighteyes gave a happy pant and signed, 'Good.'

He waited until there was good amount of honey on the plants and then proceeded to grind the rounded rock into the mixture. After a minute, he picked up the water bottle, and I could see he was going to squirt some water into it. Fearing the organisms in the creek water might be counterproductive to his planned treatment, I grunted sharply and shook my head no. I pointed at the can of boiling water on the edge of the fire and signed, 'Good water.' Pulling my sleeve over my fingers as a makeshift potholder, I lifted the can and poured some on the poultice, stopping to look at Brighteyes. His eyes remained on the poultice.

I hadn't come up with a sign for 'more' or 'go on,' but he didn't need one, simply making a pouring motion and giving a soft grunt. I poured some more and he touched my arm to stop me, signing, 'Good.' Some more rock-on-rock grinding and the poultice looked ready. I set the can on the rock and pointed at it. I mimed pouring it on my wound and reacted with mock pain, saying, "Ow, ow, ow!" I would have signed, 'We wait,' but I'd not had any luck with the concept of waiting. Instead I pointed to him, then myself, then pointed middle and index fingers at my eyes before swinging them to point at the can. Essentially: 'We look at can.'

He furrowed his brow a moment, but then gave two quick pants and nodded his head. I readied an elastic bandage to dress the wound while the boiled water cooled and then did my best to rinse the wound with the still-hot water. I winced at the pain and Brighteyes made some soothing cooing sounds while he gathered up a generous blob of the poultice. When I was ready, I pointed from the poultice to the wound and nodded. Considering the massive size of his hands and the unquestionable strength in his fingers, Brighteyes was very gentle and precise in his movements as he carefully pressed the poultice to the wound. I then bound the leg with the elastic bandage, which had the added benefit of better securing my hastily constructed splint.

When I was finished, I looked at our handiwork. 'Good,' I signed.

Brighteyes nodded, repeating my sign for *good*. Then he signed, 'I go. You sleep.'

I clapped, which seemed to be a good way to say, "I need your attention." He waited and I signed again, a simple phrase that I seemed to be using often with this furry giant: 'Thank you.'

7 A.M. WEDNESDAY

Between my journal writing in the front of the book and my sign language key in the back, I am quickly running out of pages. I will have to shorten my entries. Brighteyes is not here yet. I will finish setting up my little tent. I didn't do a very good job last night.

1 P.M.

Brighteyes returned a few hours ago with a fresh injury. He was holding his ribs and wincing. I had my suspicions about what had done this, and I gave a soft clap and held his eyes. I pointed at his ribs, patted my own, pointed at his cheek, then gingerly patted my own as if it hurt. Next I pointed off to where he had gone at night and made a soft whoop, imitating the call we'd heard the night before last. Finally I jabbed a finger toward the whooper, smacked my fist violently into my palm, then pointed at Brighteyes.

He understood. He sighed and his body sagged. He whuffed sadly and nodded. I pointed at him and then held that hand up, palm facing down, indicating height. With my other hand I pointed toward his distant attacker and then held my hand much higher. He looked at my charades with interest, nodding and grunting vigorously and holding his arms wide. I suspect there is a large alpha male out there who is not happy with Brighteyes' extended outings. We came up with a gesture for this other, which I will call "Alpha," as well as a few more signs. He has gone away again, taking my rain poncho and water bottle with him.

5 P.M.

Brighteyes has returned, my poncho held like a sack in one hand and a bundle of wood tucked under an arm. Spreading out the poncho beside me, I could see several kinds of berries, two trout, some sorrel, acorns, and the filled water bottle. I thanked him and was about to start cleaning the fish when Brighteyes clapped once. I stopped and watched him as he reached into the pile of wood he'd brought and retrieved a stout, straight branch, about five feet long. One end looked roughly honed. Going to the boulder we'd used to grind up the poultice, he scraped the tip of the branch along the rough surface as if to sharpen it. He pointed at me, rasped the point again a couple times, then came over to me. He mimed stabbing the makeshift spear into the air before handing it to me. He stepped back and began to sign.

'You friend. I give food. I give wood. I friend you.' He paused before signing, 'Alpha...' Here he shook his head vigorously. 'Alpha no friend.' He grabbed some fur on his arm and sniffed at it with wide nostrils. He pointed off and gave the sign for *alpha*, sniffed his fur again, then pointed at me.

A chill ran up my back as I nodded understanding and whispered, "Alpha smells me on you," saying it more to myself than to him.

Brighteyes raised his hand and waved several times, then signed, 'I go. I go. I go.' He is gone now and I don't know if he'll be back. It is starting to rain.

4 P.M. FRIDAY
SEPTEMBER 21, 2012

I write this now from my hospital bed. I had to beg a
nurse to dig through my ruined clothing to find my
journal. I will do my best to recall what happened. After
Brighteyes left, I sharpened the spear he gave me, even
fire-hardening the tip. The rain began in earnest, so I
dragged everything into the tent, including the fire-
wood. I went to sleep, but several hours later, a sound
woke me. The rain was coming down hard and it was
difficult to hear, but soon I heard a high whooping call.
I listened intently and heard it again. It sounded closer.

The campfire had been doused by the rain and I
couldn't make out anything in the downpour and darkness. I located my flashlight and the makeshift spear and
hunkered down in the back of the little tent. Another
call, even closer. Then I jumped as a loud clap sounded
outside the tent. Movement. I leveled the spear at the
tent opening and switched on the flashlight. Eyeshine.
A shape. I gave a simple grunt of greeting and held my
breath. The shape moved closer and waved, returning
my grunt. Brighteyes.

I crawled to the tent opening with the spear and
flashlight. He seemed on edge, looking off into the forest
and listening intently. Occasionally he would sniff the
air. "Brighteyes," I said. I was sure he had excellent night
vision, but I'd probably blinded him a bit with the light,

so I set down the spear and pointed the flashlight at myself. I signed, 'I hear Alpha.'

I moved the light enough to see him in the edge of the beam, and he nodded and signed frantically, 'Alpha come. Bad. Bad. Bad. We go. We go. We go.' He moved close and raised his palms several times, asking me to get up. He then offered his hand to me. I remember this vividly, it was such a human gesture. I took it and with his help came up onto my good leg. He tapped the flashlight and shook his head vigorously. I doused and pocketed it as he reached past me and grabbed the spear, pressing it to my chest.

Gripping his furry arm, I could feel the powerful muscle beneath, and when another high whooping cry pierced the rain, the muscles tensed. He grunted softly and we began moving roughly east. Between his arm and my spear, I was able to keep the weight off of my ruined leg. It was hard to tell exactly where we were headed in the darkness and driving rain, but I was fairly sure we would eventually reach Crooked River Road, which runs north to south through Orogrande.

We'd been walking for about a quarter hour when a terrible roar erupted from behind us. This was no hooting or whooping; it was an angry scream from a large animal. If I had to guess, the alpha male had found my tent. Brighteyes froze and we stood in the rain, listening. Another roar split the night, and my shaggy friend bent and lifted me up as easily as I might have my daughter when she was a toddler. I clutched the spear and hung on for dear life as Brighteyes crashed through the forest, making no attempt at stealth. I had no idea if we were still heading east, but at this point, all I wanted was to put distance between us and the sounds of primal rage that continued to reach our ears.

After several hours, we finally reached a dark country road. By now the rain had let up and there was a little moonlight to see by. Brighteyes set me down gently and I leaned on my spear. For a long time, we only looked at each other, man and almost-man. I felt a hitch in my chest and realized I was crying.

Finally, I signed, 'Thank you... friend.' I reached out my hand, an instinctive human gesture. He took it gently and I gripped his massive hand and gave it a shake. He whimpered softly and nodded, but our parting was interrupted by another call, this time a deep, guttural scream.

He looked back into the woods, then turned to me and signed, 'You go,' pointing north up the road, where I could see a distant light. Then he pointed into the trees to the southwest and signed, 'I go.' Then he laid a massive hand on my shoulder and lowered his face to mine. He looked into my eyes a moment, then stepped back and signed, 'You. Me. Good.' Brighteyes turned and began running into the woods, giving a loud whoop once he was some distance from me. I hobbled up the road heading for the light.

The rest is incidental. A pickup truck. A ride to the Orogrande Airstrip. A medevac to a hospital in Grangeville. And here I am. The doctors were fascinated with the poultice on my leg. There was some infection, but not nearly as much as they would have expected. The concussion worries them more—not so much because of the injury itself, but because of what I've been telling them. They wanted to know how I survived, how I managed to make it to that road. I told them. And no one believes me.

9

Russ closed the journal. There were no further entries apart from the rough sketches and notes on the various hand signals the professor had taught the Bigfoot. The story told in that little book had a ring of truth to it, but Russ knew that no one had believed Dr. Anthony Bishop. The concussion was certainly part of it. The unbelievably fantastical nature of it and the convenient fact that he had lost his cell phone—a simple way to have recorded undeniable proof—that was part of it too.

Russ had spoken briefly with the professor's university secretary and had a rough idea of what had happened next. Dr. Bishop had brought a small group of skeptical yet supportive peers out to the location to show them his campsite, and they'd found… a campsite. There was a tent, a campfire, and some of his gear, but little else. There *were* tracks. Bear tracks. The tent had been torn open, and the professor's pack, which had contained some packaged food, had been ransacked. The professor, who witnesses described as "highly agitated," pointed out that between the heavy rain and a rampaging bear, the signs of his Bigfoot visitor might have been wiped out.

He'd then walked to a flattened area next to the campfire and said, "It was here. It was right here!" His friends had asked him what he meant, and he'd described a boulder that Bright-eyes had carried over to grind a poultice.

Dr. Bishop had grown more distraught, saying something about an "Alpha Bigfoot" and suggesting this second Bigfoot had destroyed or hidden any evidence. The professor had then made loud whooping calls and clapped his hands while his friends stood in silence before suggesting they should get back to town. The professor's obsession had spiraled out of control, and soon he was let go from the university. What happened next—that was something he needed to hear directly from Sarah.

Russ looked up at her, deep in conversation with Carson and the others, gesturing passionately at points on the map. There was no doubt she believed her father's account, and after reading his journal, Russ was certain that whatever had happened to him out there in the woods, it was more than a curious bear or a weeklong concussion-induced hallucination.

Russ rose and joined them at the table, holding the little notebook up. "This is incredible. I mean… well, it's hard to believe—"

"And yet you *do* believe it, don't you?" Carson interrupted, smiling that huge smile.

"I'm not sure…"

Carson took the book and flipped through it. "I'm well aware of your skepticism in regards to the existence of Bigfoot. I was a skeptic myself… until I read this." He handed it to Sarah and continued, "My company has a small research group looking into elements of the paranormal, UFOs, and cryptozoology. I didn't expect much from them, but their financial needs were minuscule, and if even one of their investigations panned out it would be a public relations coup. About three months ago they set up a meeting with Dr. Bishop here, and I had a chance to read her father's account. I had the crypto department drop everything and begin planning this expedition."

"But everyone thought the professor was crazy. And there was no proof. As detailed as the journal's account is, you would think there would have been *something*."

"Well, that's just it, isn't it?" Sarah interjected. "Sightings all over the country over such a long period of time and very little evidence. I think the professor was right about this 'Alpha.' It was covering their tracks, so to speak. It seems to me the only way a species such as this could exist for this long without being irrefutably discovered would be if Sasquatch are cognizant of the need for secrecy. Or, at least, the elders among them are. I believe my father came across a young individual, one whose curiosity about humans outweighed his caution. And when the alpha male of the troop became aware of the amount of contact that had been going on, he took steps to correct the mistake."

"Fortunately for us," Carson said, "this Brighteyes got your father out before the alpha could get to him."

"Well, we don't know that this dominant male would have done anything aggressive," Sarah cautioned. "There is no credible account of a Bigfoot ever harming a human."

*R*age. Hunger. Pain. Thinking... hard. Family near. They are looking at me. They should stop. I could make them stop. I could—

STOP. You must protect family. You must think. So hard to think. Hand hurts. Hungry. Very hungry. Very very very very very very hungry. Family. I smell them. Hungry... I could—

NO. Never hurt family. Always protect. I am Silverback and they are mine and I must protect. But so hungry/angry/hungry/angry—

FOOD. I need food. Silk has brought nuts. Silk has brought berries. They make me vomit. They are not-food. I smell... family. NO. Not ever (not yet?) not... not sure. I smell... what else? Distant. Humans. Many humans.

AVOID HUMANS. This is the law. Always avoid humans. But I smell them. And I hunger.

I must EAT.

Russ, Sarah, and Carson had sketched out a rough time-
table for their search, and the meeting was drawing to a
close. Sarah had insisted on keeping their forays small until
they made contact so as not to frighten their quarry. Joseph
remained silent unless someone directly addressed him.
Willem Jaeger was a bit more talkative, and Russ decided he
disliked the man. It wasn't just that he hunted for sport; Russ
had hunted too many animals himself to condemn him solely
for that, though Russ hunted for food and this man clearly did
it for the fun of it. No, there was something else about the man.
He'd have to keep an eye on him.

Cameron Carson was enthusiastic and filled with boundless
energy—he was also an egomaniac and a bit of a narcissist—
and Russ felt he had a pretty good read on the man. Still, it
wouldn't hurt to pry a little.

"Mr. Carson—"

"Cameron, please."

"Cameron. I've been meaning to ask, why exactly are you doing this? I don't see any other billionaire businessmen traipsing through the forest looking for monsters. Don't take this the wrong way, but shouldn't you be on a gold-plated yacht somewhere, sipping ten-thousand-dollar champagne and counting your billions?"

Carson's shiny white teeth burst through his beard in a Cheshire Cat grin. "Never been a fan of gold... and anyone who spends more than a hundred bucks on champagne is a fool. But to your question, some time ago I grew bored with the business side of my business. Accumulating wealth, once you already have it, is child's play. I decided to branch out into what I dubbed 'adventure ventures.' Circumnavigating the globe in a solar-powered plane, mapping the Kamchatka Oceanic Trench, and then a few more... ambitious undertakings that weren't entirely successful..."

"Epic fails, as the young folk say," quipped Jaeger. "Did they ever figure out if those astronauts would be drawn into the sun?"

A rare flash of anger twitched across Carson's perpetually smiling face. "Brave men. Brave *volunteers*. If errors were made, the responsibility lies with the Maiden Galactic Division of Maiden Industries. I merely provided the capital."

"Let me get this straight," said Russ. "You take credit when it's a success and blame underlings when it's a failure?"

Carson looked Russ in the eye. He was still smiling, but there wasn't any sunshine behind it. "You've just summarized Business 101, Mr. Cloud. Don't mistake me, when a Maiden project doesn't meet expectations, I am deeply regretful and immediately take steps to ensure the failure is identified and those responsible are disciplined. And, yes, several recent ventures have generated rather bad publicity. Which is precisely why I am here! This expedition is low-risk and, in my opinion, has a good chance of success. If it fails, the worst that happens is your show gets a couple of well-funded, entertaining episodes. And if it succeeds, I will be bringing to light one of the greatest discoveries in the history of mankind."

"My *father's* discovery," Sarah said.

Cameron's smile flickered, but it quickly returned to full grin. "Of course. Without his story, we wouldn't even be here, but I will provide the world proof. Undeniable proof. A live, captive Bigfoot!"

"*If* we can do so without injuring the animal," Sarah asserted.

"Yes, of course. All precautions will be taken," Carson reassured her. "There are a bare minimum of lethal firearms in camp, and the capture team will be armed with a combination of tranquilizer rifles, net guns, and electrified catch poles. The animal will be sedated and secured in a rubberized carbon steel cage. I have every intention of procuring a live, uninjured Bigfoot."

Carson clapped his hands together and rubbed them briskly. "All right, then, I think we've done enough for now. Dr. Bishop—Sarah—if you would get your team up to speed on our plans? And Joseph, perhaps you and Russ could combine your tracking skills for a little reconnoiter around the immediate area? Assess each other's strengths and weaknesses?"

Russ and Joseph looked at each other, and a ghost of a smile curled the Shoshone's lip. "Sure. Could be fun."

"Sounds good," Russ said. "There's actually something I want to check out on the trail we came in on. I need to go over a couple things with Sarah first, but I'll meet you at the south side of camp in twenty minutes."

Joseph nodded and sauntered out the tent flap. After saying their goodbyes to Carson and Jaeger, Russ and Sarah followed.

Jaeger made no move to leave. "Don't you have preparations of your own to attend to?" Carson asked.

The Afrikaner hunter rose lazily from his chair and stretched. "The Bishop girl was quite adamant 'bout not harming the Sasquatch."

"And we won't. I'm counting on you to dart our quarry so we can capture it without injury."

"Fair 'nuff. So long as you remember the other part of the bargain. You find a Bigfoot, you get what you want. But if there's more than one… I get what *I* want."

As Sarah and Russ headed back to Sarah's tent, Russ thought about the journal and what had happened to her father. "Sarah… after your father was let go from the university…"

"Fired."

"All right, fired. After he was fired, what happened? I heard he fabricated evidence before he…" Russ trailed off.

Sarah stopped walking. She sagged, and there was a hitch in her breath as she sighed deeply. "My father made a mistake. He shouldn't have done it. I know *why* he did it, but…" She lapsed into silence.

"What exactly did he do?"

Sarah resumed walking, "Come on. I need a drink."

They reached her tent, and after setting her father's journal on a camp table, Sarah went straight for a compact trunk by her cot. Extracting a bottle of small batch bourbon and a pair of stainless steel highballs, she pointed to a camp chair.

"Sit."

As Russ sat, she poured a couple fingers and offered one to Russ. When he took it, she poured some for herself and dragged a chair next to his, setting the bottle on the ground. He raised his glass and said, softly, "To your dad."

Sarah looked at him, moisture in her eyes. She raised her glass. "To Dad."

They drank. The bourbon was good, not too sweet. Russ simply sat and waited, giving Sarah all the time she needed. Finally she downed the rest of hers and set the empty highball in the little cup holder in the arm of the camp chair.

"My dad went back to the site of his accident over and over. He never found any tracks, and no one ever answered his vocalizations. In the creek, he found that boulder he had talked about; any signs of the poultice were washed away. Dad was convinced the alpha had dragged it there. He found the spot he'd fallen from and located his cell phone halfway down the cliff. Once it was recharged and powered it up, he found the photo he'd taken when he fell. Unfortunately there was no Bigfoot in it—just treetops and sky. The branch he was holding must have given way as he took it. He told me about finding the phone, but it turns out I was the only one he mentioned it to; there being no photo in it, I think he figured it would hurt his case. My father began researching other Bigfoot sightings, interviewing witnesses and examining evidence. He took particular interest in the Patterson-Gimlin case. You've seen that film?"

"Yes. And I remember reading an article your father wrote about it. He thought the film was real but the tracks were faked?"

"Yes. He felt the men who shot the film wanted more evidence to bolster their story, so they created the tracks. The Forestry Service rangers who first arrived on the scene didn't find any footprints, but when they returned several days later, all of a sudden there were tracks. Dad never proved the prints were a hoax; it was just his opinion. He went on to support or debunk several other sightings, but he always came back to his own encounter. Brighteyes never left his mind, and he continued to travel to the site of his accident. His work at the university was suffering, and he was taking more and more time off. He should have requested a sabbatical, but he'd already taken one the year before and, in all honesty, the administration was probably tired of all the Bigfoot talk. So they fired him.

"I don't think he really cared. He had undergone the most life-changing experience imaginable and no one believed him. I remember one particular conversation. He was seething with frustration. He said, 'Dammit, Sarah! There should be proof! I had an experience unlike anything anyone has ever had. After everything I went through, everything I shared with Bright-eyes, all the time we spent in that location, there should have been *something*! It's not fair.'

"And so… since there was no evidence, he decided to manufacture it. He purchased a Bigfoot cast and made several imprints beside the creek bed near the boulder he was certain the alpha had moved. By then he already had a new cell phone, and he took several photos of these prints. Then, taking his old phone to the top of the drop-off, he staged a photo of a dense copse of trees. He hired someone to Photoshop a furry figure deep in the trees; no face or anything, just a hint of something standing upright. The next day, he brought this photographic 'proof' to a local news station, claiming he'd found his old phone with a photo taken right before the accident and that he had also found fresh prints by the creek. The station ran with the story."

Sarah sighed and was quiet for a moment. She grabbed the metal cup and poured herself another drink before offering the bottle to Russ.

He shook his head. "Better stay sober. I got a date with the world's greatest tracker, remember?"

Sarah smiled and set the bottle down before continuing. "My father was a brilliant professor of anthropology with an astonishing wealth of knowledge of Native American lore and ancient woodcraft… but he didn't have it in him to pull off a hoax. He spent his life in pursuit of truth, and when he turned to fakery, I think a part of him wanted it to fail.

"And fail it did. Within a week, we had Bigfoot enthusiasts coming out of the woodwork, declaring the tracks to be fakes. They recognized the cast and pointed out that all the 'good' prints were left feet. He had made five tracks: three left and two right. The right prints were flat and indistinct; he'd inverted the cast when making those. And there aren't many places that sell Bigfoot casts, so it didn't take long to find out that one of them had shipped a replica to my father."

A wave of guilt washed over Russ. "Sarah, that prank I pulled…"

She smiled halfheartedly and waved his apology off. "It's OK, you didn't know. It was a Patterson-Gimlin, wasn't it?"

"Yeah, molded out of foam rubber," Russ admitted sheepishly. "I screwed it onto a squeegee handle. Anyway, go on. What about the photo?"

"The photo was declared to be a hoax as well; the signs of alteration were well hidden but detectable. And finally, when the reporter from the station my father had approached came to dad's home and asked him if he could show her the photo on the actual cell phone, my father simply closed the door in her face. The local news ran a retraction, complete with some interviews with a couple Bigfoot 'experts' who mocked my father for the incompetent hoax. That night, my father…"

She trailed off and Russ leaned forward and placed a hand on her forearm. "I'm sorry, Sarah. Look, you don't have to—"

"It's all right. Need to finish." She sighed and continued, "My father had a lot of pain medication and he took an overdose. The ME thought it might have been accidental, but I know it wasn't. His experiences in the woods—his injuries—they changed him. He knew, after that retraction, that no one would ever believe him. When they found him, they found his journal and the old map from our camping trip on his desk. There was a single sheet atop them with just my name on it."

"But why? Why did he fake the evidence?"

Sarah shook her head. "I'll never know for certain, but I think maybe the reason was simple. My father saw a Bigfoot, was saved by him, communicated with him. He wanted nothing more than to share that experience with the world and was devastated when he couldn't find any proof that it happened. Why did he fake the evidence? I think he just wanted to be believed."

Sarah's eyes glistened with moisture and Russ looked into them. "Well, he succeeded. At least as far as I'm concerned. I believe him." She smiled at him as a single tear broke free. He stood and gently brushed away the tear with the back of a finger. "I gotta meet Joseph. Maybe we can find some of that evidence your father needed."

Brighteyes looked into the glade and spotted what he was looking for: a small cluster of camas plants growing in a patch of sun. Silk had wanted to remain near Silverback and had asked him to handle the foraging. He was happy to oblige. When Silverback was in a foul mood, Brighteyes tended to pick those times to melt away into the forest. The bite on the alpha's hand by a defeated enemy had likely bruised his considerable ego, and the minute he felt better, he would take it out on Brighteyes.

After a minute of sniffing the air and listening intently, Brighteyes decided he was alone and broke from the cover of the trees, heading into the glade. Gently setting down his double handful of huckleberries and acorns, he crouched and began digging up several bulbs, being careful to leave most of the younger plants. They had a unique flavor, but they did tend to cause flatulence; Littlefoot considered that a plus. Brighteyes chuckled to himself, but the laughter died off as he looked at the camas bulbs he'd harvested. They had been one of his mother's favorite foods. She had taught him where to look for them, bringing him with her on foraging trips. It was on one of those trips that tragedy had struck.

Brighteyes expelled a shuddering sigh. Still holding the bulbs, he sat down heavily in the glade. It had happened in a patch of grass and flowering plants much like this one. Brighteyes had always been an adventurous youngster, curious to a fault. His occasional encounter with humans was a source of particular fascination; it was so clear that those strange pinkish bipeds were related to the forest folk in some way. Silverback had been stern to the point of violence when he'd first heard that Brighteyes had been seeking out humans, but the young Bigfoot just didn't see the harm. Humans almost never saw him, and they were so clumsy in the woods that it was easy to spy on them with little risk.

But this wasn't the case that one fateful day. His mother, Sky, had taken him with her on a foraging trip. As she'd gathered camas bulbs in a glade, Brighteyes had gone exploring, capering through the surrounding trees. With a Sasquatch's keen hearing and sense of smell, he could range quite far and not lose track of where Sky was. It wasn't long before he'd come across a human in the near distance. He was stalking a deer! But he wasn't carrying one of those boom-sticks that most hunters carried; he had a bow. Silverback had told him about those. Long ago the native humans from the area had used these weapons. It was basically a big curved stick that threw a smaller pointed stick at high speeds. He had never seen a human hunt with a bow before, so he crouched and watched.

The human moved very slowly and quietly, drawing closer to the deer, a young buck. At one point, the animal had tensed and raised its head. The human froze, waiting patiently. When the deer went back to foraging, the hunter took two quiet steps to the side before raising and drawing the bow. There was a moment of terrible stillness, and then a wooden shaft rushed from the bow and buried itself above and behind the deer's foreleg. It bolted, running a short distance before collapsing with a shudder.

Brighteyes was so astonished he uttered an excited hoot. The human's head whipped around in his direction, and he quickly ducked behind a tree and froze. After a moment, he peeked back around the tree. The human was gone! The deer lay still; why wasn't the human going to claim it? Feeling uneasy, he scampered off into the forest, heading back to where he'd left Sky.

When he reached the glade, his mother was just finishing her camas gathering, smiling at her offspring's excited approach. Brighteyes gestured and vocalized wildly, pointing back from where he'd come. 'Human! Hunter! Kill deer!'

The smile melted from her face. 'We go! We go!' She began loping toward the far tree line, pausing to make sure Brighteyes was keeping up. As they reached the safety of the trees, there came a whistling sound and a loud thunk. Brighteyes looked up and saw a quivering arrow buried in a tree next to his mother; looking back, he saw the human. The hunter was setting another shaft on his bow.

'Run!' Brighteyes grunted. They ran into the forest. No human could keep up with a Bigfoot; soon they would be safe. There was another whistling noise.

Sky screamed. Brighteyes looked up to see an arrow sticking through his mother's shoulder. Brighteyes cried out with concern, but she kept running. They fled for their lives. The hunter did not follow.

By the time they reached the troop, Sky was having trouble breathing; the arrow had nicked a lung. Silverback removed the shaft and the family did their best to save the alpha's primary mate. Silk, a younger female, applied a poultice of various medicinal plants, but by then it was too late. There had been too much bleeding, and his mother passed away that night.

Silverback had blamed him for the encounter with the human and had beaten him near to death. Only Silk's intervention had saved him. What was worse, the alpha was right. He had let that hunter see him, had led him right to his mother. *Humans are dangerous.*

Leaving his memories behind, Brighteyes swam back to the surface of his thoughts, returning to the now. His eyes were full of tears, and in his hands was a mashed pulp of camas. *No,* he thought. Some *humans are dangerous. But some are friends. Like the hair-faced one I spent time with.*

Brighteyes gathered the acorns and berries on top of the mashed camas bulbs and carried the handful of nutrition back to the troop.

13

Already running late for his rendezvous with Joseph Washakie, Russ decided not to go back to his tent and unpack his camera gear. This would probably just be a quick jaunt, anyway. As Russ approached the southern edge of the clearing, he spotted Joseph napping at the base of a big oak and decided he'd have a little fun with the legendary tracker.

Russ moved laterally and reached the trees a hundred yards behind the oak. He could see the Shoshone's cowboy boots, one foot crossed over the other. *OK, time for a silent stalk.* Russ was quite skilled at moving stealthily through the forest and had once snuck up on a peccary in an Amazonian rainforest, getting into spear range without ever alerting the animal. Keeping an eye on the oak, he moved closer and closer, finally reaching the thick trunk. Silently counting three he tensed, then jumped around the left side of the big oak.

"Howdy, Joseph!" he called out loudly.

There was no one there. *Impossible, I only lost sight of his boots in the last few seconds! How could he have—*

A hand clapped him on the shoulder, and Russ jumped. "Howdy, yourself. That was some excellent stalking, Russ."

Joseph had just *appeared* behind him. He must have moved with blinding speed, and Russ hadn't heard the slightest rustle. "How did you…?"

Joseph smiled a crooked smile. "All us Indians are magic, I thought you knew that."

But Russ had already spotted a partial boot heel print to the right of the trunk. He knelt, touching his fingerprints to the track. "You must've moved when I moved. Came around the trunk behind me."

"Very good. You spotted that quickly." Joseph raised his boot and looked at the sole. He sucked his teeth. "I'm getting sloppy." He plucked an acorn off the ground and started off toward the trail that ran to the south. "C'mon, Survivor Guy. Let's go see what we can see."

"Sure thing, Kemosa—"

Thwack! As soon as Russ uttered the *k* sound, Joseph spun and flicked the acorn from his fingers, bouncing it off of Russ's forehead. "Ow!"

"Kemosabe is an Ojibwe word. I'm Shoshone. Every time you call me that, I'm going to bounce an acorn off your head."

"Kemosabe means 'one who looks secretly.' You're a master tracker who just snuck up on my dumb ass, so I hope you got a lotta acorns. If the boot fits…"

Joseph's impassive face burst into a huge grin. "I think I'm going to like you, Russ. OK, 'Kemosabe' is fine. But if I ever hear 'Tonto' leave your lips, I'll kick you in the *wea.*"

Russ laughed. He sounded out the word: "Way-ah. Did you just teach me a Shoshone naughty word?"

Joseph just smiled and headed south toward the trail. They soon reached the spot where Russ, Sarah, Liz, and Bud had hiked, and Joseph stopped. He scanned the trail and stooped, coming up with a wad of gum, which he inspected and sniffed. "Ahh… Juicy Fruit."

"That would be Liz, Sarah's assistant. Bit of a gum chewer."

"The petite one?" He glanced down and pointed. "There's one of her prints. And here… this is Sarah's boot print. She walks with a lot of purpose. The deeper one here belongs to the fat, bearded one… and this one? That's you." He stood back up and looked at Russ. "You're left-handed."

Russ stared at him in shock. "How? How could you tell that?"

"Simple," Joseph deadpanned. "I watched how you held the professor's journal when you read it." He lost his straight face and snickered as he strolled away. "You can't tell handedness from tracks, you asshat. Where did you learn woodcraft, *Last of the Mohicans*?"

They soon reached the location where Russ had spotted the tracks running perpendicular across the trail. Russ pointed out everything he'd gathered from his earlier examination and told Joseph about the roar that Bud had picked up on his parabolic mic.

"So, I'm thinking we follow the tracks. See if we can find these hikers. It looks like one of them might be injured… or drunk."

Joseph stood silently, an intense look of concentration on his face. Russ couldn't tell if he was listening or just thinking. Finally he turned and looked up the slope the footprints had come down.

"No. We should backtrack. Find where they came from."

"Why? We know they're probably down that way," Russ said, pointing to the west. "Why go in the opposite direction?"

"Instinct. Sometimes you have to follow what you *feel*… not what you see. I feel we need to go this way."

Russ shrugged. "All right, I'm game. Lead the way."

They made their way up the embankment to where the terrain rose gently to the east. The trail was easy to follow, the hikers having pretty much just plowed through the trees and brush.

"These have got to be the clumsiest pair of hikers I've ever seen. Maybe they were moving at night with no flashlight."

"Maybe," said Joseph, who plucked something from the low branches of a tree. It was a stocking cap.

"Who loses their hat on a branch and doesn't stop and grab it? They weren't running… the tracks aren't far enough apart." Russ stopped. *What did I see?* He took a few steps back. There—a stain on the point of a broken branch, at about eye level. *Blood?* He moved closer to it.

Joseph was focused on the cap. He sniffed it, frowned, then tossed it far away. He turned just as Russ was reaching out to touch the branch tip. "Stop!" he yelled.

Russ jumped, looking to Joseph. "Jesus! Indoor voice! Look here. I think one of them scraped their face on this branch."

"I think you're right. Don't touch it. Something is wrong."

Five minutes later, they came across a small campsite. There was a ring of stones with the ashes of a campfire on a small cleared patch of ground. A few cooking utensils were scattered beside it along with a pair of camp chairs. A green two-man tent stood on a bed of pine needles nearby, a sleeping bag poking out of the entrance, half in and half out.

"What's that smell?" Russ asked Joseph quietly.

"Death."

14

"Jerky?"

"What?"

Bud was chomping on a bag of jerky while Dhir made some last-minute adjustments to the software for the giant parabolic dish mic. He held out the bag and shook it. "Jerky. Help yourself, my man. It's teriyaki flavor. Super tasty."

"Is it beef?"

"Yeah…"

"Then, no." Dhir tapped the enter key with finality. "That should do it."

"Are we in business?" Bud asked, leaning down to look at the screen.

"Only one way to find out." He offered Bud a pair of headphones. "Have a seat. I'll test the rotation."

As Bud settled in and put on the cans, pulling up his own audio software on the computer station, Dhir sat beside him and fiddled with a pair of joysticks. "I'll start with one full rotation and then we can test the fine adjustments. Fingers crossed." He typed in a command and they both watched a small viewscreen showing an image of the dish. The dish oriented itself due north and tilted to a flat ninety-degree angle before beginning a slow rotation.

Bud listened intently as it turned a full 360 degrees. He picked up all sorts of sounds and was eager to finish the diagnostic and begin focusing on some of them. "Everything is coming through loud and clear."

"Let's test the manual controls. Got a bearing you want to play with?"

"Yeah, actually." Bud pulled up a side window with a digital map of the area that was linked to the dish. Thinking about those sounds they'd heard on the trail, he looked at the area south and west of the clearing and clicked the cursor on a random spot. It brought up range and bearing.

Dhir was leaning over, watching him. "OK, good… once you've got the location set, just hit this button here and it'll automatically track to your map point." Dhir punched the button and the Dhir Ear swung around to the southwest, the dish tilting down slightly. "It factors in the topography, too. That area is downslope, and it'll take that into account. It won't point at the ground, of course, so it will find the best unobstructed angle available."

Bud listened to the sounds. Nothing stood out at the moment. "So, how do I tweak the dish once I'm in the general area?"

"Roll over here," Dhir motioned. Dhir hated rickety camp chairs and had insisted on bringing in a few wheeled office chairs for the tech tent, complete with a rubberized floor mat to facilitate rolling. Bud trundled over to the joysticks. "The little one is for fine control. It can nudge the dish angle a little bit at a time. The one with the bulb top controls the mounting. Rotation is left/right and height up/down. Easy-peasy."

"Lemon squeezy."

Dhir laughed. "Never heard that part."

"I'm a wealth of useless knowledge," Bud said, taking a piece of jerky in his teeth and settling in to the controls. "OK, let's play." Taking hold of the joysticks, he got to work.

Sarah sat in a camp chair, going through her notes from the planning session with Cameron Carson. The man might be an egomaniac, but she had to admit he had a sharp mind and an eye for detail. The search plan he'd come up with was excellent. The Dhir Ear would scan for known vocalizations, and the drones with high-tech optics would act in tandem: the large one would search a wide perimeter while the smaller one, with its quieter engines, would move in to check out possible contacts.

Joseph and Russ would also lead small capture teams to search for tracks. If there was a Bigfoot troop within fifty miles, she was confident they'd find them; with luck, they might even find Brighteyes. She'd reviewed the pharmacological reports on the tranquilizer they were planning on using and it seemed to be the safest one available. If the capture turned lethal, she would never forgive herself. She was determined to prove to the world that her dad was telling the truth, but if a Bigfoot—*or Brighteyes*—died in the attempt... her father would probably come back from the grave and kick her ass.

Liz came into the tent with a huge green smoothie. "The cafeteria tent is *huge*! They had a whole juicing section. I got a mango carrot wheatgrass. Want one?"

"No, thanks, I'm good." Sarah had been impressed with the mess tent and was looking forward to grilled salmon for dinner; she loved salmon but never cooked it at home because it always stunk up her little kitchen. Sarah watched with amusement as Liz removed her ever-present gum, looked at the smoothie, then smushed the gum onto the side of the cup and took a long pull on the straw.

"Oh yeah. That's good." Liz basked in fruit-'n'-veggie heaven for a moment before coming over to Sarah. "Can I do anything for you, Dr. Bishop?"

Sarah had given up trying to get the young intern to stop with the whole Dr. Bishop routine. It seemed like only a few short years ago that Sarah herself had been an intern helping with an archaeological expedition in Nepal, but, yes, she was a "doctor" now. Dr. Sarah Bishop, professor of anthropology and great ape studies at USC's Jane Goodall Research Center. Still, she felt more like a young adventurer type than a stodgy dissertation-writing professor. Thank God for fieldwork.

The university had raised a collective eyebrow when Sarah had laid out her plans for this project, but then they'd learned a certain billionaire was footing the bill. When a large donation was dangled in front of the university's nose, it was decided that a search for a possible *Gigantopithecus* ancestor could fall within the realm of primatological studies. Within weeks, Sarah and her graduate assistant Liz were on a plane to Idaho.

Sarah pulled a sheet off her notepad and handed it to Liz. "Here, take this over to Bud. This is a list of grid coordinates for the first two search days. Have him plug those into his setup."

"You got it, boss!"

Liz bounded out of the tent, and Sarah stood and stretched. *Maybe I will go get a juice*, she thought. *Stroll around the camp a bit.*

Sarah stepped out into the late-afternoon sun. To her left, she could see the big parabolic dish just behind the tech tent. Occasionally it would turn or tilt a little. A moment later, one of the small camera drones took off and made a slow circle of the camp. Bud and Dhir were hard at work. Sarah paid a quick visit to the mess tent and got herself some fresh-squeezed orange juice. She exited the mess on the opposite side and noted a large, long tent. The mountainous bodyguard, Brick, and a couple military-looking types were standing in front of it.

That looks like a barracks tent, Sarah thought. After a moment, a man dressed in camo left the barracks carrying a long, black hard case. Sarah watched him go up to an adjacent tent where a man was standing, smoking a pipe. It was that Afrikaner hunter, Jaeger. The two men spoke briefly and Jaeger nodded his head toward the tent flap. The camo-clad man went into the tent before exiting it again, empty-handed. Sarah watched Jaeger finish up his pipe. Alarm bells went off in her head. *I'm going to have to watch that man.*

Willem Jaeger tapped the ash from his pipe and looked up at the sky. *Still a few hours of daylight.* Born on a large farm in the northwest corner of South Africa, not far from Kruger National Park, Willem Reiner Jaeger was descended from the earliest settlers of the Boer Republics. His father had been a renowned game hunter, and Willem had been hunting from a very early age, taking his first lion at the age of six. Since then he had traveled to every corner of the globe, hunting nearly every large animal known to man. He'd even learned to scuba dive and killed an eighteen-foot great white with a hand-load ten-gauge bang stick. Even with ear protection, he'd had ringing in his ears for weeks. Sharks, bears, tigers… and now, at last, a chance to hunt a monster of legend.

Jaeger ducked into his tent and went to the collapsible workbench he'd brought. Lying atop it was a custom-built tran-quilizer rifle. He'd practiced in similar terrain and successfully darted a huge grizzly with a factory-built animal control rifle, but the range was terrible. He might only have one shot at a Bigfoot, and he figured they'd be a lot smarter and a lot more skittish than a bear. His new weapon was a bullpup design, the magazine in the stock holding six 10cc darts. The ability to put multiple darts on target would be critical if they found an extremely large specimen. He had designed a cluster of four compressed air cartridges that could be selectively activated, one at a time or all at once. At full charge, he could almost guarantee a hit at two hundred yards in windless conditions and have a decent chance of a hit at three hundred if he arced the dart properly.

The selective four-pack would also allow him to dial back the velocity on a close shot to avoid injuring the animal. Carson had made it crystal clear that Jaeger's substantial payment was contingent on an injury-free capture. Jaeger checked the three magazines he'd loaded before snapping one into place. He peered at the little gauge he'd installed by the gas canisters; the needle was at full. Finally, he examined the short scope he'd snapped onto the Picatinny rail on top. He'd zeroed it earlier in the day and it seemed secure. Excellent. Jaeger was accustomed to simply killing what he hunted, but he did enjoy changing up his weapons for each hunt, and this one would present unique challenges. And, if they found *more* than one specimen…

Jaeger set the tranq rifle aside and picked up the locked hard case his friend had brought. He punched in the four-digit code and opened it. *There you are, my beauty.* Inside was a partially disassembled sniper rifle, a CheyTac M200 Intervention chambered for a .408 cartridge. The scope was already attached and zeroed; all he'd need to do is attach the barrel and extend the stock and it would be ready for action. He'd chosen this gem for three reasons. First, its accuracy was astonishing. Second, it was much lighter and less clumsy than most antimateriel rifles. And third, the brutal .408 round was sure to bring down a Bigfoot with a single shot. A fifty-cal would be overkill, he figured; but just in case, he'd loaded some custom-filled wildcat cartridges for a little extra punch.

Running his fingertips along the receiver, he hummed a throaty growl. He flipped the case closed and locked it. *Soon.*

15

"Hello? Anybody here?"

Russ and Joseph waited for a reply but were greeted with silence. The odor in the air was faint, but it was definitely there. Almost like rotting meat. Russ took a quick glance into the tent, but it was unoccupied. Joseph went to the campfire and placed a hand over it. Finding no heat, he scooped up some ash and let it sift through his fingers.

"The fire has been out for a long time."

Russ examined a tool belt next to a camp chair. It held several small hammers, picks, and brushes. Beside it was a cloth spread out on the ground with several small rocks arranged on it. There was a wide variety, including a split geode.

"Geologists?" Russ hypothesized.

Joseph looked around the perimeter of the camp. "There." He pointed to the base of a tree that stood on the top of a slight outcrop. A hole had been dug in the side of the outcrop, amidst the roots of the tree. A pickax and shovel lay nearby.

Looking up, Russ noted that the tree didn't look like any other tree he'd ever seen. It had the appearance of a cedar, but its branches were oddly twisted, patches of bark sloughing off like dead skin. He went up to it and reached out a hand to lay his palm on the trunk.

"Don't touch it," Joseph said calmly but firmly.

Russ froze and withdrew his hand. "What kind of tree is that?"

"I have no idea, but it doesn't belong here. Doesn't belong anywhere." Joseph crouched by the small excavation. The tree's twisted roots were gnarled in dense loops, almost as if the roots had shaped themselves around something about the size of a soccer ball. Whatever the object had been, it wasn't there now, but the shape of something spherical was quite apparent. A couple of the roots had been chopped through.

Russ looked over Joseph's shoulder. "They dug something out of there."

"Yes." Joseph rose and looked back toward the camp. The sun was low in the sky and the shadows were lengthening. His eyes went distant and he tilted his head, listening.

"None of the rocks laid out on that cloth were large enough to fit that weird root sculpture," Russ mused. He headed back to the camp. "Maybe in the tent."

Russ went to the tent opening and looked at the sleeping bag sprawled across the threshold. The top of it was outside, as if someone had crawled from the tent without getting out of the bag first. Russ looked inside the shadowy interior. On the left was a thin camp pad where the absent sleeping bag had been, and on the right was a second sleeping bag. At the back of the tent, he could see a faint greenish glow. Russ thought it might have been a dying flashlight pointing at the greenish fabric of the tent, but as he ducked inside, he could see it was emanating from a pouch lying between the pad and sleeping bag.

As he moved closer to the glow, he became aware of a sound: a barely perceptible humming that reminded him of the odd little hum that comes from some charger plugs, so faint it almost seemed like it was imaginary. And there, in the pouch, was a craggy, greenish rock. *A meteorite?* It gave off a faint glow, and as he reached for it, the humming grew louder. *It's like a single note... no, a beautiful chord...* The next thing Russ knew, he was lying on his back, looking up at the blue sky through the treetops. His thoughts were fuzzy, like he was awakening from a sound sleep.

"Russ! Look at me!"

"Wha... what happened?"

"I yanked your dumb ass out of the tent, is what happened."

"There was a rock... a green rock... and I heard... something."

"You heard it sing."

Russ sat up. "What? No. It was... humming... but it was almost like I was *thinking* the sound."

Joseph nodded. "Yes. I can feel it in the air. I know what this is, and we need to move away from it."

Russ took Joseph's offered hand and hauled himself up. Together they headed back down the slope toward the trail. Once they were about a quarter mile away, Russ stopped.

"OK, what on earth happened back there?"

Joseph was silent for a moment, sorting his thoughts. "There is an old Native American legend. Not from my people, but from the tribes near the Great Lakes. They tell of a rock that fell from the sky—a 'stone that sings.' Those who listen to its song for too long become mindless man-eating beasts. Cannibals. There are different versions of this tale, but they all involve a rock that sings a distant song and glows with a greenish light."

"A rock that fell from the sky... you mean, like a meteorite?"

"That would be my guess."

"Holy shit. It was right between their sleeping bags. They must have gone to sleep with that rock right beside their heads."

"It's just an old legend, but most legends come from a kernel of truth."

Russ looked at the sky. *Not long until sundown.* Russ thought about the trail the two had left—the uneven tracks, the lost hat. "We better follow their trail. They might be sick."

"You smelled the air in that camp. They are definitely sick."

Russ hesitated a moment. "Joseph, from what you remember of this story, do we *want* to find them?"

Joseph had no answer to that.

16

Brighteyes watched Silverback intently. The alpha's massive back shuddered with an occasional ragged breath. His breathing had become strangely irregular, almost as if his body was forgetting to breathe and then racing to catch up. The huge male was still sitting on the dead tree trunk, hunched over, his back to the troop. He had barely moved since they'd returned from the fight with the Alive-Dead not-humans.

The strange breathing was disturbing enough, but there was something else. The smell. It was a sickly-sweet aroma, like decay. Brighteyes thought of the odor on the two creatures from this morning and made a decision. They had to get away from Silverback. Leave him. Convincing Silk to leave her mate would be difficult, but he had to try. She would return any minute from her search for medicinal herbs.

Scratch was sitting behind Brighteyes, grooming him. Brighteyes turned, grunting his thanks to the teen Bigfoot before putting a hand on his shoulder. He vocalized softly, keeping his gestures small.

'Scratch. When Silk returns, we must go. We must go far.'

Scratch looked at Brighteyes, furrowing his brow. 'Why? Silverback? Silverback get better.'

Brighteyes shook his head. He had learned that gesture of negation from observing humans and liked it enough to teach it to the troop. 'No. Silverback not get better. He get worse.'

'But he is leader. He is father. He protects us. We should protect him.'

'Silverback is not Silverback. He is *other*. He will hurt family.'

Scratch was about to protest further when they heard Silk approaching. The female carried several healing plants. Little-foot clung to her back, riding her shoulders. He hopped off as she set the plants on the ground. Brighteyes rose and dragged Scratch over to her.

'Silk. We must go.'

Scratch pulled loose from his grip. 'Brighteyes says Silver-back will hurt us!'

Silk selected a handful of berries. 'Silverback is sick. I will heal his hand, but first he must eat.' She selected some huck-leberries from Brighteyes' earlier foraging foray; they were Silverback's favorite. Silk started toward the solitary figure, but Brighteyes grabbed her arm in a panic.

'No no no! There is danger!'

'He is my mate!' Silk growled, easily tearing her arm away. 'I *will* help him.'

Silk moved cautiously toward the alpha, who continued to sit unmoving on the fallen trunk. While Silverback hadn't been the most loving mate, he was a strong protector, and Silk would do her best to nurse him back to health. She came up beside him, holding a bunch of plump berries in the cupped palm of her left hand.

Brighteyes tensed, his hackles standing on end. Every instinct was telling him that this would end badly. He grabbed Littlefoot and pushed him into Scratch's grip, signaling the teen to hold the youngster. The three Sasquatch watched as Silk reached out to touch Silverback's shoulder.

Had Silk been able to see Silverback's face, she never would have touched him—never even approached him. His mouth was stretched wide in a mindless grin, eyes shining with madness. The Sasquatch that had been Silverback was no more. What sat on that log was a monster that had little memory of its previous life, no love of family, no thoughts, no feeling. All that remained was a terrible need to feed. Silk's fingertips brushed its shoulder, and the hunger awakened. It sniffed the air. *Meat.*

Silk chuffed softly and held out the handful of berries. Her mate responded with a long, low growl. The guttural noise built to a snarl as Silverback's face slowly turned to her, eyes glaring hungrily, lips pulled back from canines, teeth locked together in a feral grin.

Silk was momentarily frozen in shock, and a moment was all it took. The thing that had been Silverback lunged and snapped its jaws at Silk's hand, catching the pinky finger in its gnashing teeth. She cried out in fear and jerked her arm back, the finger tearing free from her hand. The beast slowly rose from the tree trunk, casually chewing the severed finger as he turned the rest of his body to face his prey. It was then that Brighteyes struck.

Brighteyes had known something terribly wrong was going to happen but also knew he might not be strong enough to prevent it. Earlier in the day, as his fear had begun to grow, he had found a large, heavy branch and kept it close at hand. As Silk started forward, he had pushed Scratch and Littlefoot behind him, hefting the branch in his powerful grip. When that terrible low growl had begun, Brighteyes had moved to close the distance, but he wasn't quick enough. He watched in horror as the thing chomped down on Silk's finger, tearing it from her hand. As she cried out and staggered away, Brighteyes tightened his grip on the branch and cocked his arms back. When "Silverback" rose, Brighteyes swung with all his might. The branch smashed into the creature's shoulder, the wood exploding into chunks from the impact. The blow spun its shaggy bulk around, sending it to the ground. Brighteyes grabbed the terrified Silk and pulled her along. 'Run!' he called out to Scratch, who scooped up Littlefoot. The four Sasquatch fled into the trees.

The massive beast rose clumsily to its feet, staggering as it worked to regain its balance. Its prey was escaping! It planted its feet and let loose a roar of rage and hunger, the terrible sound splitting the late-afternoon air and sending flocks of birds fleeing into the sky.

17

Willem Jaeger puffed at his pipe, enjoying the mild flavor of the Van Erkom tobacco. His brother in South Africa sent him a couple bags of Fox every month, and the aroma and taste always took him back in time. His father had smoked this blend and gifted this very pipe to him when he went off to university. Jaeger looked up at the sky. Dusk was not far off. Motion caught his eye, and he stepped away from his tent into the open. *There.* A cloud of birds, several separate flocks, were rising into the sky above the trees to the northwest.

Something spooked them. I wonder... Jaeger thought about the expedition schedule and shook his head. The methodical, grid-like search was going to test his patience. He longed for the hunt. The spot, the stalk, the kill. Something had startled those birds, and it might be worth taking a look. Probably an elk or a bear. *Excellent. An evening hunt will give me my fix. And if it's our mysterious quarry, even better.* Jaeger would relish a chance to solo-hunt the legendary beast. A last look to the northeast and he made his decision.

Tapping out his pipe, he looked toward the barracks, zeroing in on a poker game at a card table off to the side. Cameron had hired quite a few mercenary types for this expedition, and one of them was making a second salary, courtesy of Jaeger. Manfred was an old hunting pal, and Jaeger had made sure he was hired on. As the men finished a hand, Jaeger caught Manfred's eye and nodded his head toward his tent before ducking inside.

Jaeger put on his safari vest and belt, preloaded with some select gear. He grabbed the tranquilizer rifle, adding the spare dart magazines to his vest pockets.

Manfred came into the tent. "What's up, boss?"

"You and I are going to do a little recon. Hold this." He handed the tranq gun to Manfred then plunked the black hard case onto the table. Punching in the code, he opened it up and quickly assembled the CheyTac rifle.

"Expecting to kill something, boss?"

"Hope springs eternal, Manfred. Here, switch." He traded the sniper rifle for the tranq gun. "Best to keep up appearances. Pocket those extra mags." Jaeger went to the tent opening and looked out. A shirtless Brick was arriving at the barracks, toweling off his massive form after a workout in the weight room tent.

"I got my own gear back in the barracks. You want me to fetch it?"

"No, best not. Carson's five-ton flunky just showed up, and I'd rather we kept our little expedition a quiet two-man affair, *ja nee*? This way."

Jaeger led Manfred to the rear of the tent and the two men ducked out a flap in the back.

Bud finished inputting the last of the coordinates as Sarah entered the tech tent. Further back in the tent, Dhir was showing Liz his drone control station.

Bud spun in his chair. "Hey, Sarah, just FYI… I've picked up a few civilian groups out to the west and northwest. From the sound of it, maybe some hunters or campers… and I heard some kids singing a song. Maybe scouts?"

"I'm thinking we might not have the woods all to ourselves, after all. Did you let Carson know?"

"Yeah… he wasn't too happy about it. They're pretty distant, though. It actually helps eliminate a few spots, assuming Sasquatch will avoid humans. Anyhoo, I can begin audio sampling whenever you want. Where do you want me to start?"

Sarah looked at one of the screens in front of Bud that displayed a digital map. "That vocalization you heard on the hike—if you had to guess, where do you think that came from?"

Bud looked at the screen, scrolling and zooming the map a bit. With the mouse, he dragged a box around an area on the map. "Somewhere in here would be my bet. I wasn't pointed at the sound source at the time, so this would be a rough estimate."

Sarah looked at the area, south-southwest of base camp. The digital map overlaid the topography, and she scanned the numbers before pointing at a spot. "Here, the base of these two slopes. Probably a creek there. Take a listen along this contour."

As Bud began to punch in coordinates, a squeal of delight drew Sarah's attention to the drone station. Liz was gripping the joysticks like a gleeful kid, and Dhir was "helping" over her shoulder, his hands on hers.

"Easy does it. Nudge your right stick forward a little."

Sarah could hear the buzz of one of the smaller drones above the tent. The camera feed was excellent, the image very clear.

"OK, Liz… now let's gently rotate." He took her left hand and slowly pushed it to the right. "This is your yaw. Watch the monitor and you can see how fast you're turning."

Liz chewed her lower lip in concentration. Sarah looked at a larger set of controls off to the side. "Have you flown the big one yet?" she asked.

Dhir kept his focus on Liz's driving lesson as he answered. "No, not yet. I'll go install the fuel cells after dinner and we'll take her up first thing in the morning."

Liz giggled. "This is amazing! How am I doing?"

"You're a natural," Dhir replied. "Sarah, I might need to borrow your assistant from time to time."

But Sarah didn't hear him; she was focused on the camera feed. "Wait!" *There was something…* "Go back. Right… rotate right."

Dhir was about to take over, but Liz effortlessly rotated the image back.

"Stop. Right there. Dhir, can you zoom in?"

Dhir thumbed a scrolling wheel and the view shifted.

Sarah stared at the image. "That motherfucker…"

Liz glanced quickly back before returning her eyes to her controls. "Is that the creepy hunter guy?"

Cursing, Sarah grabbed her little pack and started for the exit.

"What's wrong?" Liz asked.

"Nothing I can't handle. Keep going with your flying lesson."

Bud set his headphones aside and started to get up. "You want me to go with?"

"No, run that audio scan. I'll be back shortly."

Sarah left and looked back toward Carson's tent. No time to find him and explain; besides, she'd prefer to handle this herself. She jogged toward the northwest tree line, the image from the camera feed vivid in her brain. Two men, one of them Jaeger, toting rifles and heading into the forest. After Dhir had zoomed in, it had been crystal clear that one of those rifles was no dart gun. She'd had a bad feeling about that man, and she listened to her instincts.

You are not *killing a Bigfoot, not if I have anything to say about it.*

18

"So… where did you learn to track?" Russ had been watching Joseph closely as they followed the trail of the two hikers and was amazed at the little details the man spotted. "I mean, I thought *I* was good…"

"You *are* good," Joseph replied. "One of the best I've seen." He stooped and looked at a spot on the ground. "Aha… Russ, what do you see here?"

Russ joined him and peered intently at the forest floor. "Nothing. I don't see a thing."

"Excellent. There was nothing there." Joseph's lips turned up in a half smile. "I think you knew that, but you've been doubting yourself. I've seen you hesitate before pointing things out to me. You have good instincts, Russ. Listen to them. Just because your ratings are down doesn't mean you're losing your touch."

"You've watched my show, you said. Watch any of my competition?"

Joseph blew out some air with a disdainful sound. "Which ones? Wolf Wallace's *Man vs Nature*? *The Naked Survivalist*?

Or *The Mormon Family Robinson*? They may have better show-manship, but those clowns don't have the survival skills you've got in your pinky. And all that phony urgency they put in… if I see the phrase 'The team must…' in the episode summary, I turn the channel."

"You still haven't told me where you learned how to track."

"Would you believe me if I told you my skills were passed down from a nineteenth-century Shoshone shaman to my grandmother and through her to my father?"

"Wow… really? No, wait… you're bullshitting again."

"Very good, grasshopper. See, your instincts are good. My father was a potato farmer. A very successful one… until his farm was destroyed by toxic runoff from a nearby Superfund site. An abandoned phosphate mine contaminated the ground water with selenium. Anyone eating those potatoes would probably wind up with selenium poisoning. We were living on the east side of the Fort Hall Reservation, and after the farm failed, we moved into town and worked on a relative's farm."

"So, you're a farmer?"

"No more than a kid who works a paper route is a journalist. It was just something I did growing up. As for the tracking, well… it started with chickens."

Russ chuckled. "You tracked chickens?"

"Nope. Weasels. And a coyote or two. A neighbor's chickens were being eaten, and I offered to help find the culprit. I learned I had a knack for it."

"So, you just sort of taught yourself?"

"Well, I did have some inspiration." Russ waited while Joseph looked at him for a moment with a deadpan expression. "Sherlock Holmes."

Russ started to laugh but stopped himself. "Oh, wait… you're serious."

"Growing up on the res, there wasn't a great deal to do, and it was a rare week for me that I didn't finish a book or two. I particularly enjoyed mystery writers, and Arthur Conan Doyle was a favorite. When I offered to help solve 'The Case of the Murdered Chickens,' it struck me how Sherlock's techniques were a perfect fit for tracking. Observation, deduction, and instinct. Once you know *what* to look for and have become skilled at spotting the signs, it becomes a simple matter of analyzing what you see and inferring what it means."

Russ had spotted movement above and glanced up through the tree canopy. "I'm observing a turkey buzzard up ahead. Deduction, Holmes?"

"Elementary, my dear Watson," Joseph said, equal parts playful and somber. "Something's dead."

19

The ravenous beast followed the scent of its former kin. With every passing moment, it gained greater control of its massive limbs, the earlier clumsy movement giving way to a savage grace. Despite this, its prey was outpacing it, and a mindless rage merged with the all-consuming hunger. Suddenly, the monster stopped and sniffed the air. Another scent. *Humans. Near.* It turned toward this newer, closer source of food. Despite its huge size, the creature moved quite stealthily on its padded feet. Though most of its mind was gone, it instinctively sensed a quiet approach would result in more meat. It sniffed the air again, pinpointing the humans. *Eat.*

"Randy. Keep your head down, bro," whispered a corporate douchebag named Trent.

"Sorry, man. Whoa… shouldn't've had those last two beers," slurred his slimeball coworker Randy.

"Where's your goggles, bro?"

"Aw, man, they sucked. I wanna be able to see those mutha-fuckers when I shoot 'em."

Randy and Trent were hunkered behind a fallen log, paint pellet guns at the ready. Somewhere out there were their two opponents. The boss of their startup hedge fund had decided to send them on a corporate wilderness outing for team building exercises. Apparently, shooting each other in the face with paintball guns would foster a competitive *esprit de corps*. The four young men had expected to go to some swank paintball resort, but their CEO had driven them to a remote rest area and told them to take a quick bathroom break. When they heard the SUV crunching away on the gravel, they rushed back from the trees to find four packs of gear and instructions. Basically: "Go out there and build some character!"

A hundred yards away, a white-collar sociopath named Chet and a narcissist asshat named Chad readied their weapons.

"OK, dude, I'm gonna flank those fuckers," Chad said quietly. "When I flush 'em, you light 'em up!" Chad played a lot of *Call of Duty* and thus believed himself a tactical genius.

Chet turned his perfect features toward his teammate and smiled impassively. *Chad is such an idiot.* "Roger that, buddy," Chet replied.

"Oorah!" Chad grunted loudly, destroying all semblance of stealth. He circled to the left, moving in a low crouch. *I am a fucking ninja*, he thought.

Across the way, Trent watched Chad's blond mop of hair bobbing through the brush as he tried to sneak around them. "That moron thinks he's a fucking ninja," he whispered to Randy. "Hold the fort, bro. I'm gonna bag me a junior partner."

Randy went for a fist bump, but Trent was already moving away. Randy popped his earbuds in and cranked up some Kanye West. He looked to the sky and noted the sun was getting low. *Happy Hour's almost over*, he thought. *Better gas up.* He pulled a can of cheap beer from a cargo pocket and tried to open it quietly. It made the same noise every beer can makes when you open it.

Randy, you idiot, thought Trent before realizing that Randy would make excellent bait for Chad. He hunkered down and waited.

Chad heard the beer can's *psht* and turned toward it, slowly raising his paintball gun. *Big mistake, pal. In war, you gotta keep your head.*

Unfortunately, Chad did not get to keep his head. A massive set of jaws, yawning wider than would seem anatomically possible, crunched down on the top of Chad's blond head, removing the crown of his skull and half of his brain. The ruined remnant of the Chadster collapsed to the ground.

The gigantic undead Sasquatch chewed the chunks of bone and brain and looked at the corpse. The urge to gorge was tempered by a rudimentary concept in its decaying mind: *No. First... kill all. Then eat all.*

Trent heard rustling from a very thick stand of brush, about where Chad should be. He leveled his gun. *Come to Papa, blondie.* There. The branches were moving. Trent applied a little pressure to the trigger. *Like shooting fish in a—WHAT THE FUCK IS THAT?*

A gigantic shaggy thing burst from the brush, striding right at him. Instinctively, Trent opened fire with a rapid burst, peppering the creature's hide with splotches of green. It didn't even flinch as the stinging pellets struck it, and Trent suddenly realized he didn't have an actual gun, he was shooting at this walking nightmare with a fucking toy. He turned to flee.

Pain was a thing of the past for Silverback. It ignored the little green things the human shot at it and reached its prey in seconds. As the man turned to run, the monster reached out and snagged his forearm, wrenching the entire arm out of the socket. The severed limb's hand, still gripping the paintball gun, clenched in a death spasm. As Silverback beat the Trent-meister to death with his own arm, the gun wildly spewed green pellets into the trees.

Chet heard Trent's death screams and immediately assumed it was a brilliant ploy to draw him into the open. *Nice try, Trent.* The psychopath-in-training hunkered down, waiting for a shot.

Randy didn't hear Trent's death screams because Kanye West was loudly singing into his ears about a "gold digger." But while Randy didn't *hear* anything amiss, he did *see* something. Two splats of green paint smacked into the log he was crouched behind. *Green. Wait. Aren't we green?* He removed his headphones and yelled, "Hey, Trent? Are we green?" as he turned toward where he'd last seen Trent.

Something sailed through the air toward him, and Randy reflexively reached out and caught it. It was an arm. *Wha...?* He looked up from the arm to see a massive apelike horror crashing through the trees toward him, its jaws dripping with blood. "Ahhhhh! Devil monkey!" Randy screamed. Before it reached him, Randy vaulted over the log and ran. "Chet! Chad! Omigod, help!"

Chet coolly sighted along his paintball gun as Randy ran headlong toward him. *Another feeble ploy*, he thought and popped off a single aimed pellet. The missile went straight into Randy's unprotected eye. "Aiiieeee!!" Randy screamed, his vision blurred with neon green. Blinded by pain and paint, he continued his headlong rush, stopping only when he collided with the stout oak tree right beside Chet.

Chet rose from his hiding place. *Damn, that was a good shot.* He went over to the stunned Randy. "You should have worn goggles," he said matter-of-factly. More rustling in the brush, coming this way. *Trent, you're making this too easy.* Chet crouched and raised his weapon just as a huge mass of fur and fangs tore through a bush. *That's not Trent* was the last thought the Chetolator had before his head was ripped from his shoulders. His goggles did not help him.

The Randy-man didn't have to wait long before joining his friends. A foot the size of a skateboard pulped his head into the forest floor.

20

"**...a**nd the good news on that front is that the astronaut's families have finally agreed to our countersettlement."

Bill Singleton looked up from his digital tablet at Carson. The dapper little man had exchanged his immaculate suit for a pair of chinos and an expensive dress shirt. *At least he's rolled the sleeves up,* Carson thought. "Excellent. I was hoping that whole debacle would just... go away." Carson paused before sighing and asking, "Where is the spacecraft now?"

Singleton tapped the screen a couple times. "Just over two million miles from Venus. The craft is not expected to enter the planet's gravity well and the sun will not be in its trajectory."

"Deep space, then."

"Yes, sir." Carson spun his forefinger, signaling Singleton to continue with the list. "Item three: the Mosquito Eradication project. Additional mutations have occurred and—"

"Skip that item."

"Yes, sir. Item four: the preorders for the new Maiden Tablets have exceeded expectations. However, the engineers still haven't quite figured out a few bugs with the photovoltaic charging case."

"Dammit, that solar charger cover is the whole draw for the thing! Without that, it's pretty much the same as the last BrightPad!" He gestured at the tablet in Singleton's hands. "Is that the prototype I gave you?"

"No, sir, this is the previous model."

"Why the hell are you using that? Where's the newest demo model?"

"It spontaneously combusted, sir."

Carson stood up and paced. "Fire the head engineer and promote whoever seems the least incompetent. Is there an item five?"

"Yes, sir. The publisher for your latest autobiography would like you to come to New York to record the audiobook."

"Oh dear God, I don't want to do that."

"Sir, they were quite adamant that titles sell better when the author does the narration."

"I don't care. I don't wanna sit in an airless booth for four days hoping my stomach doesn't rumble. Get some celebrity to do it. Billy Bob Thornton, he's good. Ooh! Or that guy that played that cranky doctor, House. I like his voice. Get House to do it."

"Hugh Laurie is British, sir."

"So? Have him talk like House."

"I'll see what I can do. Oh, and you asked me to look into the civilian activity to the west?"

"Yes. What the hell, I thought we had this whole forest to ourselves, and then that audio engineer tells me there are several groups traipsing about."

"Yes, sir. I've determined that the Park Service opened up a new series of trails just last week. It was buried on a website and I'm afraid we missed it."

"Well, make sure to let the men know. Last thing I need is some trigger-happy mercenary tranq-darting a Cub Scout."

Just then a ruined voice crackled from the front of the tent. "Mr. Carson, it's Brick."

"Come on back, Brick."

The tent flap split apart as the colossal man pushed through into the main part of the tent. A woman in a tank top and camo pants entered with him, her bare arms and neck festooned with lurid tattoos. Each of them carried a duffel bag.

"Mr. Carson," Brick rumbled, "this is Katya Volkov. She's the expedition armorer. We've brought the capture gear you requested."

"Ah, good. Use the map table there. Bill, why don't you grab some dinner? Bring me back a wrap or something."

As Singleton bustled out of the tent, Brick and Katya plunked their duffels down on the long table and began extracting various items. While Brick started screwing together several thin lengths of metal pipe, Katya held up a bulky rifle with an odd cone at the end of the barrel. She spoke, a pronounced Russian accent forcing Carson to listen carefully.

"This is a net gun." She picked up a small black cone with a semiopaque end; Carson could see a bundled net within. Katya snapped it into place within the odd-shaped barrel. "The net is propelled with a powerful burst of compressed air. The shape of the barrel imparts a spin, and the net will unfurl and entangle its target with the help of several peripheral weights. It is shit at anything other than close range, but anything it envelops will have a hard time getting untangled. The net is

made of polypropylene mesh—very difficult to cut or break."
She removed the net cartridge and turned to Brick, who was
modeling a long pole with a noose at one end and a trigger
grip at the other. "Brick?"

"This is a catch pole—though the boys are calling it a shock
pole. You loop the noose around an animal's neck or limb…"
Katya held up a tattooed arm and made a fist, and Brick "captured" her arm. "You give it a pull and the noose pulls taut.
Now, here's the fun part. Take a look at the end of the pole,
close to Katya's arm."

Carson leaned in and spotted two small metal studs on the
tip of the pole. "What am I looking at?"

"Those are electrodes, positive and negative. If you need to
enforce compliance on the trapped animal, you push the pole
against the critter"—Brick pressed the pole tip against Katya's
arm—"and you pull this trigger."

"Do it and I kill you," said Katya impassively.

"She would, too," Brick chuckled. "Triggering the shock
pole generates thirty thousand volts. We had the techies amp
the juice up from what it's usually set at. It can run contin-
uously for about twenty seconds. Should cause the animal's
muscles to seize and may even knock it out."

"But it won't kill it," said Carson, more of a statement than
a question.

"Not likely; it is just a scaled-up version of a Taser," said
Katya, freeing her hand. "I tested it on Brick. He was fine."

"Still wish you'd given me a little more warning," he grumbled, setting down the pole and retrieving a lightweight rifle,
which he handed to Katya before diving back into the duffel
and coming up with what looked like a target pistol.

"These tranquilizer guns will be our main mode of capture," Katya said, holding up the rifle. It was very simple in construction, with a short scope on top and a small compressed air canister in front of the trigger guard. "The rifle is accurate up to seventy meters, the pistol half that. We will be using a common tranquilizer used by zoos for larger primates."

"How long does it take for a dart to have effect?"

"Depends on the size of the animal. One dart might take twenty minutes or so. Multiple doses will increase the effect, but too many could be lethal."

"Then make sure we've got strict trigger discipline with those. If anyone kills my Bigfoot, they're gonna wish they'd never been born. You have collected all contraband weaponry? I know mercs love their toys."

"Yessir," Brick rumbled. "Most of the men had followed your instructions, so there wasn't much. One fella refused to give up his Tavor assault rifle, so I was forced to disassemble it with the help of his jaw."

"Is he hurt badly?"

Katya snickered knowingly and Brick shrugged. "They got soup in the mess tent; he'll be fine."

"There are only a couple shotguns and hunting rifles in camp in case of bears," Katya said. "Brick and I will carry sidearms, but only to use as a last resort."

"What about Jaeger? What is he using?"

Katya's eyes shone and she practically salivated as she described the special tranquilizer rifle the Afrikaner had designed. "It is a thing of beauty. He was supposed to be here for this briefing, but we couldn't find him."

"Fuck 'im," Brick growled.

21

Brighteyes signaled the troop to stop and hunker down in the lee of a huge tree. He could no longer detect their pursuer's scent and was pretty sure they'd lost Silverback. Except it wasn't Silverback, not any longer. Whatever it was, they had to get away from it, and he had been pushing them at a breakneck pace. Scratch and Littlefoot gratefully sat on the ground, but Silk kept going, as if she hadn't heard him. She had been in a great deal of pain from the bite, but in the last span of time she had ceased gripping her wounded hand and had become less communicative. Brighteyes went after her and gently touched her arm. She stopped and looked at him in confusion.

'Brighteyes?'

'We rest. You sit with Scratch and Littlefoot.'

She allowed herself to be led to the tree where she sat heavily. Brighteyes knelt beside her.

'Tired,' she grunted.

Brighteyes looked at her hand and caught a whiff of an odor that sent a chill through his body. *No. Not Silk.* He rose and took hold of Scratch's shoulder. 'Watch Silk. I get medicine.'

'Silk is sick,' Scratch responded. It wasn't a question.

'Yes. We will make her better.'

Brighteyes headed back the way they'd come. Perhaps it wasn't too late; the bite had occurred not long ago. He'd seen the yellow flowers of the yarrow plant a little ways back; he quickly found the spot and tore up several plants, shoving some of the leaves into his mouth. Chewing, he returned to the family and handed some yarrow to Scratch; together they prepared a paste of the medicinal plant. Silk sat quietly, her eyes distant, her ragged breathing all too familiar.

Brighteyes cupped the mass of chewed yarrow in one hand and gently gripped Silk's wrist with the other. 'Silk?'

Silk didn't look at him but knitted her brow at the sound of his voice. 'Silk. Yes. I am Silk,' she rumbled.

Brighteyes took a deep breath and drew her wounded hand closer. He knew that putting a mass of yarrow right onto the torn stump of her little finger was going to be extremely painful, but it had to be done. Whatever happened to Silverback was happening again, and he had to stop it.

'I am sorry,' he said and pressed the poultice onto the wound, tightly gripping her hand in his.

Silk's powerful muscles tensed and her eyes went wide. Brighteyes held on for dear life as she bared her teeth, tilted her head back, and let loose a tremendous roaring scream.

"What the hell was that?" Manfred asked in wide-eyed awe.

"Shh!" Jaeger hissed, raising a hand to signal "stop."

They stood in silence, listening intently. Again, a screeching roar echoed through the trees. This time Jaeger was able to estimate distance, but due to the terrain, he knew it was too far away to get an accurate bearing. Somewhere to the west and maybe two miles away, but that was a very rough guess.

When there was no third roar, he turned to Manfred and eyed the CheyTac he carried. "Chamber a round, Manfred. We're going hunting."

Manfred racked the slide and double-checked the safety. "What the hell *was* that?" Manfred asked.

"That was no animal I've ever heard in my time on this earth. My guess is that's our Bigfoot."

"Your guess would be right," said a feminine voice from behind them.

Manfred jumped but Jaeger simply turned and looked at her as she came around a tree about twenty yards back. "You've a light step, Dr. Bishop. I thought I heard something but figured it was a squirrel. It's nearly sundown; what exactly are you doing out here?"

"I could ask you the same question," Sarah said as she approached them, a determined look on her face.

"Reconnaissance."

"Really?" She held his gaze and pointed to the rifle in Manfred's hands. "Well, then, you won't be needing that."

Jaeger gave her a brittle smile. "Come now, Dr. Bishop—there are bears in these woods. It's always prudent to bring adequate protection—"

"Then you should've brought a shotgun. *That* gun is for putting rounds through an engine block." Her voice took on a steely tone. "We are here to capture a Bigfoot. We will not kill one, not even *injure* one. That rifle goes back to base camp… now."

Jaeger admired the fierce determination in her eyes. "Or what? I take orders from Cameron Carson, not from you."

"If that rifle doesn't go back to camp, I guarantee you the next 'order' you get from Carson will be to tuck your safari hunter ass into a chopper bound for home, because he'll have to choose whether he wants me on this expedition, or you. And I guarantee it isn't gonna be you."

Jaeger knew she was right. Carson wouldn't even be here if it weren't for Sarah and her father. Furthermore, Carson wouldn't be too pleased to hear Jaeger had taken it upon himself to make a foray without his knowledge. He sighed.

"*Blerrie hell.* All right, girl. You win." He went over to Manfred and pointed him back toward camp, walking with him a ways. "Take the gun back to camp, put it back in its case, and lock 'er up." He leaned close and muttered, "Commandeer that large drone. Hook the case to it and be prepared to send it to my GPS coordinates. *Ja nee?*"

Manfred nodded. "Got it, boss," he said and headed back to camp.

Sarah watched Jaeger closely as he returned. He still had a high-tech-looking rifle, but she had noted the cluster of compressed air cartridges and knew it to be a dart gun of some kind. "Now what?" she asked.

"You know as well as I. If that was a Bigfoot call, I'm going after it. And I won't insult you by suggesting you go back. I know you'll just follow me. Besides, you clearly know your way around the woods, and I can always use a second set of eyes and ears."

Sarah thought a moment. She would have liked to have Russ or Joseph along, but they had gone off to the south. "Shouldn't we call Carson?"

Jaeger snorted. "The sun's going down, and by the time he gets a large group together and sends them tromping into the woods, we'll have found our quarry. You know as well as I, for an animal as elusive as this, less is more. If we need to call for assistance, we'll do it later."

"Fine." She thought a moment. "Sasquatch have an excellent sense of smell. We need to stay downwind, so we should—"

Jaeger chuckled, "I have done this sort of thing before, you know." He gestured. "We'll loop a little north and head toward the sounds from there. I take it you're familiar with the creature's calls. Anything you can tell me?"

"Yes, actually. That cry was unlike anything I've heard from one before, but if I had to guess, I'd say it sounded like it was in pain… or angry."

22

Russ and Joseph approached a clearing and both stopped dead in their tracks. They had easily followed the trail the two geologists had left, and it had led them straight to the clearing up ahead. What brought them up short was sound. More to the point, the absence of one sound—no birds, not a peep—and the presence of another—the buzzing of flies. Joseph slowly drew his large hunting knife, and Russ gripped the walking stick he'd found. Wordlessly they moved apart before stealthily entering the clearing.

Carnage. That was the only way to describe the scene that greeted them. There were bodies lying on the ground. Or what was left of them. Two bodies had been torn open, and it looked like something had been feeding on them. Intestines were protruding from one's body cavity. The flies were all over these two corpses, but as for the other two, they were completely devoid of flies. One corpse's head had been caved in and the other had no head at all. The odd decaying odor that had been present in the geologists' camp was here too. Noting a couple cameras on the ground, Russ bent to retrieve one but stopped suddenly when he saw what was next to the camera.

"Omigod. A Bigfoot track!"

Joseph was slowly scanning the clearing. "Yes. There are many." He pointed. "They came from the northwest and they returned the same way. Two individuals. One much larger than the other."

Russ examined a pair of tracks more closely. The light was fading fast, but he could still make out some features. "These scuff marks. They were running when they came into the clearing, walking when they left it." He looked at the corpses. "Do you think…?"

"I have never heard of a Bigfoot attacking a human. And there are no tracks beside those two," Joseph said, gesturing to the half-eaten shapes on the ground. "But these *other* two… yes." He pointed to a large track next to the headless corpse. Chunks of skull and brain matter were clearly visible within the huge footprint. "This one for sure."

Russ was crouching by the other one and examined a large club-like branch. It was coated in blood at the thicker end. "Looks like Bigfoot went all Captain Caveman on this one."

Joseph thought a moment. "I don't think those two were human any longer. At least they didn't smell human to the Sasquatch. Even the flies are avoiding them."

"We're out of our league here, Joseph. Better call Home Base." There was no cell signal out here, so Russ pulled out a little walkie he'd been issued. Nothing but static. "We're downslope here and probably out of range. You have a sat phone?"

"No, but maybe these men did." The Shoshone headed over to a couple packs lying next to the tree line that had probably belonged to the first two victims. He dug through them and found a couple hefty flashlights. "No phones, but these will come in handy. We can detour north, follow those Bigfoot tracks. That will bring us upslope and closer to base camp. We can try the walkie again then."

Russ sighed. "All right, Kemosabe. But do me a favor, put an edge on this with your pig sticker, OK? I'm feeling a little unarmed at the moment."

He handed over his walking stick and Joseph whittled it into a rudimentary spear as Russ stooped and picked up one of the cameras. The battery was dead, but the other one had a little juice left. He pulled up the last video and viewed it.

"Night vision camera. Holy shit, it's the *Spook Stalkers*!"

Russ watched the video. He couldn't stand those guys, but evisceration was a bit harsher than they deserved. He fast-forwarded a bit and watched as the camera swung away from some annoying selfies and focused on a staggering figure emerging from the woods. The camera operator offered assistance, but then the unknown man charged. A stream of liquid, probably pepper spray, came from behind the camera and hit it in the face, but it kept coming. The camera fell to the ground, and there was a lot of screaming. Russ rewound the video a few frames at a time and paused it when the attacker's face was nearly filling the screen. Though the greenish tint of the camera distorted the image somewhat, one thing was clear: that thing was barely human. Its face was twisted into savage rage, and the eyes were empty and feral.

"Umm... Joseph, the legend about that singing rock turning men into mindless cannibals...?"

In the gathering gloom, Russ turned the viewscreen toward Joseph, who looked at it closely before shining a flashlight beam on the bodies of the two geologists. "Looks like one legend took care of the other."

"Wait a sec. This camera still has some charge left." He quickly shot some footage of the bodies and the tracks before powering off. "Better save some battery in case we find our furry friends."

"*Friends…* let's hope so." Joseph handed Russ the simple spear he'd fashioned and began following the tracks into the tree line to the north. Despite the twilight shadows, the trail was not hard to see, the two Sasquatch not having traveled with their usual stealth.

Russ followed, stooping to pick up a small can of bear repellent. *Must've been what was sprayed in the video. Might come in handy, though I have a feeling bears are probably the least of our worries.*

23

Whatever had happened to Silverback was happening to Silk, and the change was occurring much more quickly. Brighteyes gathered up Littlefoot and handed him to Scratch. He hated leaving Silk here, but he couldn't risk her harming the two youngest troop members. He crouched by Silk but kept his distance. He chuffed softly and Silk slowly turned to him, her face at war with itself.

Silk's eyes went to the children and took on a mad gleam, her lips drawing back. 'Hungry,' she growled. Brighteyes tensed, but just as quickly the terrible stare evaporated and Silk gave him a desperate, sorrowful look. 'Go! Silk hurt you! Silk… not Silk. Go. Go!' She gripped her head in her massive hands and shrieked.

Brighteyes rose quickly and pushed Scratch and Littlefoot ahead of him to the south. 'Run!' he grunted. 'Run!' As they dashed into the trees, the shrieking continued.

"*Kak!* That's close." Jaeger crouched and unslung the tranquilizer rifle from his shoulder, flipping off the safety.

Sarah stopped and crouched low as well. The keening shriek was higher-pitched and more ragged than the last time, and there was something about it that filled her with fear. The two of them had circled through the woods, trying to home in on the first calls they'd heard. The sun was down now, but Jaeger had insisted they keep the flashlights stowed. Sarah was fine with that. Her night vision was pretty good and the moon was nearly full, so they could make out the trees ahead with little difficulty. They listened intently. Another shriek, farther away.

"It's moving." Jaeger gestured ahead and to the right. "Uphill, that way." He was about to move out when they were greeted with another sound, echoing through the night. Sarah furrowed her brow in confusion.

"What the… drums?"

"Drums?" asked Dhir.

Bud handed a second headset to Dhir. "Listen for yourself!" Bud had been zeroing in on a strange shrieking howl to the northwest when he'd started picking up the sound of drums.

Dhir put on the headphones and listened. "Bongo drums. I had a roommate who had some. I got a *new* roommate the next semester."

A new sound. "That sounds like a flute or something." Suddenly a shriek was heard over the headphones. "There's that vocalization again. What the hell is going on out there?"

Wavy Davey and Doobie leaned into their bongos, building to a crescendo. Moonpie warbled on her recorder, dancing like a satyr around the drumming boys and their little campfire, her dreads twirling. If they hadn't been playing so loudly—and toking so heavily—they might have heard an eerie screech emanating from the woodsy darkness.

Now, the screeching stopped. The creature that had been Silk ceased its cries of pain and madness and went silent, its brain now filled with *hunger*, the desire to *feed*. And there, up ahead—a small flickering light. In the recesses of Silk's twisted mind, the beast remembered. *Fire means humans. Avoid humans! Hide from humans!* Then the new instincts washed over those thoughts. *No. Eat humans.*

A final furious flourish and Wavey Davey brought his drumming to a stop.

Doobie thumped his drums a few more times, reflexes slowed from a generous helping of Purple Urkel. "Righteous," he slurred. *Time for a fresh roach.*

Moonpie ceased her twirling and tilted her face to the night sky, soaking up the moon's rays. "Can you feel it? The night *wants* us." Moonpie had enjoyed a hefty dose of ecstasy.

Wavey Davey wobbled to his feet. He'd been shrooming and had felt a bit of a freak-out coming on, but the furious drumming had brought it down to a manageable level. "Need to piss," he managed, staggering into the trees and out of the light of the fire.

"Don't let the night fuck you," Moonpie giggled.

Wavey headed down a little slope and noted a particular tree that he was pretty sure wanted him to piss on it. "Your wish is my command, tree." As Wavey released a stream of rainbows at the base of the tree, he became aware of a presence. Zipping up, he saw a large shape detach itself from another nearby tree and move toward him. It stopped a few feet away, looking down at him. Wavey could hear a deep, rhythmic breathing. *Whoa, these mushies are primo*, he thought. Wanting a better look at his vision, he dug a lighter out of his pocket and flicked a flame to life. A huge, gorilla-like face grinned down at him. It was so real. "Whoa, epic. O Monkey God. What wisdom do you have for me?"

Silk imparted wisdom in the form of a clawed hand, whipping across Wavey Davey's face, tearing deep gouges in his cheek and snapping his neck with a brutal crunching sound.

Back at the campfire, Doobie fired up a masterpiece of toke-itude, taking a deep drag of some Alaskan Thunderfuck. Moonpie was across the way, hugging a pine tree in a manner that was turning Doobie on. A twig snapped behind Doobie; Wavey was back. "Dude, you have got to try this Thunderfuck, man," he croaked, holding the smoke in. He offered the roach back over his shoulder, continuing to stare through the flames at Moonpie as she energetically communed with nature. Something took the roach. And his hand. Jaws clamped down, severing the hand to the wrist. Paralyzed with shock, Doobie could only stare at the geysering stump, drops of blood hissing as they hit the flames. He gathered air into his lungs to scream, but since they were already busy holding in the Thunderfuck, he burst into a brutal coughing fit instead.

Moonpie heard the coughing and looked back toward Doobie. She saw an immense, shaggy shape coming around the campfire. It was chewing on something bloody and was coming right for her, growling low in its chest. Terror broke through her rapturous state, and she instinctively gripped the recorder in her hand. Suddenly a phrase entered her mind: "Music soothes the savage beast." She raised the recorder and began to play.

Alas, the old adage was better phrased thus: "*Good* music soothes the savage beast." Moonpie had a tin ear and was downright terrible. While the first few notes seemed to momentarily calm the creature, the missed A flat enraged it. A powerful hand gripped the recorder and rammed it straight into the back of Moonpie's mouth, punching through and crunching the mouthpiece into the spine at the base of her skull. The night returned to blessed silence. Except for the eating noises.

The silver-backed monstrosity was devouring the last hedge fund employee when the grizzly showed up. Wildlife officials said there were no grizzlies in the area, but no one had bothered to inform this one of the fact. The huge bear had smelled the fresh meat and moved in to join the feast. It smelled the Bigfoot, and while its odor was a bit odd, the bear was not concerned. These gentle giants rarely ate much meat and always melted away into the forest when a hungry grizzly arrived on the scene. Confident and eager to feed, the big male grizz moved in. The Sasquatch did not run. It raised its blood-soaked face from the abdominal cavity of the carcass, a length of intestine dangling from his mouth as it chewed. Seeing the bear, it stared and began to growl, still chewing the guts. The grizzly stopped in its tracks, hackles rising. Something was very wrong with this Sasquatch; maybe it had that sickness that sometimes drove animals mad. Still, the bear's blood was up; perhaps an aggressive display would suffice. It rose on its haunches, standing over eight feet tall, and let loose a roar. The crouching beast chewed and swallowed its current mouthful before rising to its full height of nearly ten feet. It swelled its massive chest and bellowed a horrifying sound, half roar, half scream.

The bear dropped to all fours and ran. The ravenous creature kept screaming as it watched the bear flee. The big *juicy* bear, full of *fat* and *meat*. It gave chase.

Russ and Joseph reached a level spot and immediately saw signs of Bigfoot habitation. In the light of their flashlights, they could see more tracks, smaller than the ones they'd followed. One set looked to be quite small, about the size of a young man's. Joseph shined his light on a bedding of boughs and pine needles.

"A nest," Russ murmured in wonder, pocketing his flashlight and powering on the Spook Stalkers' camera to get some footage.

"Yes," said Joseph. "I've never actually seen one, but Dr. Bishop showed me pictures."

"Sarah said they're rare because Sasquatch always clean up after themselves, leave no trace. They must have left in a hurry."

Joseph aimed the flashlight beam at a dead tree trunk. Slowly he circled around it. "Blood. A pool of it here, next to a track from the large Bigfoot. And some more here." He pointed alongside the dead trunk.

Russ set aside his spear and joined him. Pointing the camera at the scene, he spied something on the top of the trunk in the camera's night vision. "Hair. A lot of it. Kind of silver-gray. We should collect some for Sarah," Russ said, reaching for it.

"I would not touch it." Joseph's cold voice stopped him.

"Why not?"

"Something is very wrong here. Can you feel it?" Joseph was following some tracks that led away from the tree trunk, heading to the northwest. "They were running. Why were they running?"

As if to answer the question, a roar sounded from the trees to the west. It was followed by the sound of something large crashing through the trees and brush, heading right for them.

"Incoming!" hissed Joseph, drawing his long knife. Russ looked at the trees nearby. Deciding there was too little time to climb, he dropped the camera and dug the flashlight and pepper spray from his pocket.

Another roar tore through the night. The sounds of an onrushing creature increased and a huge brown bear burst through the brush, coming up short at the sight of two humans and their flashlights. Russ aimed the bear repellent, but before he could depress the trigger, another shape appeared in the gloom and hurled itself onto the grizzly.

For a moment Russ and Joseph could only stare in amazement as a gigantic Sasquatch grappled with the powerful bear. Russ shined his flashlight beam on the struggle and a chill ran up his spine. The creature was clearly a Bigfoot, extremely large, probably male. It looked very much like the artistic renderings he'd seen, but there the similarities began to skew south.

Its silver-gray pelt was matted and patches of it had fallen out. There were several splotches of bright fluorescent green on its face and chest. *Paint?* Shining in the moonlight, blood coated much of its face and arms, and its eyes glowed with a mad gleam, its lips pulled back from savage-looking canines. The skin of its face seemed to be... rotting? And the stench... it reeked of decay, much like the smell in the geologist camp only many times worse. Sounds of feral rage gurgled from its massive vocal cords.

The shaggy horror managed to grab hold of the bear's upper and lower jaws with its powerful hands and began opening the grizzly's mouth beyond the point its anatomy would allow. The grizz tried to transition from fight to flight, but the Sasquatch's grip was too strong; the bear uttered terrified gurgling bellows as its jaw muscles started to split.

Joseph gaped and uttered a single word: "*Wendigo.*"

Russ blinked. "Umm... *now*! We go now!" He snatched up his spear as they turned and ran east toward the base camp, dodging trees and vaulting stumps. Behind them they heard a loud crunch and the sound of tearing flesh as the beast ripped the bear's head apart. Russ exchanged the repellent for his walkie-talkie. "Base camp! Base camp, do you read?"

25

Sarah and Jaeger could just make out a campfire through the trees. They were moving without flashlights, relying on the bright moon overhead. Whatever had been making that eerie call had gone quiet. The drums and some kind of horrible flute were also silent now, and voices carried through the night air, though they were not close enough to make out words.

Jaeger suddenly held up a fist. "*Skort!*" he hissed, slipping into his Afrikaner dialect. The word was apropos; it meant both "look out" and "something is wrong." He squinted into the darkness, listening intently.

"It's just a bunch of drunk kids," Sarah whispered. "If there's a Bigfoot nearby it's going to avoid that fire."

"That's what I'd've figured," Jaeger responded softly. "But it's not." He listened again and they both heard a distant rustle. "I think it's right outside their camp. We need to move closer—"

And that was when the screaming started.

"Stay behind me, girl." Jaeger immediately began moving fast and low. Ahead, a huge shape moved across the fire, blocking its light for a brief moment. The flute started up again but abruptly stopped. As they drew closer, they heard other sounds. Tearing, ripping, slurping… eating sounds.

Sarah followed right behind the Afrikaner hunter as they neared the little camp but froze when she saw what was making those sounds. A huge shaggy shape was hunched over a body on the forest floor, its face buried in the corpse. It jerked its head from side to side and the dead body's limbs flopped limply about. Even at this distance, there was a sickening smell of decay—but that corpse was freshly killed. When a horrified gasp escaped Sarah's throat, the shape stopped its feast, raising its head and slowly turning toward her.

My God, it's a Bigfoot, and yet… The thing that was staring at her certainly looked like a Sasquatch—its dark brown hairy pelt, the shape of its face—and from its build, Sarah thought it to be a female. But there was a *wrongness* about it. This was no gentle berry-eating forest dweller. In the light of the campfire, the eyes shone with a feral light, its face twisted into a savage rictus. A low rumbling growl grew in its throat as it slowly rose from its crouch. The growl crescendoed and then broke into a full-throated roar. It started toward Sarah but stopped short as two small darts slammed into the side of its neck, burying themselves up to the tailpiece tufts.

Jaeger had watched the beast carefully as he circled around it. *The thing's gone rabid*, he thought, wishing he had something more than the high-tech dart gun. As the beast turned and focused its attention on Sarah, he raised the gun and flipped the selector switch to sync all four compressed air cartridges. At this close range, he only needed one cartridge to guarantee a hit, but he wanted to hit as hard as he could. With a full charge, he might be able to kill it. He aimed for the neck and the gun gave two staccato pops, sending the darts straight into their target. At this range, they'd have the impact of a bullet, and the double dose right into the neck should have an immediate effect.

The effect was not what Jaeger had hoped for. The pain of the hits did not send the creature running away in surprise; instead, the impacts caused it to whip its head to the side and zero in on Jaeger. The sedative appeared to do nothing and it charged toward him. Jaeger had faced a charging water buffalo without losing his cool, and he quickly raised the rifle to his shoulder and emptied the remainder of the clip, sending four darts in a tight pattern into the monster's chest, right where a primate's heart should be. The burst staggered it, but that was all. It didn't even bother trying to remove the projectiles as it charged forward again. Jaeger ran.

Sarah watched Jaeger emptying his clip into the beast before running for his life, and she quickly took the opportunity to do the same. She ran down the hill, trying to put as much distance as possible between herself and that nightmare Bigfoot. Something had corrupted it. No eyewitness, no shaky film footage, had ever described anything like what she'd just seen. Sarah cursed herself for pursuing Jaeger from camp so quickly, having left without a radio or sat phone; no call for backup would come from her. She knew Jaeger had one, and surely he would call for help… if he survived.

Jaeger dashed through the forest, occasionally jinking around larger trees or jumping over deadfalls in the hopes of slowing the beast or tripping it up. There was no time to attempt to load another magazine, and he doubted there'd be much point anyway, the way it had shrugged off the darts. He could hear it cracking branches and smaller trees as it slowly gained on him. It didn't seem to move with much grace. That could have been the sedatives, but Jaeger didn't think so. While clumsy, it still moved with the same power and speed as before, and he was certain he was not going to outrun it. Since a Sasquatch was likely a form of primate, Jaeger figured that escaping up a tree would be a one-way ticket. He had a good eye for terrain, and in the moonlit gloom, he was pretty sure there was a steep drop-off ahead.

Jaeger had no time to weigh the pros and cons; he simply made his decision. Dashing for the edge of what he hoped was more drop-off and less cliff, he dug in a cargo pocket and grabbed a powerful LED flashlight. He reached the edge and looked down. Steep, but survivable. He tossed the empty dart rifle aside and turned, spotting the giant shadow closing in. Thumbing the flashlight on, he focused the bright beam in the horror's face. Its eyes shone madly in the light, blood-soaked teeth gleaming. It kept coming. Keeping the beam right in its eyes, he counted three, then tossed the flashlight to its left. The huge head turned, tracking the light, and Jaeger jumped.

It took all of the Afrikaner's concentration to keep from tumbling as he slid and ricocheted down the steep slope, grabbing roots and an occasional thin tree to maintain a controlled descent. Occasionally he bashed a random body part as he fell, then finally he came to an abrupt halt as he impacted with the valley floor. He lay still, listening intently, ignoring the pounding of his heart.

There was too much foliage to make out the top of the cliff, but he could hear an occasional grunt or growl from above. Finally a shrieking roar of frustration split the night air. Jaeger tensed and waited. If it managed to find him down here, he was far too banged up to escape a second time. Another roar, this time further away. Probably going after Sarah. *Shame, that. The gal had fire in her.* Jaeger let out the breath he'd been holding. Still lying flat on his back, he pulled out his portable GPS and two-way radio. He didn't want to risk any illumination from the light on the GPS screen or any noise from the radio, so he waited, listening to the receding calls from the creature above while he catalogued his aches and bruises.

Sarah continued to run. She had strapped on a headlamp she carried and risked turning it on once she was fairly sure she was far enough away. Far in the distance behind her, the creature bellowed an angry call. Once the initial panic of her escape had worn off, she'd started to think. The Sasquatch she'd seen must have been insane. With a brain similar in structure to a human's, it likely had some of the same vulnerabilities to psychological problems as its less hairy cousins. As a primatologist, Sarah had seen numerous examples of mental illness among captive populations of apes and monkeys, and there were certainly instances of disturbing behavior in the wild. Sarah thought of the mother/daughter pair of chimpanzees, Passion and Pom, that Jane Goodall had studied. They had displayed shockingly aggressive tendencies, killing and eating the infants of other females in the troop. This cannibalism occurred so frequently that there was some debate whether a primate form of psychopathy was at work.

Might that have been a psychotic Bigfoot? It was reckless to anthropomorphize too much, but what she had seen in that creature's eyes looked like madness. Another possibility:

rabies, or some form of environmental toxin disrupting the brain chemistry. The one thing she couldn't figure out was how six tranquilizer darts had had no discernible effect. She had used a tranquilizer on primates herself, and that dose would have outright killed a full-grown mountain gorilla. She supposed the darts could have contained expired or evaporated drugs, but somehow she doubted Willem Jaeger would have made such an oversight.

Sarah stopped to check the small compass she carried on a lanyard. She had been heading south, directly away from the deranged Bigfoot. At some point, she would need to turn east to get to the base camp, but for now she would put a little more distance between herself and…

Flashlights! Ahead, two flashlight beams danced through the trees. Someone was running northward. She didn't want to call out in case the creature was closer than she thought, so she ran on an angle to intercept them. *They'll see my headlamp in a second*, she thought.

"Sarah?" an out-of-breath voice said from ahead.

"Russ! Thank God!" Her headlamp illuminated Russ and Joseph as they came to a halt, gasping for breath. Everyone doused their lights so as not to further blind one another.

"We've got to get out of here," Sarah panted.

"You've seen it, too?"

"I've been running from it for the past fifteen minutes."

"Wait… where was it?"

Sarah pointed back the way she'd come. "I was tracking it with Jaeger when it attacked us. It killed a bunch of campers just as we found it."

"Was its fur silver-gray?" Russ sounded perplexed.

"No. Dark brown."

Joseph spoke up. "There are two."

"The one that attacked me had something terribly wrong with it," Sarah said quickly. "It was *eating* people. Sasquatch are omnivorous and eat far more vegetal calories than meat, and even then they usually only eat fish or scavenge carcasses. I think it was insane or rabid."

"No," Joseph said quietly. "They are Wendigo."

Russ turned to him. "That's what you said before. What does that word mean? Is it Shoshone?"

"No. Ojibwe. You remember the story I told you of the singing stone twisting man into a mindless cannibal? The Wendigo is a creature from a different legend, but I'm beginning to see a pattern. It too is known for being a cannibal, craving human flesh, but it is said to be many times the size of a man. You could become a Wendigo by eating human flesh or by being possessed by a demonic spirit that could enter your mind in a dream."

"You think that whatever affected those geologists has changed these Bigfoots."

"Yes. I think this happened before, long ago. Now it is happening again."

"Hang on, what geologists?" Sarah asked.

Russ started to explain but Joseph interrupted. "Let's get moving first. We don't want to be caught between those things. Keep your lights off; there's enough moonlight to see by."

As they began to head east, Sarah said, "I didn't bring a radio. Did you call the camp?"

"Yes," Russ answered. "Carson's getting a large group together. With luck they'll reach us before these 'Wendigos' do."

Sarah suddenly remembered what had been bothering her. "Jaeger shot that thing with six darts full of tranquilizer and it didn't even slow it down. Do your legends have an explanation for that?"

Joseph thought for a moment as they trudged through the moonlight. He thought of the smell that had emanated from the geologists and the giant silverback; he thought of the look of the attacker's face in the Spook Stalkers' video; and he thought of the geologists' bodies and how the flies had avoided them.

"I don't think these Sasquatch are truly alive. But I don't think they're exactly dead either."

Russ was incredulous. "Wait… are you saying they're some sort of Zombie Bigfoot?"

26

When Bud had focused the parabolic microphone on the drumming, he'd quickly determined that it was probably a bunch of college kids out for a deep woods adventure. Whatever had been making that strange vocalization had gone silent, and Bud was about to swing the dish away, figuring the drums would scare away most creatures. But then his headphones were filled with screaming and several monstrous roars. Bud grabbed a Post-it and quickly wrote the bearing and estimated distance, then tore off the headphones and started for the exit. "Dhir, get on the Ear, I've got to find Carson!"

Dhir and Liz looked up from the thick drone instruction manual they were studying. "What is it?" Dhir asked.

"It sounds like something is attacking a group of campers to the northwest. I've got the location locked in, but if the sounds move, do your best to track them."

As Bud exited the tent, he was met with a hive of activity. Groups of rough-looking men and a few women were gathering nearby, many of them wielding dart guns and capture poles. One heavily tattooed merc woman held a bulky gun with a cone-shaped barrel. A man was loading the cone with a bundle of netting. Bud had been so focused on the audio coming in from the woods that he'd missed all the commotion.

As he entered Carson's tent, the billionaire was haranguing his huge bodyguard. "What do you mean, you can't find him?"

"I checked his tent, checked the mess, called his radio… nothing. That buddy of his, Manfred, he's gone too." Brick folded his thick arms across his chest. "Betcha Jaeger went out on his own. I told you not to trust that weasel."

"Dammit, we've got a definite sighting and I need my best shooter. And Dr. Bishop is AWOL as well."

Bud cleared his throat and the two men looked at him.

"Mr. Carson, Sarah headed into the woods a couple hours before sundown. She spotted that safari hunter fellow and another man going into the woods and went after them. She seemed kinda pissed."

Carson gritted his perfect teeth. "Shit. I do believe Mr. Jaeger has gone rogue."

"You don't need him, boss. You got me. My boys and I will bag your Bigfoot, don't you worry."

Carson turned to Bud. "Mr. Sorenson. You came in with a look of urgency. I take it you've picked up some activity to the southwest?"

Bud looked puzzled. "Wha… no. The *north*west. We heard a large animal roaring and human screams, at these approximate coordinates," he said, handing Carson the Post-it.

Carson furrowed his brow as he took the Post-it over to the map table, motioning Bud and Brick to join him. He looked at the map and put the Post-it on a spot to the northwest of their clearing. "Is this about right?"

Bud looked at the spot and gestured to either side of it. "Yes, sir. The terrain might affect the bearing somewhat, and the distance is difficult to pinpoint exactly, but I'm fairly sure it's within a quarter mile of that spot." His eye was drawn to another part of the map. There were a couple wooden pawns from a chess set at a point on the map to the southwest of camp; a little further to the west of the pawns was a black king. "What are those?" Bud asked.

"Those two pawns are Russ and Joseph. They were out on a little scouting mission, and as luck would have it they ran into"—he tapped the king—"a Bigfoot. Evidently a very large, very aggressive Bigfoot. They radioed for help and are on their way back." He grabbed a rook from a cluster of spare chess pieces. "We're going to meet them *here*," he said, plunking the rook down midway between base camp and the pawns.

Carson tapped the Post-it Bud had brought with a well-manicured fingertip, thinking. "Roaring and screaming?" Bud nodded. "Is it possible it's a bear or cougar?"

"I don't think so. I came straight here, so I didn't run a full analysis, but I've been listening to Bigfoot screams for weeks in preparation for this expedition; if I had to lay odds, I'd say it's a Sasquatch."

Carson whispered, "Is it possible?" He grabbed a black queen and set it down on the Post-it. "Brick, we're going to split into two teams. Handpick a third of the crew and have Katya lead them northwest to those coordinates. Have them keep radioing Jaeger. I'm betting he's in that area." *And those might have been his screams*, he thought. "And maintain my nonlethal protocols. Darts, net guns, and catch poles only." Carson turned to Bud and smiled. "Mr. Sorenson, Dhir told me you have an excellent portable microphone system?"

Bud hesitated. "Yes. But it's nowhere near as good as—"

"Dhir will man the primary parabolic. Since you know what to listen for, you're going to help guide the second team. You're going to find *that*," Carson said, pointing at the black queen. "Brick, you're with me. Let's move out."

Manfred reached the tree line and was greeted by a camp buzzing with activity, the tents lit up by klieg lights. His radio suddenly crackled to life.

"Manfred, this is Jaeger. Are you at the camp? Over." Even over the crackly connection, Manfred could hear the adrenaline in Jaeger's voice.

"This is Manfred. Affirmative. Just reached the camp. Over."

"*Goed…* good. I'm gonna need the rifle, Manfred, and I'm gonna need it fast, *ja nee*? Attach the hard case to the big drone and get those techies to fly it to a clearing next to me. It's got night vision lenses, and the landing zone I've found is plenty roomy, so they should have no problem. Send it to the following coordinates…"

Manfred grabbed a pen from a pouch and wrote the information on his wrist. "Got it. I'm on it, boss. Will call you when it's on its way. Over."

"Make it *fokken* snappy. I'm not alone out here, and the dart gun is for *kak*. Jaeger out."

Manfred scanned the tents. Brick was marshalling the mercs to a central point in the camp. The route to the drone pen was clear, but there was no way he could reach Jaeger's tent unobserved; besides, Jaeger had stressed speed. *So, no hard case. I'll just have to improvise.* He hefted the big rifle, running through the gloom at the edge of the camp to reach his target: a large white drone, the name TED stenciled on the bulbous nose of the vehicle. The drone had been designed to carry a small payload, and there were a number of containers intended for it stacked to the side. He found one with internal padding that could fit the fully assembled CheyTac and quickly loaded it with the rifle and spare magazines. It was a simple matter to secure the container in the sling beneath the main fuselage, just to the rear of the lens turret. It looked like the sling was attached by clamps that could be released quickly. That would come in handy.

Entering the tent, he saw Carson's techie sitting at a laptop with a pair of headphones on. Manfred wasn't sure if the young man was Pakistani or Indian. At the rear of the tent was that beautiful young Latina that worked for the Bigfoot scientist.

"Oy! Attention." Dhir removed his cans and looked at him. Manfred continued, "I've got a priority mission for the big drone." He strode to a pad of paper and transferred the information from his wrist before tearing off the top sheet. "Boss wants it sent to these coordinates, ASAP."

Taking the paper, Dhir looked at him in confusion. "Carson didn't request any nighttime drone flights. Sarah convinced him to minimize their use after sundown to avoid spooking any Sasquatch in the area."

"Change of plans." When Dhir started to protest, Manfred leaned in close. "This isn't open to debate, friend."

Dhir sighed and scanned the coordinates. He rose and went to the drone controls, handing the sheet to Liz. "Would you enter these into the autopilot, please?" He sat and started up TED's engines, running a quick test on the optics. "Switching to night vision." His primary viewscreen went to a greenish gray. Manipulating the controls, he brought the drone up a couple feet to a low hover. "Hang on. We're about fifty pounds over default weight." He turned to Manfred. "You add something to the drone?"

"Medical supplies," Manfred said. "Time is of the essence, my friend, so get that bird in the air now."

Dhir shook his head as he typed in a few adjustments. "Added weight affects the range and flight characteristics. Good thing I caught that. Liz, watch and learn. I'm going to bring her above treetop level manually, then we'll engage autopilot to bring her to the coordinates."

Liz rolled her chair over next to him. "What do we do when it gets there?"

Dhir looked back at Manfred. "Good question."

"There will be a small clearing. Set her down, release the payload and you're done."

Liz elbowed Dhir. "Easy-peasy," she said, trying to ease the tension in the young man.

"Yep," he said simply.

"What's the ETA?" Manfred asked.

Dhir glanced at a readout. "About six minutes."

"I'll radio ahead, let them know the drone is on its way." Manfred exited and put some distance between himself and the tent. He raised the radio and thumbed the push-to-talk button. "Jaeger, this is Manfred. Over."

After a moment came a response. "Jaeger here."

"It's on its way. Should be at your location in six minutes. Over."

"Roger that, Manfred."

"Oh, and boss… something is happening at the camp. If I had to guess, I'd say Carson is about to make a push into the woods."

"Really? OK, see if you can find out where they're headed. Thanks again, Fred. Jaeger out."

Manfred turned to go and came face to chest with Brick. The huge bodyguard clamped a viselike hand onto his shoulder. "Well, well. Jaeger's flunky. Been looking for you," the huge man rumbled, his gravelly voice carrying an undertone of menace. "Where's your pal, Manny?"

27

Brighteyes ran through the moonlit forest, Scratch close behind. Littlefoot clung to the back of his shoulders, occasionally whimpering near his ear. They had left Silk (*not-Silk*) far behind, but a roar to the south told Brighteyes that the thing that had been Silverback was not far away. They had to keep moving or they might become trapped between the two. Scratch stumbled on a root and Brighteyes reached out and steadied him.

'Tired,' Scratch vocalized.

Brighteyes grunted his understanding but then continued, 'Not yet rest. Must go.'

'Miss mother,' Littlefoot sniffled from behind.

Brighteyes whuffed an agreement and reassuringly stroked the hair on one of Littlefoot's arms that was hooked around his neck. As they continued to move through the forest, he took a moment to scent the air. The breeze had shifted, coming in from behind. Brighteyes didn't like traveling with the wind at his back; if something was up ahead, he'd have to hear it or see it. His night vision and hearing were good, but with the heavily forested terrain and the ground thick with pine needles, they might be right on top of danger before he detected it.

No sooner had he thought this than a trio of humans appeared not ten strides away! Startled, Scratch leaped back with a little yelp. The humans seemed just as surprised as they were. One of them, a female with blond hair, made a noise very similar to Scratch's cry. Everyone froze for an instant and one of the males clicked on one of their handheld lights, shining it on the three Sasquatch. The other male said something.

Brighteyes was tempted to try a threat display. If they could frighten the humans away, they could continue forward, but he couldn't put the two youngsters at risk. He grunted to Littlefoot and Scratch and made use of his special sign language.

'Danger. We run.' Just as he turned to flee, the blonde female spoke a word he understood.

"Brighteyes?"

The instant Sarah spoke the name, the adult male Bigfoot froze and looked at her. His brilliant blue eyes glittered in the bright beam of the flashlight; she immediately saw why her father had chosen that name for him. She reached out and nudged Russ's flashlight off to the side so as not to blind the trio of Bigfoot.

When they had come upon them, the impulse had been to run, but Sarah immediately knew that this trio were not the same as the ones she and the others had seen. When Russ illuminated them, Joseph had said simply, "They are not Wendigo."

It was at that moment that the adult male had made several hand gestures to its younger companions. Sarah had immediately recognized the sign language; those hand signals were in the back of Dr. Anthony Bishop's journal. They were among the simple series of words and concepts that he had developed with Brighteyes. Sarah had been fascinated with the rudimentary drawings and had committed them to memory.

Now, as the male looked at her, she said, "Russ, turn your light on me." When she was lit, she quickly signed, 'Friend.'

Brighteyes uttered a surprised panting grunt and gently lowered to the ground the youngster who was clinging to him. The other young Bigfoot, probably a teenager, stood behind Brighteyes, looking around the big male with a mixture of fear and curiosity.

Sarah pointed at Brighteyes and repeated his name, nodding to him in an exaggerated manner before shrugging. If she was ordering things correctly, he should interpret this as, "You are Brighteyes. Yes?"

The Bigfoot grunted once and mimicked her nod. He pointed at her and shrugged.

"Sarah," she said, tapping her breastbone with a finger. Sarah trembled, filled with a rush of excitement. Here she was having a conversation with a Bigfoot, just as her father had done, and it was the same individual! And yet, a part of her had *hoped* this meeting might occur, had, in fact, *planned* for it. This was why she'd guided Carson's expedition to this area. And it was why she'd made sure to always carry a certain item on her person.

She shrugged her little pack from her back and removed a small rigid envelope. Taking two steps forward, she said, "Brighteyes," and signed, 'Look.' She opened the envelope and laid one of the contents on the ground in front of her. Stepping back, she directed Russ's flashlight onto the object: a photograph of her father.

Brighteyes took a few tentative steps forward and crouched. Though he wasn't human, there was no mistaking the wave of emotion that swept across his apelike features. He reached out with a fingertip and touched the photo and made several attempts at a word. 'B… B…' He looked at Sarah and tapped the photo before tugging at his facial hair.

She laughed. "Beardface?" she asked.

Brighteyes grunted happily and nodded. 'B! B!' he voiced again.

Sarah moved forward cautiously, casually signing, 'Friend.' Brighteyes watched her carefully but didn't rise from his crouch. She set the second part of the envelope's contents on the ground: a photo of her father at an earlier age, holding a chubby little girl on his hip. In the short time her father had been with Brighteyes, they'd come up with a very limited vocabulary suited to the situation they were in at the time. He had not attempted to teach anything like *father, daughter,* or *offspring.*

Sarah pointed at the contents of the photograph, saying, "Beardface… Sarah." She tapped her breastbone again, repeating, "Sarah."

Brighteyes looked puzzled, but only for a moment. Suddenly his features opened up and he nodded vigorously, tapping his index fingers onto each photo of Sarah's father, grunting, 'B!' Then he touched the photo of the little girl with one finger and pointed at Sarah with the other.

"Yes!" Sarah said, smiling broadly and nodding her head, gathering up the photos.

"I can't believe this," Russ stammered.

Joseph had been watching Sarah's gestures and copied the one for *friend* as he stepped forward. He then named himself and Russ, signing their friendship again.

Brighteyes rose and grunted, nodding his head. The littlest Bigfoot clung shyly to his leg, but the older youngster stepped around Brighteyes. Sarah figured him to be a teenager. The teen thumped his chest and astonished Sarah as he signed to her with great facility. 'You see me. I friend.'

Sarah laughed, delighted. 'I see you. You good.'

The teen panted happily, nodding and signing back, 'Yes! I good.' Gaining confidence, the young Sasquatch stuck out an arm and offered his hand.

Sarah gaped in amazement. The handshake her father had exchanged with Brighteyes when they'd parted—had Brighteyes taught that custom to this youth? She reached out and took the proffered hand, giving it a firm shake.

Russ was about to remind Sarah that they needed to keep moving when a terrifying roar echoed through the night, coming from the west.

The smallest Sasquatch looked terrified, and the teen released Sarah's hand, looking around wildly. Brighteyes signed to Sarah, pointing back toward the terrible sound. He continued signing and picked up the youngster.

Sarah translated for them: "He says that that roar is from the 'alpha.' He says 'bad,' 'danger,' and 'not good'… 'not friend.' He says we should go. He's very emphatic about going *right now*."

"Your furry friend has the right idea," Russ said, clicking off the flashlight.

"You said the creature that attacked that bear was silver or gray?" Sarah asked.

"Yes," Joseph said, already turning to go. "And much larger than Brighteyes."

"That would be the alpha of their troop. Older great apes develop gray hair just like we do. The individual that attacked Jaeger and me was a female." Sarah grunted once to draw Brighteyes' focus, then signed, 'You. Me. *We* go.' She pointed a finger and swept it behind them, signing, 'Bad,' then repeated the gesture ahead to the east and signed, 'Good.'

Brighteyes grunted and nodded, pushing the teen gently ahead of him. Joseph was already scouting ahead, and Russ and Sarah walked alongside the trio of Sasquatch. Together, the two species headed east.

28

Jaeger heard the loud buzzing hum approaching from the southeast and quickly spotted the silhouette of the drone as it traversed the moonlit sky. He descended from the tree he'd been hiding in, a precaution in the event the rabid Bigfoot returned. He had not heard its weird shriek in some time and he assumed it had headed south. As soon as he was properly armed he would track the beast and bag the ultimate trophy. The large drone reached the clearing he'd designated and its three propellers brought it to a hover. *Probably going manual,* he thought. Jaeger stepped out from under the trees and waved his arms, knowing the night vision in the drone would spot him easily. It slowly lowered itself to the ground, and after a moment, the latches holding its payload released and a container thumped to the grass. Jaeger gave a thumbs-up, followed by a circling hand motion, letting the drone know it could return to the air.

As the drone roared back into the night sky, Jaeger crouched over the container. It wasn't the rifle case he was expecting, but when he popped it open, he was pleased to find the CheyTac

Intervention within. He put the spare mags in his vest and removed the big rifle, extending the stock. Flipping on the Pinnacle night vision monocular he had attached to the scope, he raised the rifle to his shoulder and scanned the slope he'd slid down. There. A route back up. Smiling, he lowered the rifle. *All right, Bigfoot. Let's try this again, shall we?*

Liz watched over Dhir's shoulder as the drone hovered, the greenish-gray camera feed showing a man removing a large rifle from the container. Dhir had zoomed the image in before setting the drone's autopilot to return it to base. They watched as the man raised the gun to his shoulder, sighting on the hillside nearby.

"Medical supplies, my ass," Liz muttered.

Dhir sighed. "I was pretty sure that goon was full of shit, but I'm mildly allergic to conflict with guys with guns."

Liz leaned close to the monitor. "Hey, that's the creepy hunter guy! Where's Sarah?"

Dhir zoomed back out and flipped on the infrared, scanning in an arc around the drop zone. There were no other heat signatures in the vicinity. "I don't see her. Why don't you call her on her radio?"

"I tried that earlier. She left it behind when she ran after that guy. Where is she?"

He got to his feet and placed a comforting hand on her shoulder. "Liz, Sarah struck me as pretty badass. I wouldn't worry yourself too much. I bet she headed back when the sun went down." He offered his chair to Liz. "Here, why don't you make sure TED gets home safely? Just engage the autopilot and she'll do the rest. I need to man the Ear and check in with Bud."

Liz plopped into the chair and punched the autopilot, watching the camera view swing away from the rifle-toting figure. She checked the various readouts; speed and altitude were normal, no mechanical issues. Liz looked over at Dhir and smiled. The nerdy young guy was kinda cute. She was pretty sure that teaching her how to fly the drone was his form of flirtation. *Beats buying a girl a lousy drink*, she thought. Dhir glanced up from the sound detection systems and caught her looking at him. Both blushed and returned to their controls.

The camp outside their tech tent had become eerily quiet after Carson's men had headed into the forest. Dhir set the parabolic microphone to scan the area where the billionaire's group had gone, then grabbed the two-way radio that Bud had left him before leaving with the other group. He thumbed the push-to-talk.

"Bud, it's Dhir. You there, Bud Buddy?"

Bud's radio crackled to life on his belt and Dhir's voice broke the quiet. The heavily tattooed female merc named Katya whipped her head around and glared at him. The woman's lantern jaw held so much tension it looked like she chewed nails in her spare time. "Turn that off!" she hissed. "You're supposed to be *listening* for noise, not making it!"

Bud handed his parabolic to one of Carson's goons and unclipped the radio from his belt. "It's the tech tent back at base camp. Could be important," Bud replied. He turned the volume on his radio down and answered the call. "Hey, Dhir," he whispered. "Can't really talk. What's up?"

"Just checking in," Dhir replied. "You hear any more of those weird animal sounds?"

"Not yet. I think we're about halfway to where we heard the drums and screams. You got the Dhir Ear aimed toward Carson's gang?"

"Yes. I'm scanning the area in front of him, near where Joseph and Russ called in from. I'm to call them if I hear anything Bigfooty."

"Good." Bud looked at Katya, noting the pulsing muscle in her cheek. "Hey, Dhir, I gotta run, and we're gonna need to go silent. Keep your channel open, and if I need you I'll call. Over and out." Bud made a visible show of turning the radio off.

Katya hefted her net gun and signaled him to move forward. Bud retrieved his parabolic gear and stepped to the front of Katya and the other two men, sweeping the microphone ahead of them. Nothing unusual reached his ears—no roaring, no screaming. He had to admit he was relieved.

Cameron Carson flipped his night vision goggles up and let his eyes readjust. The moon was bright enough that he didn't really need them. He looked around at his group. Brick was right next to him, never far from his employer. The other seven men in the group were spread out around them.

Carson had been adamant that the Bigfoot must be captured unharmed, and all were armed with nonlethal weapons. One had a cone-barreled net gun, two had dual-purpose capture pole shock sticks, and the other two had tranquilizer rifles. The sixth was a cameraman; he would be filming this historic capture… and making sure the world saw Cameron Carson right there in the thick of it. Carson himself had a dart pistol. The one exception was Brick, who had insisted on bringing his Desert Eagle .50 hand cannon. "Just for bears," he'd promised.

One of their number was completely unarmed: Manfred. Brick had "persuaded" the man to confess to his earlier stroll in the woods with Jaeger. Carson's bodyguard had recommended they keep him close at hand to keep an eye on him. Jaeger's lackey was sullen, but the man was a professional. He made himself useful, lugging some of the group's gear.

Carson lit the glowscreen on his wrist-mounted GPS and checked their location. Brick held a hand up and the group stopped, waiting. Satisfied with the reading, Carson darkened the screen. He motioned everyone closer and spoke softly. "We're about a half mile from where Mr. Cloud sighted the Bigfoot. Spread out in a line to improve our spotting range. I'll keep us on the correct bearing." He grinned, his pearlescent teeth shining in the moonlight. "Gentlemen, with luck we'll make history tonight." He flipped his goggles back down and began walking. Brick silently directed the others to their positions, and the group headed into the gloom.

29

"**O**nce there was a boy who went digging in his garden for carrots for an evening stew. He wished he could have some meat in his stew, but he was allllll out of rabbits."

"Eww, who eats rabbits?" asked one of the Cub Scouts.

"Your mom," replied another, eliciting snickers from the other scouts.

"Shut up and let me tell the story!" Justin the scoutmaster spat. He leaned forward into the firelight and glared at the Cub Scouts, the campfire shining in his thick glasses.

Oh God, not this story again. Miguel watched Justin's dangling neckerchief, willing the campfire to reach out and ignite the fabric. *The guy is such a tool*, the assistant scoutmaster thought. He'd been asked to "chaperone" Justin's camping trips after some parents had complained about his aggressive behavior. Miguel figured the guy had grown up in a "spare the rod, spoil the child" household. Short-tempered and socially inept, the scoutmaster loved yelling and belittling and could be a little rough when disciplining an unruly scout, claiming it "built character." Miguel had a sneaking suspicion that at his core, Justin just hated children.

Shifting on his camp chair, the scoutmaster continued the story. "So, as I was saying... the young boy needed carrots from his garden. He pulled up one carrot. He pulled up another carrot. He grabbed a third carrot and pulled, but it wouldn't budge. He yanked with all his might and suddenly it tore loose! But it wasn't a carrot. It was a toe. A big... hairy... toe."

"Eeeew," said the kid who was squeamish about rabbit-eating. Another scout silenced him with a brutal arm punch.

"The boy looked at the toe. 'Oh goody!' he said. 'Now I will have some meat for my soup.' He took the big hairy toe into his house and made a delicious stew of toe and carrots."

This time Squeamish Scout only managed to open his mouth before another arm punch cut him off.

"After his meal, the boy went to bed. No sooner had he closed his eyes than he heard a deep, spooky voice out in the garden. 'Where's my big hairy toe?' it growled. The boy was scared. Whatever was out there, it sounded big. Thump, thump, thump. It walked up onto the porch. 'Where's my big hairy to-o-oe?' it growled again. The boy pulled his blanket up to his nose, hoping it wouldn't open the door. Then he heard the door cre-e-e-e-eak open. 'Where's my big hairy to-o-o-oe!' it growled even louder. The boy pulled the sheets over his head, cowering in his bed."

Miguel yawned. *Bed. That boy had the right idea.* Their camping spot was on a new set of trails the Park Service had just opened up, and the hike up here had been more strenuous than expected. They needed to get some rest. Thank goodness Justin was almost to the jump scare. He always did it the same way. One more "where's my to-o-oe," and he'd scream "Here it is!" and throw a chunk of potato at whichever kid looked the most scared. Problem with the storytelling logic—the boy in the story *ate* the damn toe, so what the fuck was Justin throwing? The idiot must've mixed up his spook stories. Just then Miguel spotted movement behind Justin. Frozen with fear, he gaped in amazement as something huge emerged from the trees and shadows.

Justin kept soldiering on. "Clomp, clomp, clomp. The big thing stomped over to the boy's bed. 'Where's my big hairy to-o-o-e?' it growled, leaning over the boy."

Suddenly the entire scout troop screamed in terror and scattered.

"That's not the punchline, ya idiots!" Justin yelled. "Get back here and let me finish! Miguel… what the hell's the matter with you?"

Miguel was staring over his shoulder, mouth open, eyes wide with fright. Behind him, Justin heard a deep, burbling rumble, coming from several feet above his head. He slowly turned and looked up into the dripping jaws of a gigantic nightmare. His scoutmaster training kicked in and galvanized him into action. Unfortunately, that action was to throw the chunk of punchline potato he'd been holding. It bounced off the shaggy beast's chest with all the effect one would expect from an ounce of potato striking a ten-foot zombie Bigfoot. The creature's response was considerably more effective; it swung a fist in a long-armed sledgehammer blow, crushing Justin's skull and shattering half the vertebrae in his spine. The greatest chiropractors in the world would have thrown up their hands and entered the priesthood if they'd witnessed it. Miguel scrambled back in a crab walk, grabbing a flame-tipped chunk of kindling as he went.

The creature tilted its mad face to the moon and opened its jaws. A bloodcurdling roar tore loose from its lungs, shattering the night sky.

30

They had just spotted the light of the campfire when they heard the first screams.

"Those are children!" Russ yelled. Joseph was off like a shot, running toward the flickering light. Russ turned to Sarah. "Stay here," he said before dashing after Joseph.

"Fuck that," Sarah muttered. She started to follow, but a bloodcurdling roar came from the direction of the fire, followed by more screams.

Brighteyes signed, 'Alpha!' and looked ready to run.

Sarah clapped her hands at Brighteyes, grabbing his attention. 'Help! Help humans!' she signed frantically, pointing toward the terrified cries.

Brighteyes made an unhappy sound, looking uncertain. He pointed to Scratch and Littlefoot.

He doesn't want to endanger his troop, Sarah thought. She couldn't blame him. "OK, Brighteyes," she said and signed, 'I go,' before dashing toward the sounds of frightened children.

When Russ caught up with Joseph, the Shoshone was gathering up three frightened Cub Scouts, keeping them low in the brush near the campsite. Fifty yards away, the monstrous silverback Bigfoot was feasting on the ruined neckhole of a dead adult, the corpse dressed in a scouting uniform. A second man was holding a burning branch, ready to fend off the creature if it finished its grisly meal. Two other kids were behind him and the little group was slowly backing away.

Russ knelt by Joseph and addressed one of the Cub Scouts, who seemed slightly less petrified by fear than the others. "We're here to help; we're gonna get you out of here. Those scouts with the torch guy, is that everyone?" Russ was afraid some scouts might have run off into the forest.

"Yeah, there's five of us scouts," the kid said, clearly scared but holding it together. "That's Miguel," he added, pointing at the man with the torch.

"OK, good. What's your name, kid?"

"Tyler."

"All right, Tyler. You're in charge. Keep your scouts together." He put a hand on Joseph's shoulder. "Joseph, take the scouts east. I'll get those two and catch up with you. Here." He handed Joseph the two-way radio. "Call Carson. His group is probably halfway between here and the camp." The monster suddenly belched and tossed the half-eaten corpse aside. Growling, it advanced on Miguel. "Go, Joseph! Get them to safety!" Russ ran toward Miguel, hefting his "spear." *Who am I kidding, I've got a pointy stick.*

Brighteyes was in torment. He knew he should protect the youngsters of his troop, but those humans were his friends.

That thing that had once been Silverback would hurt his new friends, would *kill* them. They didn't carry boom-sticks. They had no chance. Brighteyes grunted in frustration. It was Scratch who decided his course of action.

The teen Bigfoot tugged his arm and signed, 'Those humans are friends. We must help!'

Brighteyes vocalized and signed to Scratch, 'You must stay. You protect Littlefoot. I go help humans.' He turned and ran toward the roaring sounds. The monstrous alpha sounded angry.

Scratch watched him dash away. Though not related by blood, he had always considered Brighteyes as an older brother. He couldn't let him face this danger alone. Lifting Littlefoot up, he boosted the little Sasquatch into a tree and signed, 'Stay. Climb. Hide. I go help Brighteyes.'

"Jeezus, what the fuck is this thing?" Miguel cried, poking his burning branch at the monster. The flames seemed to confuse it somewhat; it swiped at the branch with a blood-soaked hand, but Miguel kept it just out of reach.

As Russ ran up alongside him, he was shocked by just how big this horrifying alpha was. His sharpened stick wasn't going to be of much use. Suddenly, he remembered the bear spray he'd picked up from the Spook Stalkers. Digging it out of his pocket, he yelled to Miguel to hold up the torch. *I hope this brand's flammable*, he thought, raising the canister and aiming it through the flames. When the beast lunged again, Russ mentally crossed his fingers and depressed the trigger.

A gout of flame shot through the torch and engulfed the creature's face. Some of the liquid stuck and flames licked around its monstrous features; the smell of burning hair filled the air. Strangely, it didn't cry out in pain or run away; instead it looked around, waving its hands in front of its face like it was swatting at bees.

"Russ!" Sarah cried as she ran up.

Russ glanced at the blazing Bigfoot face and realized it was probably reacting to having its sight disrupted by all the flames. "Sarah! Joseph has the other scouts. Let's get out of here. I don't think that trick is gonna hold it for long."

As if to confirm his statement, the twisted Sasquatch suddenly swatted itself in the face with a flattened palm, snuffing out a portion of the flames. Miguel yelled, "Shit!" and grabbed one of the Cub Scouts by the arm while Russ got the other. The beast smacked at its face again as the group turned and ran for their lives.

Sarah could *feel* when the creature took off after them, its tremendous weight shaking the ground as its huge feet pounded into the earth. *The length of its stride... we're not going to make it.* "Russ! It's going to..."

She was interrupted by a bloodcurdling scream. Miguel was to her left, and in her peripheral vision she saw a massive hand reach out and grab him by the top of the head the way Shaquille O'Neil might palm a basketball. It stopped Miguel in his tracks and lifted him bodily in the air, his feet momentarily pumping away as if he were still running. The Cub Scout he'd been dragging with him fell to the ground.

Sarah stumbled to a stop and went to the boy, looking up at the shaggy nightmare. A few small flames still flickered in the hair surrounding its face, the fire reflecting in the beast's shining eyes. It held Miguel high, turning him slightly before taking a bite of his stomach cavity. Sarah felt her sanity slipping as the sight made her think of a Roman emperor eating a bunch of grapes held above his head. Miguel's screaming abruptly stopped as he lapsed into shock.

Russ turned back, gripping the other scout by his arm. "Sarah! For God's sake, run!"

Sarah hauled the other scout to his feet just as the creature tossed Miguel aside, the man's intestines unspooling briefly as the Sasquatch continued chewing a mouthful of guts. Its ravenous gaze locked on Sarah and the scout, and it *grinned*, a low burbling rumble sounding in its chest.

I'm going to die, Sarah thought as it started slowly forward. An odd acrid smell stung her nostrils as it drew near.

Suddenly, Sarah became aware of pounding footfalls, and a blur of brown flashed into view. From out of the shadows, Brighteyes rushed straight at the monster, barreling into it with lowered shoulder. The beast was caught off guard and, despite its size, was bowled over, tumbling into the forest floor a few yards away.

Sarah turned and ran, dragging the scout with her as she caught up with Russ. A terrible shrieking howl sounded from behind them.

Brighteyes recovered his balance and looked for a weapon. He would have had little chance against the massive alpha before the change; now, with its mind and body corrupted, he suspected it would be even more dangerous to confront hand-to-hand. It shrieked a weird sound as it regained its feet, and Brighteyes grabbed the only thing in reach, a dead branch half-buried in the litter of needles on the ground. The freakish giant charged and Brighteyes swung his pathetic club, the rotten wood exploding in a cloud of sawdust and splinters as it struck the alpha's outstretched arm.

The monster hurled itself at Brighteyes, bearing him to the ground. Its attack had a mindless ferocity, and Brighteyes was just able to grip one of the creature's wrists while clamping his other hand onto its throat, muscles straining to keep its ravening jaws from sinking into his flesh. He squeezed with all his might, trying to choke the creature, but it seemed to have no effect. *It is too strong*, he thought. He hoped Scratch and Littlefoot would not wait for him. He should have told them to run. Already, Brighteyes could feel his own powerful muscles tiring; his attacker seemed immune to fatigue. It was only a matter of time.

A dark shape leaped onto the alpha's back, grabbing fistfuls of hair in one hand and pounding on the creature's head with the other. The alpha roared in fury and twisted its head to the side, snapping its jaws. Scratch held on, grunting aggressively. Raining blows on the side of Silverback's face, Scratch's punches met with the beast's teeth, and a canine tore into the flesh of his forearm. He howled in pain but hung on.

Just when it looked like the beast would kill them both, a human came to their aid. It was the male who had been running a moment before. He had returned, holding a sharpened stick high above his head. 'Silverback' was on top of Brighteyes, its legs on either side as it straddled him. The human rammed the stick straight down into the beast's calf. It had little discernible effect; it continued snapping back over its shoulder at Scratch. *This thing feels no pain*, Brighteyes thought. The spear stood straight up out of the meat of its calf, and a course of action came to him.

He vocalized, 'Scratch! Let go!' As the young primate dropped off the creature's back, Brighteyes released the creature's throat, grabbed the shaft of the spear, and shoved it into the ground with all of his might. That got the alpha's attention, and Brighteyes was just able to scramble out from under it. It grabbed at him, but its leg was now pinned to the earth. It didn't seem to be completely aware of *why* it couldn't move and kept mindlessly swiping at him. Brighteyes watched the human male running, signaling for him to follow. He grabbed hold of Scratch, who was nursing his arm, and the two of them ran after the human. Behind him, he could hear a wet sucking sound; looking back, he witnessed Silverback rising to his feet, pulling the spear partway out of its leg until the tip came loose from the ground. Fortunately, the mindless beast tried to break into a run without removing it entirely and promptly tripped itself up with the shaft of the spear.

Brighteyes grunted and signed frantically, 'Where is Littlefoot?'

'He is safe. He hides in tree.' Scratch was clearly in pain but was keeping pace.

Brighteyes panted in frustration. He would get Scratch to safety before returning to the forest to find Littlefoot. The little Sasquatch was an excellent climber, the best in the troop; he should be able to stay out of reach if Silverback found him. *Or Silk. Silk is still out there.* Brighteyes pushed that thought away and kept running, slowly gaining on his new human friends.

31

"This is Joseph Washakie, does anyone read?" The radio at a mercenary's belt crackled to life, the voice coming over the channel panting with exertion.

Brick signaled the group to halt, grabbing the radio off the man's belt and tossing it to Carson, who caught it smoothly and responded, "This is Carson. Joseph, where are you?"

"About a quarter mile from the base camp. We're coming in hot, Mr. Carson. That Bigfoot Russ told you about? It attacked a group of Cub Scouts. We rescued as many as we could. Russ and Sarah are not far behind me. I can hear their voices."

Carson cursed. Civilians in the middle of his capture attempt! He imagined the headlines if a bunch of adorable Cub Scouts were torn apart during Cameron Carson's latest project. "Joseph, where is the Bigfoot?"

"Not sure. I haven't heard it in a while, but I don't think it's far behind us. Something's terribly wrong with it, Mr. Carson. It's a man-eater." Joseph wasn't about to explain the whole Wendigo legend; there was no time. He had to make the man understand that a nonlethal capture attempt was not in the cards. And there was another concern: "Listen to me… there's more. Sarah found Brighteyes."

Carson stared at the radio for a moment. "Say again, Joseph?"

"The Bigfoot from her father's journal, Sarah found him and two others. She was able to communicate with them."

Carson's heart skipped a beat and a toothy grin split his beard. "That's amazing! Can she bring them to us?"

"Mr. Carson, this other Bigfoot, it's a huge mindless predator, and everyone in this forest is in danger. We've got to kill it before we even think about anything else."

Kill it? I don't think so, Carson thought. Even if this Sasquatch had lost its mind, it wouldn't matter once it was locked in a cage. And if it was chasing Joseph and the others… "Brick! Put a strobe up in that tree," he said, pointing at a nearby oak. Brick whistled to one of the men, who scrambled up and set it.

Joseph's voice came again, "Mr. Carson? Did you hear what I said?"

"Yes, yes, we'll be ready for it. Look to your east. I've got a strobe up. Let me know if you can see it."

There was a pause, then, "Yes. I can see the flash in the trees. I'll wait for Russ and Sarah to catch up, then we'll come straight to you. Over and out."

Carson tossed the radio back to Brick and looked around at the men. "Take up positions, gentlemen. We're about to bag a Bigfoot."

Jaeger spotted another track and crouched low, scanning ahead with the scope on his rifle. A light rain had just begun to fall, and the reduced moonlight interfered with the range of the night vision; nevertheless, the beast had not been hard to track. It seemed to be moving heedlessly through the forest, leaving a trail of footprints and fur. If he hadn't been so banged up from his impromptu trip down the side of the cliff, he might have caught *die fokker* by now. Seeing nothing, he lowered the rifle and listened intently. In the distance ahead, he thought he heard voices.

"I've got something!" Bud called out. He immediately cringed at the sound of his own voice. After so many long minutes without any noise at all, the sudden burst of sounds in his earphones came as a surprise. He forgot himself and let his excitement get the better of him.

"Shut the fuck up," Katya hissed. Moving closer to him, she asked, "What kind of noise?"

Bud pressed an earphone tight to his head. The light drizzle was causing a lot of ambient interference. "Rustling. Breaking sticks. Something's moving through the brush. Whatever it is, it's big."

"Where is it?"

"It's close. Coming fast!"

"Get ready, boys," Katya whispered. "We're about to have company."

The noise moved off mic to the left, and Bud slowly turned his wrist, tracking it. "It's almost on top of us!"

"I hear it," Katya said, flipping the safety off of her net gun.

The loud rustling continued for a few seconds more and then abruptly stopped. The mercenaries looked about nervously. The few with night vision goggles peered into the gloom, the trees and drizzle reducing their range of sight considerably.

"Where is it?" Katya whispered urgently.

Frustrated, Bud swept the parabolic in a short arc. At this close range, with all the mercenaries about, it was tricky to… *Wait a minute. Deep, ragged breathing.* "There! It's right—"

Suddenly, a huge shaggy shape burst through the trees right next to one of Katya's men, grabbing him in both its massive hands and lifting him off the ground. Katya, acting on reflex, fired the net gun at the creature, the weighted net expanding as the compressed air thrust it from the cone-shaped barrel. The hasty shot engulfed the hapless mercenary the beast was holding, only partially ensnaring Katya's intended target. Jerking its arms to the sides, the creature ripped the man in two, the net holding the grisly remains loosely together. It tossed the mess aside and turned toward Katya.

Terrified, Bud stared at the gigantic figure. About eight feet tall and covered in brown fur, it certainly looked like a Bigfoot, but its features were twisted into a wild-eyed, slavering monstrosity that would have been at home in a nightmare. Katya tossed aside the empty net gun and unholstered a Glock, but the beast covered the distance to her in two strides and she was only able to get off two shots. The bullets struck the creature in the chest and had no more effect than the rain. Before Katya could fire a third time, the monster grabbed her by her outstretched arm and swung her bodily against a tree. Katya's impact with the stout pine produced a symphony of wet crunching noises. The remaining merc raised his rifle and shot a tranquilizer dart into the creature's side. It didn't seem to notice as it tossed Katya's pulped form aside and turned to face the man, growling low and actually appearing to grin. As the merc desperately tried to reload the bolt-action rifle with another dart, Bud turned and ran for his life, throwing aside his sound detection equipment. He didn't need his gear to hear the screams.

"The drone is approaching now, Dhir."

"Thanks, Liz." He'd asked her to let him know when it was about to reach the camp to avoid blowing out the Dhir Ear. The three large prop engines wouldn't play nice with the sensitive microphones. He powered the system off and came over to watch the feed over Liz's shoulder. "You want to bring her in?"

Liz turned her head and looked up at him, smiling broadly, eyes shining with excitement. "I'd love to! But doesn't it just use autopilot for landing at its takeoff point?"

Dhir leaned over her and punched a button. "Not anymore. We can always turn it back on if we need it."

Liz put her hands on the controls, took a deep breath, and started to bring the drone in. Dhir occasionally gave instructions—a verbal nudge here, a helpful hint there—but by and large, Liz flew the big vehicle smoothly to its target. She brought it to a hover and slowly lowered it to its spot behind the tent. Once she powered off the rotors, she let out a pent-up breath.

"Brilliant, Liz. You've got a knack for this." He gave her shoulders a playful squeeze.

"Ooh, that's nice… I think my whole body tensed up when you turned off the autopilot."

"Well, we can't have that. I need my pilots relaxed." Dhir kneaded her shoulders a few more times before remembering the Ear was off. "One sec, let me power the mic back up." He flipped a couple switches and heard something coming from the earphones lying on the desk. Lifting them to his ears, he felt his own body tense up. His ears were filled with the sound of screams and a bestial roaring.

32

The rain had picked up as Russ and Sarah caught up with Joseph and they quickly conferred together. Brighteyes and Scratch stood some distance away. Several of the Cub Scouts looked ready to bolt again at the sight of the two Sasquatch, but the scout who had been with Sarah quickly spoke up.

"They're good guys. They saved me!"

Sarah joined in. "They are friendly, I promise. The other one, the big one that attacked us? It's sick." She turned to Russ and Joseph and spoke softly. "It might not be far behind. You keep going with the kids. I've got to talk with Brighteyes."

Russ shifted uncomfortably. "I don't want to leave you here."

"I won't be long, I swear. I don't want them going with us. Carson's men might shoot them. I just need to explain what I want them to do."

Russ nodded. "OK, but please hurry. That thing nearly killed you."

With that, Russ and Joseph ushered the scouts with them toward the strobe in the distance.

Sarah approached the two Sasquatch. Brighteyes looked very anxious and worried. He signed, 'Little Bigfoot hide,' and pointed back the way they'd come. 'I afraid little Bigfoot.'

Sarah looked at Scratch. The young primate was holding his forearm, wincing in pain. She pointed at him and signed to Brighteyes, 'He hurt. We must go. Must run.' She thought about the group of men up ahead. Joseph said he'd warned Carson there were friendly Sasquatch, and she was pretty sure most of his men would be armed with nonlethal weaponry; that being said, all it would take was one nervous goon with an itchy trigger finger. A single tranquilizer dart hitting Brighteyes or the injured one would be a death sentence if the alpha caught up with them. *No… better if they stay hidden.*

Sarah pointed toward the strobe and signed, 'Humans.' She pointed that way again, then shook her head and pointed two fingers at her eyes before pointing at the Sasquatch. The meaning: "They no see you." She pointed that way again before miming a hunter shooting a rifle, making a little gun sound.

Brighteyes uttered a sharp pant and nodded. He pointed at himself and Scratch, then extended a finger and moved it in an arc to the side of the strobing light. He signed, 'We go. We hide.' Pointing toward the strobe, he signed, 'Humans no see.'

Sarah nodded and signed, 'Good.' She repeated the arc he had made. "Go around," she said. He nodded back and started ushering Scratch toward a point just south of the strobe. Suddenly a tremendous roar tore through the sound of the rain. 'Run!' she signed to the two Sasquatch before rushing after Russ and Joseph. Another howl came from behind, this one rising to a shriek. It was getting closer. Spotting the others in the distant gloom, she called out to them, "Russ! It's coming!"

Carson heard the terrible roars and shrieks. Even at this distance, the sound froze his blood. Softer, high-pitched screams—the Cub Scouts, he guessed—echoed through the forest. They sounded close. The rain was coming down harder; pinpointing noises was difficult and the range of the night vision goggles was drastically reduced. The flashing strobe added an eerie, nightmarish quality to the scene.

Carson's radio crackled to life. "Mr. Carson, this is Dhir. There's something right ahead of you. It sounds like—"

Carson punched the talk button, cutting him off. "We can hear it, Dhir. Stay off the channel, we're going silent. Carson out." He turned the radio off and handed it to Brick.

Brick crouched beside the billionaire behind a fallen log. The bodyguard had suggested Carson perch in a tree, but that wouldn't make for good film. The cameraman was a few feet away, camera pointed ahead toward the approaching sounds. Carson fished a little key chain fob out of a pocket and depressed the button on it. He'd wanted a way to silently signal the cameraman when he wanted to be filmed, and Dhir had rigged a simple system for him. When Carson pushed the button, a small pager would silently vibrate. The cameraman jerked, startled; everyone was on edge. He quickly swung the camera to Carson, raised a finger while the low light lens focused, then dropped the finger.

"This is Cameron Carson, speaking to you from the Maiden Bigfoot Expedition," he began, speaking in a loud whisper. "Our scouts report a large male Bigfoot heading our way. Initial reports indicate that this individual is unusually aggressive. The men of the expedition are spread out around me—"

Suddenly, his monologue was interrupted by a stampede of terrified Cub Scouts, who emerged from the forest ahead at a dead run. Sarah and Russ were herding the kids, keeping them in a cluster between them; Joseph brought up the rear. The cameraman swung his lens to the group.

"It's right behind us!" Sarah gasped.

"We need to get these kids to safety," Russ rasped, catching his breath.

"We *all* need to get to safety," Joseph said gravely. "This creature is not natural."

Carson snorted. "Of course it's not natural, it's a Bigfoot! It's what we're here for!"

"If you won't run from it, you must kill it."

"I came here to capture a Bigfoot, and that's exactly what I'm going to do. Now, get those children back to the base camp."

Joseph knelt by the fallen tree and looked Cameron Carson in the eye. "Mr. Carson, this beast is not to be trifled with. It is not natural. If the legends I have heard are true, you may not be *able* to kill it, let alone capture it. You need to retreat."

"*You* need to step back," Brick growled, grabbing the Shoshone by his jacket. "Mr. Carson gave you an order. Keep your Indian mumbo jumbo to yourself and get those kids to the camp!"

Joseph grabbed the man's massive forearm and broke his grip with a simple twisting motion. Furious, Brick started to reach for him again, but an ear-splitting howl trumpeted from the shadows. A sharp crack followed, a tree trunk splintering in the near distance. Joseph vaulted the dead tree and ran toward Russ and Sarah. "Go! Get to the camp!" he shouted.

Sarah started forward, angling herself to the right of the group. Brighteyes and the younger Bigfoot should be off to the side, and she wanted them to be able to follow her. Assuming they were watching, she pointed toward the camp three times in an exaggerated fashion. "Come on, Russ!"

Russ looked back at Carson's group. He saw a man wielding a pole with a loop on the end, another with what was clearly a dart gun. "They're all going to die," he said to himself.

Kill them all! The thought rose in what was left of Silverback's mind. It still had rudimentary thoughts. Predatory thoughts.

The emanations from the meteorite that had utterly destroyed the minds of the two geologists had done so by altering cells within the hapless humans; these mutated cells had then been passed on to Silverback. But Sasquatch were not human. They shared enough of the same DNA that the "virus" had changed the hapless alpha into a twisted man-eating beast, but this was no mindless zombie shuffling along at a snail's pace. While it had lost some of its agility, this zombie Bigfoot could still move with great speed, and it still possessed basic cunning. It wanted to eat... but the concept of eating and the concept of killing had become linked in its rotting brain.

Kill all...then feast! The creature sniffed the air, its excellent sight peering through the rainy gloom, noting the humans spread out before it. A strange light tucked into the crook of a tree branch pulsed intermittently, illuminating its prey. It was about to charge, but a tiny remnant of cunning bubbled up. These humans knew it was here. They were waiting for it. It took intense concentration, but the monster managed to dredge up a plan.

It looked around and found a small boulder. Pulling it loose from the forest floor, it held it overhead and then pitched it at the one of the humans. The rock hurtled through the air, going unnoticed until just before impact, the strobe light's sudden pulse revealing it the instant before it crashed into one of the men with a dart rifle. There was a sickening crunch as the man's rib cage popped inward. The man gurgled a surprised scream, his lungs filling with blood. Silverback growled with pleasure as the humans reacted in surprise, looking toward the stricken man. It charged, giving a passing push to a dead tree still clinging to verticality.

Although one of the mercenaries had been looking through a thermal monocular, the man saw nothing out there in the trees. No surprise there; Silverback no longer generated body heat. Thus, a whooshing sound, a crunch and a gurgling death rattle were all the warning Carson had before the gigantic Bigfoot charged out of the forest. A loud cracking and splintering accompanied its headlong rush, and a tree fell onto one of the catch pole men, knocking him to the ground and breaking his legs. The beast was almost on top of the merc with the net gun before he fired. The range was too short for the net to unfurl, and it simply thudded into the Bigfoot's chest before the creature whipped a clenched fist into the man's head, bursting it apart like a flesh piñata.

The remaining dart man, perched in a low branch, fired and reloaded, fired and reloaded, the darts zipping into arm, side, neck. Still unarmed, Manfred scrambled to the man who'd been crushed by the boulder, picking up the dart gun and adding his own volley of flying syringes. The monstrous alpha ignored them and turned toward Carson and Brick. A noose looped over the creature's head from behind and pulled taut as a merc managed to get a catch pole into play. He triggered the Taser tip on the end of the pole and rammed it into the beast's neck, sending thirty thousand volts into it. Its shaggy hairs standing on end, the shock caused its muscles to seize up but seemed to cause it no pain.

Slowly it moved forward, dragging the man and his pole with it. Carson fired several small darts into the Bigfoot from his tranquilizer pistol as it advanced. The merc in the tree, his darts exhausted, jumped down and grabbed the other catch pole, looping it onto one of the monster's arms. He flipped the juice on and added his voltage to the first. To his credit, the cameraman kept rolling, though he began walking backward, ready to bolt. Brick leaped over the dead tree and drew his Desert Eagle.

"No!!" Carson cried, "don't kill it!"

Brick glanced at his employer, then made a decision. He tossed the heavy pistol to Carson. "Here. Got a feelin' you're gonna need it." He pointed at the cameraman. "Stop backing up and keep rolling. You run, and I'll kill you myself." Brick stripped off his tactical vest, revealing a taut middle-aged body still bulging with huge muscles.

Brick Broadway had been a sensation on the wrestling circuit in the '90s. He'd never forgiven his managers for concocting his Broadway-dancer-themed persona, having to wear spangly outfits and being forced to sing show tunes in his atrocious voice. True, he'd made a mint. He became a favorite jobber to the fans, having to lose matches right and left; this stuck in his craw because Brick was fairly certain he could've taken every single wrestler in the business in an unstaged fight. He'd finally left wrestling after he suffered a severe spinal compression in a mixed match. He'd been choreographed to lose to a petite redhead ring girl turned wrestler named Strawberry Poundcake. Given the comical size difference between them, Brick essentially had to throw *himself* all over the ring. Halfway through the humiliating match, he'd decided he was going to quit the biz, but while he was thinking of whether he'd like to retire to a ranch or an island, he'd allowed his concentration to slip. When the time came for Strawberry Poundcake to execute her "Berry Pound" maneuver, a flying scissors from the top turnbuckle, Brick Broadway started to turn the wrong way and his neck was viciously twisted. When he went into the controlled fall, he landed badly. He got his wish. He never wrestled again, having been almost crippled by a five-foot-tall kewpie doll. After months of physical therapy, Brick went back into the workforce as hired muscle. The pay wasn't as good, but he never had to lose another fight.

And now, here was the ultimate fight. Brick glanced back and made sure the cameraman was rolling. *Wait until the world see this footage*, he thought. He took a couple steps toward his massive foe. This was one of the few times Brick had had to look *up* at an opponent. The beast stood nearly three feet taller than Brick's seven-foot height. Carson's two surviving goons still had hold of the beast's neck and arm, sending electricity into its body; Brick had asked one of the men what would happen if he grabbed hold of someone while they were being shocked and he'd been reassured that as long as he didn't touch the electrodes or anything between them, he'd be fine. He knew the batteries would run out of juice any second, so he'd have to act fast.

The Sasquatch locked eyes with Brick, its demonic features stretched into a rictus from the high voltage. With its free arm, it took a clumsy swipe at him. Brick ducked the blow, cocking his fist as he weaved to the flank of the beast and slammed a rock-hard fist into where he figured its kidney would be. It was like punching a bag of cement and had no noticeable effect. *The tranquilizer darts don't seem to be doing anything either*, Brick thought. He punched the creature again, dancing around behind it when it took a backward swipe at him. At that moment, the shock pole looped around its neck exhausted its battery. *Now or never.*

"Pull its arm back!" he yelled at the catch pole man latched onto the forearm. The man turned, propping the pole across his shoulder, and pulled with all his might. His efforts barely moved the beast, but they distracted it. As it turned toward that arm, Brick leaped onto the creature's shoulder, latching a sleeperhold onto its neck. *Everything's gotta breathe*, he thought, hanging on for dear life. The merc with the neck noose lost his grip as Brick's muscular frame collided with the pole.

Tucking Brick's huge pistol into his waistband, Carson dashed for the net gun, signaling to the cameraman to follow. He hesitantly did so, keeping a healthy distance. Brick was locked onto the creature like a tick, but even with a seven-foot muscle-bound man on its back, the thing remained upright. Carson lifted the gun and grabbed one of the canisters from the fallen mercenary. *How the hell do you load this thing?* he wondered. Fumbling with the bundled net, he tried jamming it into the end of the net gun's cone-shaped barrel. He looked up at the monstrosity. *And how long are those damn tranquilizers going to take?*

The Sasquatch struggled, one arm still snagged and electricity continuing to run through its muscles. It roared in frustration. Brick held on for dear life, squeezing his chokehold tighter as the strobe light in the tree illuminated the struggle in psychotropic flashes. Pumped with adrenaline, he gave a triumphant roar of his own. This was the most exhilarating fight of his life! Lost in the moment, Brick defaulted to what his character usually did in the ring: he started belting show tunes. Specifically, "Everything's Coming Up Roses." His ruined voice butchered the song, but Brick didn't care; after today he would be a legend! The sleeperhold had been in place for a good thirty seconds; with no blood to the brain and no air to the lungs, it was only a matter of time.

But the zombified Bigfoot no longer breathed, no longer needed blood in its brain. And as for the darts, how do you tranquilize the dead? Brick pushed his gravelly voice up to the money note, and it was at that moment that the battery ran dead on the second shock-stick. Things happened very fast.

The beast twisted its wrist and grabbed hold of the catch pole, wrenching it from the goon's grasp. Jabbing the end of the pole to the left, the creature skewered the other remaining merc, ramming the blunt end of the steel rod through the man's chest. The one who'd lost the pole made a run for it but wasn't fast enough. The creature swung the shish-kebabbed man back around, and with a squelching sound the corpse flew off of the pole, bowling the fleeing man over and knocking the wind out of him. The pole's noose snapped and flew off of the creature's arm.

Then it was Brick's turn. Brick Broadway took his final bow and he did so at about sixty miles per hour. The Bigfoot didn't know what a piledriver was, but still managed to replicate the iconic wrestling move quite by accident. Reaching back over its hairy shoulders with its long arms, it peeled Brick off of its throat with ease, whipping him forward over its head. Continuing the motion, the ten-foot monster swung him down, the momentum bringing the shaggy beast to its knees as it drove Brick headfirst into the forest floor.

In a children's cartoon, Brick might've been stuck in the earth like an ostrich, feet kicking in the air, mumbling garbled curse words into the soil. This wasn't a cartoon. Brick's skull held together long enough to penetrate the earth, but then his entire spinal column accordioned in upon itself, producing an abrupt chorus of crunching, snapping, and splattering. A neck injury had forced him to retire from wrestling… this one retired him from life.

Carson stared in horror as his mountainous bodyguard was reduced to a lifeless rag doll. Shaking himself out of shock, the billionaire spotted Manfred. The man looked like he was ready to bolt. "Manfred! Load this!" Tossing the net gun to him, Carson drew the Desert Eagle. The cameraman chose that moment to get some point-of-view B-roll of a headlong run through the forest, leaving everyone behind. The Sasquatch released the floppy corpse of Brick Broadway and advanced on the other remaining mercenary who was staggering to his feet.

As Carson raised the unwieldy pistol, the Sasquatch reached the stumbling merc and grabbed hold of one of the man's arms. Carson took aim and fired. He'd never fired a .50-caliber pistol before and was not properly braced; the recoil whipped the Desert Eagle back into his forehead and it flew out of his grip. The heavy round tore into the monster's chest, punching a hole through to the other side. *At least I'll have a dead Bigfoot to show the world*, he thought, shaking his head to clear it from the unexpected blow from the pistol.

The creature stopped its rampage for an instant, looking down at the hole before turning its gaze on Carson. A slow burbling rumble vibrated in its chest as it grabbed the other arm of the mercenary it was holding. Never taking its eyes off of Carson, the monster calmly ripped the hapless mercenary open like a gory zipper, taking a bite from the corpse's interior before tossing the lifeless hunks to either side. Chewing the mouthful of flesh, it walked slowly forward, reaching up to snap the neck lasso, the catch pole thumping to the ground behind it as it advanced.

Carson's life flashed before his eyes. He'd had a good run: fame and fortune, yachts, private islands, countless beautiful women (and a few men), and so many exciting adventures. True, he'd had some spectacular failures, but there had been many successes: The North-South Circumnavigation, the Wingsuit Space Jump, and breaking the underwater speed record in his one-man submersible. *Well, this will be one for the record books. Death by Bigfoot. Pretty good way to go. TMZ will love it.* But as he tried to come to terms with his impending doom, his attention was drawn to the creature's mouth. As its canines punched into the mass of guts, streams of blood and scraps of flesh falling from its lips, Carson had an epiphany. "I don't want to be eaten," he said out loud.

Neither did Manfred, who finally managed to click the net canister into place, raised the gun to his shoulder, and fired. A burst of compressed air propelled the weighted net outward, the odd shape of the barrel imparting a spin that unfurled the heavy nylon fibers. The net engulfed the creature, snaring and tangling its arms and one of its legs. Its eyes went mad with rage and it unleashed a horrifying screech, flecks of human flesh spewing free from its teeth.

Carson and Manfred ran for their lives. Both men knew the net wouldn't hold it for long.

Littlefoot huddled high in the tree, pressing his body against the trunk as the rain came down all around him. He'd lost track of how long he'd clung to the rough bark.

He had listened in terror as the sounds had drifted down from the campfire atop the nearby rise: the frightened screams of the little human children, the death shriek of a human adult, the horrible roaring of the thing that had been Silverback, the angry bellow of Brighteyes as he came to the rescue of his human friends. He had relaxed somewhat when he heard Brighteyes' grunts and human voices moving away to the east. They had gotten away from the monster; the little Bigfoot was sure of it. It was only a matter of time before Brighteyes and Scratch came back for him. But as time passed and the rain picked up from a drizzle to a steady drumbeat, Littlefoot began to wonder. Had Brighteyes left him, too? Silverback had attacked them… Silk had driven them away… perhaps something had happened to make Brighteyes abandon the youngest member of the troop.

Littlefoot shivered and strained his ears, listening. He'd lost track of the others some time ago. Suddenly, a terrible roar echoed through the trees. The sound came from the direction Brighteyes had gone. Another roar and soon the night filled with other sounds: a tree falling, humans yelling, humans screaming, humans dying. And a loud report: one of those human boom-sticks. A final roar and the night was quiet again.

A soft mewling sound escaped Littlefoot's throat. He was alone. He couldn't stay in this tree all night and even if he did, he was afraid Silverback would find him before Brighteyes could. The little Sasquatch made a decision—he would need to find the others on his own. He carefully descended the tree and dropped quietly to the needle-strewn ground. He began to run, angling toward where he had last heard Brighteyes. The rain should cover the sound of his footfalls, and he could move very fast in the forest. He kept a close eye on nearby trees, knowing he might need to climb to safety if he caught Silverback's corrupted scent on the air.

Gonna die gonna die gonna die gonna die... Bud huffed and wheezed his way up another rise, careful not to slide on the rain-slicked slope. He'd lost track of how long he'd been running. He stopped to catch his breath; there hadn't been any screams or roars in some time. *Thank God for small favors. Maybe I lost it.* That hope was shattered as a distant shriek reached his ears. *Or not. If it catches my scent...* Suddenly, a crazy idea formed in his head. He unclipped his radio and opened the channel to the tech tent. He'd not been able to get through before, but this rise might give him a good line of sight back to base camp. "Dhir? Liz? It's Bud. Do you read?"

After a brief pause, the radio crackled and Liz's voice came on the channel. "Bud! It's Liz! Where are you?"

"Liz, I can't tell you how great it is to hear your voice. Listen… our group was attacked by a Bigfoot. I got away, but I think it may be after me. Is Dhir there?"

"He's out back refueling TED. Bud, we think Carson's group was attacked too. We picked up horrible sounds on the Dhir Ear, but then it all went quiet. The rain is making it hard to pick up subtler sounds. Dhir wants me to send the drone up to see if we can find them."

"I don't suppose I could twist your arm and get you to send it for me instead?" Another distant shriek. This one startled him, and he let out an involuntary yelp. Was it closer? Hard to tell in the rain. "That thing is hunting me. You've seen my physique… I'm not exactly marathon material, and I don't think I can outrun it. Speaking of my physique… that two-hundred-pound payload Dhir mentioned… is there any wiggle room?"

Good meat. Good meat. Silk gnawed on the severed leg, tearing a mouthful from the meaty thigh. She had plenty more to eat back at the site of her attack, but she'd spotted the fat human scurrying away, and after gorging herself on mercenaries for a few minutes, a murderous little voice in her head had reminded her of that plump still-mobile morsel. She'd torn off a leg from the nearest corpse for a travel snack and begun to hunt in the driving rain, scenting the air.

No smell! Water from sky make hard! Momentarily blinded by mindless rage, she swiped a gnarled hand through the air, tearing at the falling raindrops. She shrieked in frustrated fury, the sound echoing through the trees. She started forward again, sniffing the air, thinking of that juicy round human. *Hungry. Still hungry. Always hungry.* She took another bite of the leg. *Good meat… but fat human better.* She shrieked again, and this time her ears picked up a tiny little yelp. *Fear. I hear fear.* The half-eaten leg dropped from her fingers and she began to run.

Jaeger came upon the ruins of Katya's men… and Katya. Her broken body lay at the base of a stout tree. *Shame, that. She'd been an impressive woman.* No sooner had he thought this than she opened her eyes and coughed a bubble of blood.

"Jaeger," she choked. As he moved toward Katya, her eyes fell on the massive rifle he carried. She smiled a bloody-toothed smile. "Ahhh… good. You brought your toy. Fucking *kill* it, Jaeger. None of that dart shit, blow a fucking hole in it!" The exertion of pushing those words out was too much; her chest spasmed and a torrent of trapped blood flowed from her mouth as her eyes glassed over, staring off through the trees.

He crouched by her. No need to take a pulse, that much was clear. He let his eyes drift to the side, following her life-less gaze. There. A huge footprint. He glanced back at Katya. "Thanks for the assist." Rising, he quickly spotted more tracks, the increasing rain making it easier as the softening ground gave way under the beast's great weight. A shriek sounded in the distance, and he went into a slow trot, spotting signs of the creature's passage as he went. *I'm coming for you, my beauty.* As he moved through the woods tracking his quarry, he debated where he would put the rifle round. This was going to be his greatest hunting trophy; he didn't want to make things *too* difficult for the taxidermist.

34

"There's the camp!" Russ said with some relief. The small generator-fed flood lights shone through the remaining trees and driving rain.

Sarah looked off to her right. She'd lost track of Brighteyes and Scratch, but she sensed they weren't far. Peering into the gloom, she lost track her footing and stepped into a knee-high puddle of mud, catching herself in time to prevent a complete face-plant. "Shit."

"Looks more like mud," Russ said wryly. Sarah gave him a look, and he grasped her forearm and affected an atrocious British accent. "I would have spread my gentleman's cloak over that puddle, milady, but I seem to have left it behind," he said, pulling her up out of the muck.

"My hero," she drawled dryly as she regained her feet. She wiped a muddy hand on Russ's shirt. "You sure know how to show a girl a good time."

Russ was working up a witty retort when a hurled acorn bounced off his noggin. From up ahead, Joseph gestured for them to get moving. "Less flirting, more running, Kemosabe."

He returned to herding the group of scouts to the edge of the camp's clearing.

Russ rubbed his forehead. Sarah snickered and gave him a shove as she trotted after Joseph. "Shake it off, Survivor Guy," she tossed back over her shoulder.

In minutes they reached the base camp. By now everyone knew something terrible had happened out in the forest and people were milling about. Most of the soldier types had been with the two groups, and Russ spotted one of the camp cooks holding a shotgun, looking nervously into the tree line. *Guy made me a killer omelet*, Russ thought, *hope he's as good with a shotgun as he is with a spatula.* The cook spotted them as they entered the clearing and shouted something back toward the lines of tents. A moment later, Bill Singleton came into view. Carson's tidy little assistant had ditched his dress shirt and chinos and was now dressed in what looked to be a tailored safari outfit. He had a radio in each hand and looked absolutely frazzled.

"Joseph! Dr. Bishop, Mr. Cloud... thank God you're all right! Did you see Cameron? I've been trying to reach him, but there's been no answer in quite some time."

Joseph led the group of scouts up to Singleton. "We passed Mr. Carson and his men. He seemed determined to capture the beast. From the sounds we heard behind us, I doubt they were successful."

Singleton's eyes teared up and he was speechless for a moment. "Oh dear me," he managed.

"Mr. Singleton, we came across this scout troop and we need to get them out of here. Are the helicopters inbound?"

Singleton hesitated. "Umm... about that. The rain is bad enough here, but the conditions at the staging area in Lewiston are much worse. Strong winds and lightning. One of the helicopters attempted a takeoff and had to put down hard. We're on our own, I'm afraid."

Joseph thought for a moment. "The ATVs. We had a few of those ferried in, didn't we?"

Singleton nodded eagerly. "Yes, four. I've got them gassed up and ready to go."

"All right, set three aside in the middle of camp. Pick one of your best men to drive one of them. Make sure he's well armed." He looked to the scouts. "Do any of you know how to drive an all-terrain vehicle?"

Tyler's hand shot up and another boy said, "My dad's got two of 'em, we drive 'em all the time."

"OK, good. Each of you take an ATV. The rest of you double up on the back. For now, best to stay in camp, but if one of those things shows up I want you all to haul ass away from here. Got it?"

The scouts all nodded and Joseph turned back to Singleton. "What sort of weaponry do we have?"

Bill swallowed. "Not much. Carson was adamant about not injuring any Sasquatch and was concerned about trigger-happy mercenaries with high-powered weapons. I've distributed what little we have, mostly shotguns and a couple hunting rifles. I've got them spread around the perimeter."

"All right, that'll have to do. Just make sure whoever's with the scouts has got something decent."

Sarah was impressed with how quickly Joseph took charge. She noticed Russ was rummaging through some equipment next to a tent. He had a length of paracord around one shoulder and was stuffing a big flashlight, a hatchet and a couple spades into a duffel.

"What are you doing?" she asked.

He looked up at her and grinned, then called over to the Cub Scouts, "Hey, Tyler, what's your motto?"

"'Do your best,'" the boy said proudly.

"Wh… really? No, no… the other one."

"Oh, you mean the *Boy Scout* motto. 'Be prepared.'"

"Bingo, that's the one!" He held up the duffel. "Just a few things I wish I'd had earlier."

Just then, Dhir appeared at the corner of a nearby tent. "I thought I heard your voices! Thank God you guys are OK! Listen, Bud just called. The northern group was attacked. He's on the run and Liz is sending TED in for him. It'll strain her payload limits a bit, but I think she can carry him."

"The big alpha couldn't have gotten both groups," Sarah mused. "That attack must've been from the female."

Heads turned as everyone heard movement in the woods. The shotgun-wielding cook raised his weapon, but Joseph calmly pressed the barrel down. "It's Carson."

Carson and Manfred and the cameraman stumbled out of the forest. The billionaire looked shell-shocked. Singleton ran up to him, taking his employer by the arm. "Bill… they're all dead. The Bigfoot… it was… a *monster*."

"I warned you it was not natural," Joseph said softly.

Carson quickly regained his composure. His ambitious mind churned and quickly turned to thoughts of how he might salvage things. "Give me a situation report," he demanded of Singleton.

While Singleton conferred with his employer, Manfred skulked off between a pair of tents. Coming across a scared-looking young man with a pistol in his hand and a radio on his belt, Manfred helped himself to both. The confused kid's look of protestation evaporated at the sight of Manfred's glare, and he scampered away. Manfred opened the channel that he and Jaeger had agreed upon.

"Willem? It's Manfred. Are you there?"

There was a long pause and then Jaeger's voice came out of the radio in a harsh whisper. He sounded out of breath. "Jaeger here. Bit busy at the moment, Manfred."

"You need to hear this, boss." Manfred quickly recounted what had happened to Carson's group. There was a pause.

"So… there's two of them," Jaeger said quietly. "And from your description, I'd say yours was a mature male. I'm thinking the one that attacked me is its mate. I'm tracking it now."

"How do you know it's female?"

"Just a feeling. I didn't exactly check under the skirt."

Manfred thumbed the talk button. "Carson sent a group to link up with you. Katya's leading it."

"Katya *was* leading it. I found what was left of them a few minutes ago."

Manfred received the news like a punch in the gut. He and Katya had shared a bunk more than once, and he had a soft spot for the feisty ballbuster of a woman. Without realizing he was doing so, Manfred strode toward the woods, aiming for the spot where he and Jaeger had entered earlier. Gripping the pistol tightly, he asked, "Where are you, boss? I'm going in."

"About a klick and a half northwest of camp. Don't do anything stupid, Manfred. I'll bag this bitch."

Just then a loud buzzing sounded from behind Manfred. Turning his head and peering through the rain, he watched the large drone take off and skim over his head, angling up over the treetops.

"Willem…. you've got incoming."

Brighteyes crouched in the tree line at the edge of the clearing, watching the humans. Scratch sat on the needle-strewn ground beside him, staring off into space. Brighteyes listened to the young Bigfoot's labored breathing for a moment before grunting softly and nudging the teen. Scratch looked up at him for a moment before shivering and looking back at the ground. He gathered a handful of pine needles and let them sift through his fingers before looking at his hands as if he were unsure of what they were.

Brighteyes felt a chill as he watched his companion. The confusion, the listlessness… he feared what was coming. He sniffed the air. The Alive-Dead smell was faint… but it was there. He looked back at the human camp. Sasquatch medicine hadn't helped Silverback and Silk, but maybe the humans had something that could heal Scratch. He spotted the young female human, daughter-of-Beardface. Looking around, he saw a couple small stones. He took aim and gently tossed a rock toward her. The rock arced through the air and bounced off the ground at her feet. He watched her look around, searching for the source of the stone. He threw another.

35

Littlefoot continued to scamper through the rain. He was disappointed that he hadn't come across Brighteyes and Scratch; on the other hand, he hadn't run into Silverback either. If he couldn't find Brighteyes, maybe he could find a human. The ones they'd met earlier had seemed friendly, and while Silverback had beat it into their heads—sometimes quite literally—that the troop should always avoid humans, Littlefoot had gone with Brighteyes on a couple of his adventures and didn't see what all the fuss was about. As long as a human didn't have a boom-stick, they weren't likely to be a threat. Plus, humans had food and Littlefoot was *soooooo* hungry!

The little Bigfoot sniffed the air, but the rain made scent-searching all but impossible. He hopped over a fallen tree but landed on the edge of a rock, stubbing his toe so hard his vision went white for an instant. Surprised by the burst of pain, he involuntarily cried out, his little voice making a shrill squeal. He sat down and rubbed his toe, lower lip trembling. Suddenly, in the distance, something responded to his call with a soothing trio of hoots. It wasn't a terrifying roar, like

Silverback had made. No, this sounded like… *Mama?* But Silk had changed, hadn't she? Brighteyes had made them run away from her. The trio of hoots came again, still very distant. She didn't *sound* sick. *Maybe Mama is better…* Littlefoot gave out a call, almost a short chirp. Then he listened.

The thing that had been Littlefoot's mother heard the second shrill chirp, and slowly its lips curled back from its teeth in a leering grin. When Silk had heard the young Bigfoot's first sharp cry, some residual instinct led it to return the call with a motherly response. It didn't know why it had done it, but some form of terrible cunning had urged her to do it again. And now her former offspring was calling out for her. *Yes… call again. Call for your mother.* The creature stood, swaying gently on its feet at the top of a rise. Pursing its lips, it let out another trio of hoots. A moment passed; another distant chirp. The horrible grin returned to its face, and it began loping down the hill.

Bud shivered, leaning up against a tree, doing his best to keep out of the rain. It had been pouring minutes before, but it seemed to be letting up a bit. After his first conversation with Liz, he had found an area where the trees opened up somewhat. Calling her again, he had done his best to give Liz some landmarks to send the drone to. With the rain lessening, she should be able to spot him with the suite of lenses in the drone's camera pod. Suddenly, no more than a hundred yards away, a short high-pitched squeal pierced the night. He jumped but then calmed. Whatever animal that was, it wasn't his huge man-eating pursuer. *Probably a rabbit getting skewered by an owl*, he thought. He peered into the rainy night sky, searching for any sign of TED the drone.

A trio of hoots echoed in the night and Bud jumped again. *OK… that… that sounded like a primate. Not an* angry *primate, but…* The call came again, but he was pretty sure whatever was making that sound was some distance away. Now, a chirp! Very close. Bud crouched by the tree and listened as hooting answered chirping and then… there! A small figure moving through the brush. It looked about human-sized. Taking a deep breath, he raised his flashlight. *I hope I don't regret this.* He flicked the light on. Fur, eyeshine—a baby Bigfoot!

He expected it to run, and while it did look startled for a moment, it quickly relaxed and raised a hand to its eyes, shielding them from the flashlight's glare. He quickly swung the light to the side and watched in amazement as the little animal walked cautiously toward him, gesturing with its hands. Holy shit. Sign language! Bud had read Sarah's journal on the flight to Boise, and he recognized some of what the little Sasquatch was doing from the crude drawings on the last pages of the journal. He quickly propped the flashlight bulb up against the tree so it gave off some general illumination. His sudden motion caused the little figure to freeze, but Bud quickly made his own response, aping one of the young Bigfoot's gestures. 'Friend.' He pointed at himself, repeated the gesture, then he simply waved.

The fuzzy creature made a happy panting sound and approached, gesturing again. Bud caught *yes*, *friend*, *good* and *human*. Then it rubbed its tummy and shrugged.

"Oh, you're hungry? You came to the right human." Bud was a walking snack machine and quickly dug through a cargo pocket. Remembering a particular TV commercial, he pulled out a bag of beef jerky. "If advertising is to be believed, you'll like this." He handed the Sasquatch some jerky and the little creature happily took a bite… chewed… abruptly stopped chewing… then made a face and spat it out. "Well, what does Madison Avenue know?" Bud said, diving back into a pocket for something else. *All kids like sweets*, he thought and dug out a candy bar. "Sorry about the jerky, buddy," he said, unwrapping the candy bar and holding it out. "Try this one on for size."

Littlefoot gingerly took the candy, a bit gun-shy after the salty leathery thing. He took a dainty bite. Eyes going wide, he took a bigger bite, nodding vigorously and gesturing, 'Good! Good! Good!'

Finishing the sugary treat, he pointed at the flashlight and then at himself, then clapped his hands.

Bud chuckled and picked up the flashlight, gently handing it to the youngster. The animal took the flashlight, turned it sideways, then deftly flicked it off…on…off…on. "Well, I'll be damned," Bud whispered. The little Bigfoot began dancing about, shining the flashlight to and fro. Bud laughed and did a little jig of his own.

Just then, a buzzing roar came from the sky. The drone! Bud squinted through the drizzle and spotted it. He turned to his furry companion and gently clapped before holding out a hand. The Bigfoot obligingly plopped the flashlight into his hand and he quickly aimed it at the drone. He flicked the flashlight off and on, and the drone slowly homed in on its light.

Littlefoot, far from being frightened of this human machine, jumped up and down excitedly, slapping his palms on the ground. He stuck his arms out and spun once and then gestured, a bit of sign language he himself had taught the troop for when they saw human helicopters: 'Maple seed machine!'

The big drone slowly lowered itself to a clear spot, and as the engines quit and the blades began to slow, a voice came out of a speaker in the nose of the drone. "All aboard for Liz Air!" The camera suite rotated as a different lens came into play. "Bud, I'm so glad you're…" The voice trailed off. "Is that… is that a baby Bigfoot?"

"That would be a yes. Wave to the nice drone, little Bigfoot." Bud signed, 'Friend,' pointed at the drone, again signed, 'Friend,' then turned to the drone and waved at its cameras. The furry little creature toddled up alongside him and enthusiastically joined in the waving.

Liz burst into laughter. *She really has a cute little laugh, even when it's coming out of a one-ton tricopter,* Bud thought, grinning ear to ear.

"Well, hello, little fella," said the drone.

Bud handed the flashlight back to Littlefoot and went forward to open up the clamps to the payload sling. While the little Sasquatch returned to his game of "shine the light on everything," Bud came around to the nose of the drone. "OK, you sure this thing'll hold me?"

"Yes. Dhir said the two-hundred-pound payload number is just the factory specs. Given the short distance to camp, it won't be a problem."

"OK. Lemme say goodbye to my little friend." Bud went to the frolicking fuzzball and clapped his hands. He waved, then pointed to himself before signing, 'I go.'

The little Bigfoot looked sad for a moment and started to reply, but then a loud trio of hoots sounded from the shadowy trees at the top of a nearby slope. Bud jerked, startled by the call. It was close! Littlefoot started toward the sound, looking unconcerned and gesturing for Bud to follow. Bud stayed where he was as the youngster reached the bottom of the rise and chirped. Branches cracked as something huge moved out of the gloom. Littlefoot flipped on the flashlight and shined it at the crest, and in that pool of light, a nightmare visage appeared. In the glare, its eyes shone with madness, a horrible facsimile of a grin stretching across its face. It strode toward Littlefoot, but suddenly its features softened and it let out a mournful *hoot hoot hoot*. Littlefoot, confused, emitted a short chirp. In a flash, the creature's face stiffened into a horrible open-mouthed roar and it charged!

Bud dropped and rolled under the drone, yelling, "Start 'er up! Start 'er up now!" The engines whined and the blades began to chop the air.

Liz's voice called out from the nose speakers, "Oh my God, it's huge!"

Littlefoot turned to run but only managed to get two steps before the monster swung an arm and backhanded the youngster, sending him tumbling down the hill. The beast growled a long, low growl, dripping with undertones of sadistic pleasure as it stalked slowly toward the prone little form. The flashlight Littlefoot had been carrying rolled to a stop nearby, throwing an eerie glow across the ground and partially illuminating the scene.

As Bud struggled with the payload sling he watched help-lessly, the scene playing out at a weird angle from his position under the drone. The little Sasquatch wasn't moving. *That thing must be its mother. It's going to eat its own child!* Tears in his eyes, Bud watched as the beast came within ten feet of the baby, streams of saliva dripping from its gaping maw.

Suddenly a man appeared on the rise and gave a sharp whistle. The creature stopped and turned to face the new-comer. There was a blinding flash and a deafening gunshot, and a sizable portion of the creature's lower back exploded outward in a spray of blood and tissue.

Jaeger had been following the beast closely since it began making those hooting calls—calls that he could only describe as motherly. He didn't have line of sight, but he had a clear trail to follow as the huge beast snapped branches and left deep prints in the mud. There were other sounds: a chirping creature that seemed to be responding to his prey's calls; then a human voice… male; finally, the unmistakable sound of that big drone that Manfred had told him was inbound. Jaeger took it all in as he stalked his quarry.

There! A huge shadowy form in the distant trees. He raised the CheyTac to his shoulder, the greenish night vision just picking up a flash of movement before the beast was obscured once again by forest. He cursed and quietly moved forward, keeping low. *Was that a flashlight?* He saw a beam dancing through the trees. Again, the triple hoot. Very close, this time. He moved closer, then things began to happen very quickly.

He heard motion, a cracking branch, another trio of hoots, a tiny chirp, and then an earth-shattering roar. Jaeger burst into motion, discarding stealth as he darted through the trees, heading for a small rise in the terrain.

Cresting the rise, he raised the rifle and took it all in from the scope: drone to the left, a man underneath it; a prone shaggy shape on the ground; and there, fully in the open, the gigantic rabid Sasquatch that he'd been tracking. He quickly dropped to a rice paddy marksman's squat, bracing his elbows on his thighs. A sniper might have instinctively settled the crosshairs on the back of the creature's head, but Jaeger had the instincts of a hunter with a love of taxidermied trophies. He aimed at the middle of its back, but then realized the beast had a fairly hairless chest and belly. *A messy exit wound on the front of my trophy? No, that won't do at all.* Keeping the crosshairs low on its body and applying gentle pressure to the trigger, Jaeger gave a loud, piercing whistle. The Bigfoot stopped in its tracks. When it turned to face him, Jaeger finished the trigger pull. The huge rifle bucked, the hefty .408 round punching into the creature's chest and tearing out the back. Staggered, the monster looked down at itself before pitching forward on its face.

"Bud? Bud, what's happening?" Bud could just hear Liz's transmitted voice over the sound of the drone's engines. The camera suite swiveled around, facing backward under the drone's body. "You're not strapped in!"

"It's OK," he shouted. "Someone shot it. Jaeger, I think. It's down." He carefully rolled out from under the drone, keeping a wary eye on the whirling props. Rising to his feet, he looked at the drone. "Liz… keep the engine running." He took a few tentative steps toward the huge shape, facedown on the forest floor. It wasn't moving. *And neither is the little one*, he thought. He headed for the youngster just as Willem Jaeger came down the little hill, rifle over his shoulder, a huge grin on his gaunt face.

Blowing out all his pent-up adrenaline in one percussive exhalation, he stopped a few feet away from the fallen Sasquatch, shaking his head in stunned disbelief. "Phwaw, would ya look at the *groot* beastie!"

"Are you sure it's dead?" Bud asked nervously.

"Pretty sure I took out the spine." Jaeger raised the night vision scope and trained it on the giant beast's torso, watching for movement. "*Ja*, it's dead. Not breathing."

Bud quickly knelt by the Bigfoot child and sighed with relief. The little one *was* breathing.

Jaeger looked over at them, which was disconcerting since he did so through the rifle's scope.

"The little one alive?" When Bud nodded, Jaeger chuckled. "Well, looks like Carson'll get a live specimen after all." Jaeger knelt by his prize—the greatest safari trophy in the history of hunting. *Where am I going to mount this beauty?* he thought. The lower back had a large exit wound, but he was fairly sure it had been a clean entry wound. He set his rifle aside and grabbed hold of the creature's arm.

"Wait. What are you doing?" Bud asked, alarmed.

"Gonna roll 'er over, see what kind of damage the bullet did going in." The lanky Afrikaner's ropy muscles strained and the body started to shift. "Don't suppose you feel like lending a hand?" he asked, his voice tight with exertion.

But Bud was already moving back toward the drone, dragging the unconscious Bigfoot youngster with him. *I know it's dead. I saw the blood, I saw it fall, I saw it wasn't breathing,* he thought. *But I have a very bad feeling…*

With a final grunt, Jaeger flipped his kill over. *What the…?* His "kill" was grinning. Its bloodshot eyes stared straight up into the night sky, raindrops striking the unmoving orbs, the fallen flashlight's glow reflecting off their surfaces. As Jaeger leaned in for a closer look, the eyes suddenly whipped to the side, locking on to him.

"Kak!" Jaeger started to go for his rifle, but one of the beast's hands shot out and grabbed him by the throat, a low gurgling growl emanating from its chest.

Bud stared in horror as the beast sat up, holding the struggling Jaeger aloft. The hunter kicked helplessly and pounded at the giant hand locked around his neck. Liz's voice crackled from the drone, distorting as she yelled into its remote microphone. "Bud! Get under the drone! Now!"

Bud started to move but then looked down at the Bigfoot child. *No… I can't let that thing eat you.* He dived to the ground and dragged himself and the little shaggy form under the drone, keeping well clear of the spinning blades. Quickly, he lifted the unconscious animal into the sling and locked the clamps in place.

"What are you doing?" Liz's voice came, the camera suite looking back at him. "That thing will kill you!"

"I can't leave this little Bigfoot behind, Liz. I'll hold on while you take off."

"Are you crazy? TED can't carry you both!"

Suddenly, a second voice came over the drone. "Bud, this is Dhir. I can floor the engines and at least get you and your friend off the ground, but there's no way TED can maintain that for long. The strain on the rotors will be too much."

"I don't need you to fly me all the way to camp, just give me a head start."

"OK… I'll get you as far as I can, then drop you off. Hang on!"

As the engines ramped up, Bud gripped the runners on either side of the payload sling, his fingers and arms feeling the buzzing vibration as the three rotor blades went to the maximum safety speed and then beyond. The drone lifted off and Bud felt his feet leave the ground. He held on for dear life, his arms straining to hold up his ample frame. *Never was any good at pull-ups*, he thought, gritting his teeth.

Looking down, he saw the horrifying Sasquatch stand up, gripping Jaeger's throat. Its arm seemed to shake as it squeezed its grip closed as tight as it could. As the tricopter began to pull away, Bud witnessed Jaeger's neck tissues and spine collapse as the beast forced its hand to clench all the way. A few strands of flesh held for an instant before the Afrikaner's body fell free from the creature's grip and flopped to the ground, his head toppling after it. Bud was grateful when TED the drone spun on its axis, allowing the nightmare scene to fade in his peripheral vision.

Thump. A second small stone landed near Sarah's feet. This time she was able to determine where it had come from. Sasquatch were known to toss rocks or sticks to warn humans they were around. She grabbed Russ by the arm and nodded for him to follow her. As they passed by Joseph, she leaned close to the Shoshone.

"We're going to talk to our 'friends.' The camp's clearly on edge… if we decide to bring them into the clearing, can you make sure no one starts shooting?"

Joseph peered back into the forest, right where Sarah had been heading. He nodded. "Ah yes, they're here. I'll have a word with Carson."

Russ looked toward the tree line. Nothing but trees. "Can you actually *see* them?" he asked.

Joseph chuckled. "No, but I can see *you*. I just observed where you were looking."

As Sarah headed toward the trees, Russ followed. He pointed back at Joseph as he went. "You and me. A new TV show, *Survivor Guys*."

"If we don't end up as Wendigo poop, I'll consider it," Joseph responded before heading over toward Carson; the billionaire was immersed in a conversation with Singleton.

Sarah approached the dimly lit tree line and quietly called out, "Brighteyes?" A rustling came from the shadows, and Sarah had a moment of panic. *What if that* thing *threw the rocks? What if that monstrous twisted Sasquatch killed Brighteyes and Scratch and it's right there, right inside the trees…?*

She let out a tremendous sigh as Brighteyes emerged into the edge of the clearing. The Bigfoot looked worried. He pointed back toward the trees, then signed, 'Sick. Humans help. Humans help friend.'

Sarah quickly translated to Russ. He dug in the duffel he'd filled and extracted a headlamp on an elastic band. Donning it, he flipped it on. "Ask him to show us?"

Sarah pointed at Brighteyes, then toward the darkness and beckoned towards herself. She pointed toward Russ and herself and then her eyes. 'Bring here. We look.'

Brighteyes whuffed and went into the shadows, retrieving his companion. The teen Bigfoot looked listless and shambled along as Brighteyes guided him over to Sarah and Russ. Pointing at the teen's arm, Brighteyes sniffed the air in an exaggerated manner and signed, 'Bad.'

Russ looked at the hairy arm and saw blood. He gently moved the hair aside, but the young Bigfoot tensed and growled low in his throat. "Easy," he said softly, withdrawing his hands. He turned to Sarah. "I wonder if he was bitten helping us with the Cub Scouts."

Sarah signed, 'Alpha.' She mimed biting her own arm before pointing at the wounded arm and then shrugging.

Brighteyes panted and nodded vigorously.

Sarah signed, 'We help.' She headed back into the trees, gesturing for Brighteyes to join her. 'We hide,' she signed before addressing Russ. "Go get Carson. Bring him over here. Alone, if possible. Tell Joseph to get a first aid kit and join us."

"On it," Russ said, jogging back to the camp periphery. Cameron Carson was in a heated conversation with his assistant. As he approached, he overheard Singleton saying, "Perhaps the National Guard, sir? There's a helicopter detachment in Boise. We should contact them now."

"Not yet, Bill! I can't have another disastrous failure, you *know* that. If we don't end up with a Bigfoot, alive or dead, then those men will have died in vain."

That's my cue, Russ thought. "Mr. Carson, I think everyone would prefer 'alive.'" Carson turned toward Russ and held up a hand to silence Singleton. "Mr. Cloud? You have something to add?"

"I have something to *show*." The billionaire seemed to have regained his composure. *Good. I want him level-headed when he meets our "friends."* "Sarah asked if you'd come join us for a moment."

Carson looked at him warily.

"I promise you, this is something you'll want to see."

"Very well. Bill, see what else you can do to secure the camp."

Russ put a hand on Singleton's shoulder. "Fire," Russ said, remembering. "It seems to confuse its vision. Give some of the men torches and set up small bonfires in front of the gaps in the tents. If the one that attacked us comes here, maybe we can keep it out of the center of camp." As Singleton scurried off, Russ called out to Joseph. "Joseph, see if you can scare up a first aid kit. I think I saw one in the tech tent. Bring it over to Sarah." He tilted his head toward the tree line and Joseph gave a nod of understanding.

"First aid kit?" Carson asked. "Is Sarah hurt?"

"No, not Sarah." Russ led Carson toward Sarah's hiding place. "Mr. Carson… Cameron, I need you to listen carefully. The Bigfoot that attacked you was an alpha male, the leader of a troop in this area."

Carson's head swung toward Russ, his pearly grin popping out of his beard. "A troop!"

"Sarah and I believe the alpha's mate is the one that attacked your other group to the north." *How do I explain the meteorite, the Wendigo legend… the fact that these things are probably zombies of some sort?* The answer was simple. *Don't* explain it. Simplify. "Joseph and I think they're rabid. They're mindless half-ton killing machines now, and we've got to put them down."

"But what about the rest of the troop? How many are there? Is this Brighteyes' troop?"

Sarah came out of the tree line as the two men arrived. She'd overheard Carson's excitement at the possibility of there being a whole troop of Sasquatch. "There are five that we know of. You read my father's journal, Mr. Carson… and I'm sure you remember his sign language at the end?" She made the gesture for *friend*. "You'll need that one." She turned toward the shadows. "Brighteyes?"

Out of the gloom, Brighteyes stepped into view. He looked at this new human. He was a hairface, like the woman's father had been. The eight-foot Sasquatch raised a hand and waved.

Carson stared in amazement, speechless. Snapping out of it, he quickly waved back and then signed, 'Friend.' "Amazing…"

he said. "The expedition is saved!" He started to turn back to camp, but Sarah grabbed his arm.

"You're not going to capture this Bigfoot. Not now, not ever."

"But… that was the whole *point*. You agreed—"

"The situation has changed. This is my friend. He saved my father's life. He saved *my* life… and Russ's life… and all those Cub Scouts. He is not going to end up in some zoo. You are going to get a camera, and you are going to get undeniable proof… excellent, unassailable video footage and DNA samples. But then they will go back to their lives."

Carson hesitated, glancing back toward the camp, then back at Sarah.

"Or I can just have them head back into the forest."

Carson looked torn. Russ stepped in. "Cameron, with the footage, DNA… and maybe the bodies of the alpha or its mate… you will make history. And, by *not* throwing a Bigfoot in a cage, you won't piss off any animal rights activists."

The billionaire sighed. "You've got a point. All right, you have my word. No capture. But where is the rest of the troop?"

Sarah spotted Joseph approaching with a first aid kit. She turned to Brighteyes and mimed biting her arm, then pointed into the darkness before making a beckoning gesture. She signed, 'Humans help.'

Brighteyes nodded, going behind a tree and bringing Scratch into the edge of the clearing. The young Sasquatch seemed withdrawn and swatted at the air as if there was a mosquito bothering him. *No bugs that I've seen, not in this rain*, Sarah thought. She turned to Carson. "There's also a Bigfoot child back in the forest. We'll need to go look for him once it's light."

"No need," said Joseph as he set down the first aid kit and crouched down, opening it. "When I grabbed the first aid kit, I talked to Dhir and Liz. They're bringing the baby Bigfoot into the camp on the big drone."

"What?" Sarah asked, incredulous. "How on earth…?"

Joseph quickly explained what he'd learned of the attack on Bud and Jaeger while he went through the kit, selecting some gauze and antibiotic ointment. He rose and showed what he had to Sarah.

Sarah pointed at the wound and signed, 'Bad,' then pointed at the antibiotic ointment and signed, 'Good.' Then she made the sign for *OK* and shrugged, making it a question.

Brighteyes nodded and signed, 'OK,' then took hold of the younger Bigfoot's arm. When the teen started to growl, Brighteyes gave a dominant grunt and smacked the youth's chest. The young Bigfoot blinked, seeming to come to its senses. It made a submissive sound and held out its arm.

While Joseph treated the wound, Carson stood in front of Brighteyes. He signed, 'Friend,' and the Bigfoot responded in kind. Delighted, Carson flashed his trademark megawatt grin but was taken aback when Brighteyes flinched.

Sarah made a soothing vocalization to Brighteyes and turned to the billionaire. "Your style of toothy grin would be considered a form of threat display in a primate. Here…" She took Carson's hand and loosely curled his fingers. "Extend your arm to him. Offer the knuckles. Keep your eyes lowered."

Carson did so. "What am I saying?"

"It's a sort of apology. And demonstrates submissiveness."

Carson chuckled. "Submissiveness isn't really my style," he said, but he did as she suggested.

Brighteyes whuffed and gently bumped knuckles with Carson. Then the Bigfoot did an amazing thing. He crouched slightly and extended his hand, offering up a very human-looking handshake.

Carson stared in astonishment. "Amazing. Your father taught him that, didn't he? I remember it from the journal." He reached out and accepted the handshake. Brighteyes closed his fingers, completely engulfing Carson's hand. His grip was surprisingly gentle. Carson pumped his arm three times and the Bigfoot released his hold. Carson laughed with delight. "Extraordinary."

"And Brighteyes has taught at least some of my father's sign language to the other members of the troop," Sarah said.

"Really?" Carson mused, looking over at the other, younger Sasquatch as Joseph completed his ministrations and left the teen Bigfoot staring off into the distance.

Joseph moved off, pulling Russ aside. "The bite was minor and it only happened a few hours ago."

"That's good, right?" Seeing Joseph's look of concern, he prodded. "What is it? What's wrong?"

"The smell. It's the same as in the geologist camp. It's faint, but it's there."

"Would antibiotics help?"

"I don't know. I—" Joseph suddenly stopped. Russ started to say something, but Joseph held up a hand, listening intently.

Carson approached the smaller Bigfoot, careful not to open his lips as he smiled a broad smile. "Hello there, young fella. Do you shake hands, too?" Though much smaller than Brighteyes, this individual was still a few inches taller than the billionaire. Carson signed, 'Friend,' then offered a handshake. The young Sasquatch raised his head and looked at him.

Scratch was listening to a tone. Was he actually hearing it? Or was it in his head? It was a humming, like a bumblebee hovering near his ear. He'd tried waving his hand at it, but the humming continued. It was getting hard to think. One of the humans put something on his arm. It stung. *They hurt you*, a voice in his head said. *Hurt them back.* Scratch shook his head. *No! Brighteyes says they help. Brighteyes says they are friends.* The voice within brushed his thoughts aside. *They are not your friends... you should... no!* As he struggled to control his thoughts, the hairface human approached. It signed, 'Friend,' and held out a hand. Scratch looked at him... looked at the hand. He remembered this human custom; Brighteyes had taught it to him. He reached out and took the man's hand. It was *warm*.

"Wow, that's quite a grip you have there," Carson chuckled as he gently pumped his arm and gave the young Bigfoot a handshake.

Sarah noticed Joseph's alert posture, his head cocked at an angle, listening. She sidled up to Russ. "What is it?" she whispered.

Russ shook his head. "I don't know. I don't hear anyth—wait. Look at Brighteyes."

The Bigfoot was scenting the air, his body tense as he took a few steps toward the tree line. Suddenly he froze and signed, 'Alpha. Alive-Dead.'

"It's here," Joseph said.

An ear-splitting roar came from the woods near the tents. Camp followers began to run to and fro. Russ and Joseph dashed toward the camp, Joseph splitting off to find the Cub Scouts and tell them to bug out. Sarah signed to Brighteyes, 'We go help!' before running after Russ.

Carson looked back toward the chaos and saw Singleton waving frantically. "Cameron!"

"Coming, Bill!" Cameron turned to run back toward the center of camp but lurched to a sudden halt. He turned to find his hand still held by the young Sasquatch. "OK, you can let go. Handshake over." He gently pulled his arm back and the creature's grip increased tenfold. Carson felt the bones in his hand grind together. "Ow! Stop! Let go!" He looked up from the crushing grasp and was met with a face devoid of any friendliness; its teeth were bared and its eyes glowed with madness. Its body seemed to vibrate with tensing muscles as a low strangled growl burbled up from its throat. "Oh my God," Cameron whispered before screaming out, "Help! H—"

The second cry for help was never completed as the young Bigfoot yanked Carson toward him and sunk his teeth into the billionaire's throat. Jerking its head back, Scratch tore a huge chunk of flesh loose. *Humans taste good*, it thought. The terrible voice inside agreed wholeheartedly.

Bill Singleton didn't see his longtime employer perish; his attention was drawn by the sight of two trees toppling to either side as a gigantic shaggy monster bulled between them, effortlessly shoving them aside and snapping the trunks. Singleton had a flashback to Sunday school—the story of Sampson, collapsing the temple by pushing against a pair of columns. *Was Sampson blind in that story? Wait… blind!* Carson's assistant snapped back to reality, remembering what Russ had said about the fire. He headed for a campfire that someone had managed to get started. "Torches! We need torches!"

A shotgun boomed from nearby; one of the cooks who'd been pressed into guard duty fired at the hideous beast. The shot was poorly aimed and served only to draw its attention to the cook. Two giant strides and it closed the distance. The cook racked the pump-action and took aim but never managed to get off a second shot. The creature swung a long arm as it took a third stride and backhanded the hapless cook with the force of a battering ram. With a wet crunch, the man went sailing backward, landing in a rag doll flop near the drone paddock, the shotgun clattering to a stop nearby. The beast roared in triumph and turned, looking for its next victim. Its eyes glittered in the light of the campfires, its pelt matted with dried blood.

Russ and Sarah reached Singleton as two men ran up, each holding a pair of torches. As they handed them out, Russ grabbed Sarah's shoulder and pointed at her tent a few yards away. "Sarah, that bottle of bourbon you had—get it!" As she dashed off, Russ pointed at the others. "Spread out, try to confuse it with the fires… and stay out of reach!"

Sarah got about halfway to her tent when she heard something running, coming closer… and growling. She turned and saw the young Bigfoot charging at her, its jaws glistening with fresh blood. *Oh God, no… not him too!* She opened her mouth to scream but a blur of motion came rushing from her peripheral vision. Brighteyes crashed into her attacker, sending it tumbling into the tent next to hers. A tent pole snapped and the entire tent collapsed in on the creature. Tangled in the tent material, it struggled, thrashing wildly. Tearing sounds and mad growls rose from the pile of fabric. Brighteyes picked himself up from where he'd stumbled and signed to her, 'Run!'

Sarah needed no encouragement. She dashed into her tent, snatching up the three-quarters-full bottle of bourbon before running back out. She was about to rush over to Russ when the sight of Brighteyes brought her up short. The big Sasquatch was straddling the collapsed tent and was doing his best to contain the younger Sasquatch, who was now going berserk, enveloped in tent material and straining against Brighteyes' grip. She came over to him and looked into the younger creature's eyes. What she saw was madness, rage, hunger. No semblance of the young primate she'd met only hours before. She set down the bourbon and laid a hand on Brighteyes' upper arm. The muscles under his hair were rock-hard with strain.

"Brighteyes…" she said. He turned to her, his eyes full of tears. In her studies of primates, she'd never seen a great ape generate true emotion-driven tears before, and she'd wondered if Sasquatch were the same. *I guess they're closer to us than I thought*, she mused as she felt her own eyes fill with tears. "Brighteyes… I'm sorry."

Brighteyes made a mewling, whimpering sound. He couldn't sign with his hands fully employed holding the ravening creature down. Sarah pointed at it, then began signing. 'That not Sasquatch. Friend gone.'

Brighteyes shuddered, took a hitching breath, then nodded reluctantly. He looked down at his former friend; it was snapping its bloody jaws at the air, straining its neck as it tried in vain to land a bite. Brighteyes gave a weary sigh and grunted several vocalizations. The mad creature hesitated for just a moment, some of the rage leaving its eyes. With stunning speed, Brighteyes released his grip on Scratch's body and planted his huge hands on either side of the teen Bigfoot's head, straining with all of his strength. It began snarling and snapping again, and suddenly the pressure on the skull proved too much; the hapless creature's head collapsed with a sudden crunch and its body immediately went still. Brighteyes raised his bloody hands and looked at the palms. A terrible wail of pain tore loose from his throat.

"Sarah!" Russ was running up. "What the hell happened?"

Weeping, Sarah staggered back from Brighteyes. "The other Bigfoot… it changed. It attacked me… Brighteyes had to…"

Russ reached out to her. "Sarah… I'm sorry…"

Before he could offer any further words of comfort, Sarah set her jaw and grabbed the bottle of bourbon from the ground, shoving it against his chest. "You wanna make me feel better?" She pointed back toward the waving torches. "Kill that fucking thing."

Tossing aside the bottle's top, Russ tore off his doo-rag and stuffed it into the bottle. "I hate to waste good bourbon, but…" He upended the bottle for a moment, soaking the cloth, then sprinted toward the sounds of combat, Sarah on his heels. Brighteyes stayed behind, overwhelmed with grief.

They reached the ring of torch-wielding men just as the zombie Bigfoot was lifting a man off the ground; the hapless soul had gotten too close trying to touch his torch to the monster's hair. His terrified scream was cut short as he lost his vocal cords—and much of his esophagus and carotid artery—when the monster took a healthy bite of his throat.

Russ grabbed Singleton's torch arm by the wrist and ignited the cloth wick of his improvised Molotov cocktail. Taking two steps toward the creature, he cocked his arm back just as the hulking beast tossed its spurting victim aside. *If this doesn't work, I'll be next.* He hurled the bottle as hard as he could. It arced through the air, flames fluttering from the cloth. *Bullseye!* he thought as it struck home... thudding ineffectually against the beast's chest before clunking to the ground. *You have got to be kidding me!* The creature looked down at the burning bottle, then slowly raised its head to glare at Russ.

"You throw like a girl," said a familiar voice. Joseph was at his side, withdrawing something from his pocket. He bounced it on his palm and Sarah recognized the chunk of white turquoise he'd used to hold down a corner of her father's map. Joseph took aim and whipped the stone like a bullet, smashing it into the bottle at the monster's feet. The bottle exploded, the bourbon splashing against one of the Bigfoot's legs, igniting it up to the knee. "Well, whattaya know? It *does* protect you from danger."

"Nice shot," Russ said. "All that practice bouncing acorns off my head really paid off."

The creature stomped around, shaking its leg. Again, it seemed more annoyed or confused at the fire than actually hurt by it.

"Did you get the Cub Scouts out?" Sarah asked Joseph.

The Shoshone nodded. "Yes, they're on their way east."

Russ looked around the camp. There were still so many people here, and Liz and Dhir were probably holed up in the tech tent, trying to save Bud. He shouldered the bag of items he'd gathered. "We've got to lead that thing away. Come on, while it's distracted by that hotfoot!" He grabbed Sarah by the hand and pulled her along, flanking the Bigfoot. Joseph ran alongside, snatching up a torch one of the dead men had dropped. They reached the tree line and looked back. The beast was stomping its blazing foot, getting angrier by the second. The rain had finally stopped, but the ground was sodden and the stomps were splashing moisture onto the flames. The distraction wouldn't last long. "Joseph, I need a few minutes. Can you delay it, then lead it that way?" He pointed into the trees.

Joseph held Russ's gaze for a moment before sighing. "All right... Kemosabe. But if it kills me, you and me are gonna fistfight in heaven."

Russ grinned. "I see what you did there. Thanks, man. Keep a torch handy so I can see where you are. Once I'm ready, I'll signal you with a flashlight." He started running, turning to Sarah as they dashed into the trees. "We need to find a good flat spot... and grab any straight branches you can find, about an inch or two thick."

Joseph slowly advanced toward the gigantic beast. *Is it truly a Wendigo? If so, how do we kill it? Can we kill it?* Wielding torches, Singleton and four other men were fanned out along the edges of the tents, doing their best to form a barrier between the creature and the center of camp. No weapons that he could see.

Carson's unwavering insistence on a nonlethal capture had fucked them royally. Joseph had an inkling what Russ was going to try, and it seemed as good a plan as anything he could think of. If it didn't work, everyone in that camp was going to die. He came within a dozen yards of the creature and stopped, taking a deep centering breath.

OK… here we go. He sucked in a full lungful of air and let loose with a near perfect Sasquatch call. He'd heard these forest creatures many times over the years and did his best to ape an alpha male's challenge, common in mating season. The creature stopped its fiery stomping and cocked its head. Joseph drew his hunting knife, holding the blade out to the right, the torch to the left. He bellowed the challenge again.

It worked.

37

Manfred hunched low in a copse of new-growth trees, peering into the darkness. He should be close now. He'd given up trying to reach Jaeger on the radio channel they'd agreed upon. He'd heard a loud gunshot that likely was from Jaeger's large-caliber rifle, so maybe he'd bagged the female. *Then why's he not answering the radio?* Manfred was about to try calling out when he heard something running. The rain had finally let up, but the ground was quite wet, muffling the footfalls. He jacked a round into the chamber of the pistol he'd "borrowed" and released the safety. Whatever it was, it didn't sound very big; soon he heard very human-sounding huffing and puffing. There! A pudgy man running full speed. *It's that audio engineer, what's-his-name... Bob? No... Bud.* Manfred stood up from his crouch. "Psst! Bud! Over here!"

The man squinted and headed his way, coming to a gasping, coughing halt by Manfred's side. He bent over, hands on knees, struggling to gather enough oxygen to speak.

"Jaeger... where is he? Did he shoot the creature?"

Bud managed to reply, his words punctuated by lung-filling gasps. "Oh, he shot it… right through the chest… then it just… got back up… and killed him."

Manfred stared, dumbfounded. "Where is it?"

The question seemed to galvanize Bud. "What do you think I've been running from?" He took off, heading toward camp. "Come on! That little peashooter ain't gonna do you any good!"

Manfred looked at his pistol and thought for a moment. *If I can find Jaeger's body, maybe I can find his rifle. Maybe I can kill that creature—be the first man to bag a Bigfoot! Maybe…*

A horrible screech ripped the night air, and in the distance Manfred heard branches snapping. All thoughts of fame and glory were blotted out by fear and a healthy dose of self-preservation. He dashed after Bud, slowly gaining on the exhausted engineer.

The man raised a radio to his head, yelling out, "Liz, this is Bud! Has the drone dropped off its package? I could really use a lift!"

Littlefoot was aware of a strong breeze blowing through his shaggy pelt. There was also a deep buzzing sound in his ears. Although the sound was very loud, it was somehow soothing. His head hurt. Maybe he should go back to sleep. *No. Open eyes.* He did so and was met with a stunning sight. He was flying! It was still dark out, but the rain had stopped and the moon was starting to peek through the clouds. He could see the trees far below. Littlefoot knew he probably should be terrified, but that wasn't the emotion that filled him. He was… exhilarated! He hooted excitedly and went to wave his arms but found he couldn't move them very much; he was tangled in some sort of bramble bush—no, it was more like vines. He started to struggle, but suddenly a voice came from nearby—human, female, and soothing.

"Hey there, little guy. Don't be scared. You're almost safe."

Littlefoot didn't understand the meaning of the words, but their timbre had a cooing quality that reminded of him of how his mother vocalized to him when he was hurt or afraid. *Mother. Silk. She attacked me!* The little Bigfoot started to whimper.

"Shhhhh… it's OK. You'll be on the ground in no time."

Littlefoot saw where the voice was coming from: a shiny "eye" that was looking at him. After a moment, it swiveled away. Littlefoot did his own eyeball-swiveling, looking around himself. *The human machine! The whirly maple seed machine!* This one seemed to have three spinning seeds helping it fly. He was underneath it, in some kind of nest. Littlefoot had a basic understanding of human vehicles. He'd seen helicopters before, and his youthful imagination had carried him up into the sky, wondering what it would be like to be on one of them. Now he knew! Littlefoot relaxed and enjoyed the ride.

Brighteyes took a deep shuddering breath and rose from Scratch's side. Even though they weren't related, he'd always considered him as a younger brother. And now he'd killed him. *No. Not Scratch.* Brighteyes understood this on some level.

Something had happened that had destroyed what made the young Bigfoot Scratch—just as it had destroyed Silverback and Silk. If anything, Brighteyes had ended Scratch's suffering by killing the *other* that Scratch had become. But that thought was of little comfort when he remembered the young Bigfoot's face… and saw his hands crushing it. *I had to. It was going to kill daughter-of-Beardface.*

A terrible roar shook him from his grief. *Silverback!* Brighteyes ran for the edge of camp, his massive feet slapping the muddy grass with wet splashes. As he neared the tree line, he could see the alpha vanishing into the trees. Ahead of the rampaging shape, Brighteyes could see a small fire moving rapidly ahead of the monster—a human with a fire stick running from Silverback. *One of my friends? I must help!* Brighteyes started to give chase, but a loud buzzing drew his attention as a dark shape topped the trees and dipped rapidly towards the camp. As it neared and was illuminated by the camp lights and fires, Brighteyes could make out a furry shape underneath the object. *Littlefoot?*

"Dhir!" Liz shouted from the tech tent behind him. "I'm back."

Dhir looked up as the large tricopter drone came to a hover above the patch of ground set aside for landing. In the cargo sling beneath the fuselage was a little Bigfoot. Dhir aimed a large flashlight up at TED, making sure its hairy passenger wasn't dangling down beneath the level of the landing gear. *No, he's tucked in. Should be safe.* Dhir noted the little animal's eyes squinting at the flashlight's glare, so he nudged the beam off to the side a couple feet. And then the little Sasquatch waved. Dhir burst into surprised laughter. He quickly illuminated himself with the flashlight and waved back.

"Liz!" he called back to the adjacent tech tent. "Looks like our passenger is safe. You're right above the landing zone. Bring TED straight down." Dhir knew that Liz would be eager to get airborne again immediately; Bud was in serious trouble. The makeshift airlift had worked with the Bigfoot child, and Liz thought she could make it work with Bud. "Don't rush it… nice and easy."

"You got it! Here we go, little fella." Liz's voice reached Dhir from two directions: from the tent behind him and from the speaker above him in the drone's camera turret. The drone came smoothly down and bumped gently on its shocks. "Thank you for flying Liz Air!"

"Cut the engines so I can free this little fuzzball," Dhir said. "Once we're clear, you can go get Bud."

Littlefoot watched the human who had waved to him waiting below, speaking human speech. The female voice responded and the whirlybird started to move downward. He watched as the grass got closer and closer. Littlefoot hooted as he reached the ground and his little enclosure bounced. The loud buzzing sound began to lessen. The human smiled; Littlefoot noted that the man's skin was a bit darker than the others he'd met today.

Once the buzzing stopped, the figure crouched down, speaking softly, and crawled over to Littlefoot, doing something to the vine-like material that was holding him. Suddenly he felt everything loosen and he dropped to the wet grass with a plop. The human crawled back out and gestured—Littlefoot recognized it as the *come here* or *follow* gesture that Brighteyes had taught him. He toddled after the friendly human but flinched when the strange device he'd ridden roared back to life behind him. He turned and watched the little whirling parts that looked like maple seeds begin to spin, faster and faster, before rising into the air. Happily clapping his palms on the ground, Littlefoot hopped about excitedly as the whirlybird banked and headed for the tops of the trees.

The human suddenly squeaked and stumbled back, tripping and falling on his ass in the wet grass next to Littlefoot, his eyes wide. Brighteyes was running toward them, arms outstretched. Littlefoot dashed forward and jumped up against Brighteyes' chest. The big Sasquatch caught him and clung to him, vocalizing softly. He set him down and signed.

'I was afraid for you! Happy to see you!'

Littlefoot gestured at himself and then pointed into the sky before flapping his arms like a bird.

Brighteyes nodded. 'I saw. You brave.'

Littlefoot puffed up with pride. 'Yes. I brave!' Then he looked around. 'Where Scratch?'

Brighteyes sagged, seeming to shrink in size. 'Scratch dead. He was *other*. Alive-Dead.' He began to whimper softly. 'I killed.'

Littlefoot staggered back. *Brighteyes killed Scratch?* He looked up at his grieving troopmate. Brighteyes was like a father to him. Silverback and Silk may have brought him into the world, but Brighteyes had been the one to *show* him that world, to teach him many things about it that the rest of the troop had little interest in. He would never have hurt his family unless he'd had no choice. Littlefoot remembered what Silk had been like when she'd attacked him. If his brother had become Alive-Dead, then Brighteyes hadn't *really* killed him.

Littlefoot came forward and clung to Brighteyes' leg, grunting softly in support. Then he stepped back and signed, 'You are good. You are father now. I love you.'

Brighteyes looked steadily at Littlefoot. He took a shuddering breath and extended his arm, offering his knuckles to the little Bigfoot. Littlefoot gently bumped knuckles with him. 'Thank you,' Brighteyes signed. An angry roar echoed in the forest, and he tensed, looking that way. He turned to Littlefoot and rested his massive hands on his shoulders. 'I must go. I must help human friends. Silverback must die.'

'I help!'

'No. You stay. Stay with humans here.' Brighteyes loped toward the tree line, heading after the mutated alpha.

Littlefoot kicked the wet ground in frustration. *I could help! I am not baby!* He stomped a little ways off and kicked at the ground again. This time his toes struck something hard that clattered across the grass. Littlefoot looked down and gasped in surprise. Near him was a dead human, his head twisted at a severe angle. *Human that Silverback killed*, he thought. *But what did I kick?* Littlefoot soon found the object. A human boom-stick.

In the forest, another enraged roar shook the night.

38

Russ and Sarah ran up an incline, stopping occasionally to grab a fallen branch or snap one off of a tree. Far behind them, they could see the flicker of a torch and hear the roar of the alpha.

"What exactly are you looking for?" Sarah panted.

"I need some level ground with a few trees close together. We'll have one chance at this, and hopefully the trees will funnel it where we want." Russ stopped and turned on the heavy-duty flashlight, sweeping the beam ahead of them. He'd been sparing in its use because he planned to signal Joseph with it. He didn't want his friend spotting the light early and luring the beast in before he was ready. "There!" Russ doused the light and ran forward toward a copse of trees.

Sarah saw the spot. "Are you planning a snare?"

"Partly. But that thing's too big for a standard snare, and I don't have any wire, just paracord." Russ went between a good-sized pair of trees, looking back toward the distant torchlight. "We need to work quickly," he said, dropping the duffel on the ground a couple yards from the two trees. "Here, take the hatchet and make eight stakes, eight to twelve inches long. Try to keep them an inch or so in diameter and sharpen one end. You need a multitool for that?"

"No, I've got a good one." Sarah swiftly laid all of the branches out and began chopping several lengths.

Russ grabbed a spade and started digging a hole, looking up toward the tree cluster, gauging distance. The night's rain made things easier, and he dug swiftly. Looking back at the hole, he chuckled ruefully. *I'll need to scale this up. That thing must be a size 40.* Digging as fast as he could, he gouged along the perimeter, widening the hole, ending with a pit about two feet across and two feet deep.

Sarah finished the last of the stakes and set them next to the hole. Russ started sticking them into the muddy sides of the hole, creating a ring of inward facing points. Sarah watched closely. "I've seen this before. In my dad's papers."

"Yep. Your father sent me the instructions for this, back during the first season of *Survivor Guy*. It's an Apache foot trap… or snare, more accurately. Hand me that paracord?"

Sarah grabbed it and started tying a knot.

"Wait, there's a knot that's best to use—"

"And that's what I'm using. Poacher's knot. I remember. I used to practice tying those knots from my dad's drawings. Here." She handed him the loop with the special slipknot. "I'll go secure the other end. One of those two trees, right?"

"Yeah. We'll need to lead it through there and over the foot trap. Its forward momentum should cinch the snare tight." Russ set the loop over the ring of sharpened sticks and watched as Sarah deftly tied off the other end of the rope. As she came back, he grabbed a thicker length of branch he'd scrounged during their short trek. "Cover the trap with some leaves or small boughs. Not much, just enough to mask it. I need to make another spear."

Sarah set to work. "If I remember right, the prey's foot goes in and the sharp points dig into the leg and ensure it goes into the snare. Then, if it tries to free its foot or keeps coming for us, the snare will pull tight."

"That's the plan," Russ said, chopping the edge of the spear into a fine point. "I should make a fire. Partly to attract it, partly to use as a weapon."

Sarah grabbed his spear. "I'll finish this up. I've only seen your show a few times, but doesn't it take a while to get a fire going?"

"Damn, you're right… and I don't have any flint and steel, so I'll have to build a fire bow and spindle. Or I could just use this." He grinned as he pulled a Zippo out of his pocket.

"Cheater," Sarah laughed.

"Hey, I've been doing the show a long time. There's only so many ways to build a fire." He quickly gathered some nearby materials. "Go signal Joseph now. The guy is fast, but I bet he's done with the whole 'bait' act."

As if to urge haste, another roar, this time much closer, echoed through the trees.

It sounds really pissed, Sarah thought.

39

onna die gonna die gonna die... Bud huffed and puffed his way toward camp. Far off in the distance, he could see lights. *And fires. A lot of fires.* He could hear the distant buzz of the drone. *It's not going to get here in time.* Manfred had quickly caught up with Bud but was now limping, having turned his ankle. *Serves you right,* Bud thought, *trying to race ahead of me and leave me for that thing.* He remembered that old joke and adapted it to his present situation: *You can't outrun a rabid Bigfoot, Manfred... I don't have to, Bud. I just have to outrun you.* Bud felt a hysterical giggle bubbling up. *At least I'll die amused,* he thought. A bone-chilling high-pitched shriek rose from behind them, no more than a few dozen yards away.

Bud yelled into his radio. "Liz! What's the ETA on that drone?"

"About three or four minutes to where I think you are. Might take a few seconds to find you with the FLIR."

"We're not gonna make it," Manfred yelled. "She's too close! I hope that thing can't climb." He hurled himself at a good-sized birch tree, scrabbling at its trunk and lower branches.

Bud tucked the radio into a pocket and followed, hauling himself up with a lot less difficulty than he expected given his traumatic memories of gym class. *Fear: the ultimate performance enhancement drug.* He climbed as high as he could but soon reached Manfred's boots; the mercenary had claimed the highest sturdy branch.

Another ragged shriek tore from their pursuer's throat. Bud twitched, startled by its nearness. Through the thick limbs of the tree, he could see a huge dark shape moving below, a few yards off. It was moving slower now, no longer running. *It's hunting us. It knows we're near.* He could hear occasional sniffs as the creature sought out their scent. *Hopefully the rain will mess with her sense of smell.* Bud had no idea if that would make any difference. He'd have to ask Joseph or Russ about that if he survived the night. The creature moved closer, near the bottom of their tree. A low gurgling growl burbled in its throat, like a demonic purr.

Manfred quietly reached for the pistol he'd snagged from that young man in camp. It was a 9mm Beretta. He wasn't sure it would do him much good, but maybe he could keep that thing from climbing up after them. He racked the slide to chamber a round; unfortunately, he'd already chambered a round earlier and a bullet popped from the ejection port. Manfred made a futile grab for it, nearly losing his balance, quickly grabbing the trunk to maintain his perch. The bullet tumbled down, hitting a couple branches on the way, the little tapping sounds seeming impossibly loud.

Bud and Manfred froze, holding their breath as the little bullet plunked to the forest floor. The monstrous purr ceased and the creature below went completely still. Then, with a terrible howl, it dashed to the bottom of their tree, grabbing at the trunk and looking up at them. The suddenness of the move ripped a scream from Bud's throat. Even Manfred gave a terrified yelp. The rain having passed, the full moon broke through the dissipating clouds. The cold light shone on the beast and reflected in its mad eyes. Its mouth stretched into a toothy grin, and the burbling low growl returned. It started to climb.

Manfred quickly scrambled around the trunk and leaned out from a branch, looking for a clean shot. "Move to your left," he yelled at Bud. Raising the Beretta, he aimed at the creature's head and popped off three rapid shots. Firing one-handed while dangling from a tree, he missed with the first two shots, but the third round struck the Sasquatch in the teeth, shattering several in a shower of tooth shards and blood. The creature let go and dropped to the forest floor. Furious, it looked up at them and shrieked, a fine mist of blood spraying from its wounded mouth, spattering the tree trunk.

"Yeah! You like that?" yelled Manfred. "Go away, bitch, or I'll give you some more!"

The huge Bigfoot grabbed hold of the tree and started to shake it. *This is not going to end well*, Bud thought. He and Manfred clung to the tree, holding on for dear life. Their tormentor ceased shaking and Bud allowed himself a fleeting moment of hopefulness. That feeling died a swift death. The beast gathered itself and then hurled its considerable bulk against the trunk, gripping it, leaning into it with its tremendous strength, roaring with mad fury. Bud heard a couple cracks. *This tree is going down, it's only a matter of time.* Bud felt the trunk fairly vibrating under his grip, but suddenly he felt the strain on the tree slacken. *Oh no, I'm not falling for that one, Universe. No way am I getting my hopes up.*

Bud's cynical thought was also a wise one. The creature made one more supreme effort. There was a tremendous pop and then a symphony of cracking and snapping sounds as the trunk split and the tree began to fall. Bud and Manfred made small adjustments, trying not to be on the underside of the tree when it hit the ground. Rustling sounds filled their ears as the tree's branches scraped through those of its neighbors, picking up momentum before it smashed to the ground. Manfred managed to stay on top and was practically trampolined off of the trunk when it bounced from the impact. Bud was not as lucky; one leg was snaked around the trunk and was crushed against the ground. He heard the crack as the bone broke and a white blaze of pain shot through him.

Liz scanned the monitor screen, searching for Bud and Manfred. Occasionally she flipped between night vision and Forward Looking Infrared on TED's camera suite. She was along the tree line that Bud and she had agreed upon, but there was no sign of them. *Wait. There. To the north.* On FLIR she could just make out a reddish blotch. She piloted the drone toward the heat source and it quickly resolved into two warm human-sized blobs. *They're in a tree! But that means...* She zoomed the camera view in and could see a huge shape at the base of the tree. *But... there's no heat.* The colorless form moved back from the trunk then rushed at it. She saw the warm infrared figures start to move in an arc to the right. *The tree is falling!* "Oh God, Bud, no!"

The being that had once thought of itself as 'Silk' gave a victorious roar and pounded its chest. The tree had crashed to the ground and now she would feast! She moved in. One human held up an object, and a bright flash and loud bang emanated from it. She barely felt the mild pushing sensation as a bullet tore into her chest. Still, the one that had hit her teeth was a nuisance; it would make tearing into flesh a little more difficult. To avoid further unwanted dentistry, the beast raised her massive hand and splayed the fingers, extending the arm out in front of her face. Silk charged, reaching the man in less than a second, taking a round through her palm as she grabbed the object and the man's hand, crushing it in her bloody grip. A sharp jerk and she tore the human's arm clean off, hurling it aside. His terrified screaming annoyed her, so she grabbed the source of the noise. Gripping the top and bottom of his jaw in her hands, she gave the human a flip-top head with one violent motion. *The other one. Kill the other one too.* She spied the second human, struggling under the tree. *Oooooh, that one looks fat... and juicy.*

Bud watched helplessly as the monster tore off the top of Manfred's head before turning its attention to him. His leg broken and pinned under the tree, he had no chance. *Unless...* He dug out his pack of jerky and tossed the contents toward the beast. It showed no interest and started toward him. *Jeez, that commercial was misleading.* Bud was momentarily fascinated by the hole in its chest, where Jaeger had shot it. *I can see through to the other side.* Suddenly the creature stopped and cocked its head. Through the ringing in his ears, Bud heard a buzzing sound, getting louder and louder. The buzzing transitioned to a dull roar, and suddenly a bright spotlight pierced the night, illuminating the Sasquatch.

"Don't worry, Bud! The cavalry's here! Ba ba, ba-ba *ba* ba... ba-ba-ba *ba* ba..."

Liz's voice! Singing the "Ride of the frikkin' Valkyries"! Her voice was projected at maximum volume from the big drone's speakers. The beast squinted, blinded by the brilliant light. The drone's engines throttled up to full power.

"Hey, bitch! Let's dance!"

It wasn't a lengthy dance. Liz brought the drone in fast, slightly off to one side. The tricopter had two of its rotary blades extending out forty-five degrees to either side of its nose. She sent TED in just off the ground, aiming the nose a few feet to the creature's right. The huge left rotor blade scythed into the Bigfoot's forehead, buzzsawing through and removing the top of its skull and half of its brain before the blades tore loose from the motor and the big drone spun wildly into a nearby tree.

Blood geysering from its topless skull, the gigantic beast slowly sank forward, crashing to its knees before toppling forward onto its face.

Bud finally remembered to breathe. He managed to dig the radio out from his pocket.

"Liz, you killed it! You… are… a goddess."

"Tell me something I don't know. Holy shit, that was wild! I'm sorry about the other guy. I was too far away."

Bud shifted, trying to get out from under the tree. A spike of pain informed him that course of action would not be happening. He grunted in pain.

"Bud, are you hurt?"

"Y'know, between having a tree fall on my leg and getting torn limb from limb and eaten… I'll take the tree. But I ain't going anywhere without some help."

"OK. I'd offer you a ride, but I'm guessing TED isn't doing very well. I lost the feed when it crashed."

Bud looked over at the wreckage of the drone. The spotlight was still on, throwing eerie shadows through the distant trees and illuminating the drone. Twisted metal; broken blades; one engine lying nearby. "Uh, yeah, TED's a mangled wreck. Break it to Dhir gently… I think he's in love with the thing."

"Oh, I dunno, I might be able to give him something else to focus on. Hey, the GPS in the drone is still working! I know exactly where you are. You hang tight, I'll send someone to get you."

Bud looked around at the eerie scene; the massive dead Bigfoot, the long shadows thrown from the drone's spotlight. "Uh… isn't there another one out here somewhere?"

"Don't worry. Sarah, Russ, and Joseph are gonna kill it," she said with forced confidence. "I hope."

40

He could hear it breathing, moving to his left. *It's flanking me.* Joseph had come to think of this corrupted Bigfoot, this Wendigo, as some form of zombie; the strong stench of decay, the ability to shrug off what should have been fatal wounds, its decidedly carnivorous eating habits… But it wasn't mindless. No, beneath the rage and ravenous hunger, there was a spark of cunning. The creature was clearly driven by simple violent instincts, but it was capable of thought. Joseph was extremely fast and agile in the forest, and while the monster would easily run him down on a flat open plain, the Shoshone had bobbed, weaved, dodged, and jumped every which way, using the terrain to frustrate his pursuer. Now the beast was trying a different tactic.

Joseph paused, panting softly as he listened. Over the gentle crackle of his makeshift torch, he could hear rustling ahead and to the left. *Yep, it's trying to quietly move around and ahead of me.* He hoped the beast wasn't moving between him and his friends. *Hurry up, Russ. I may be in good shape, but I don't think this thing gets tired at all.*

As if in answer to his thoughts, a bright flashlight beam appeared atop a low rise off to the right. It flashed on and off several times. The signal. Behind the flashlight, Joseph could make out the flickering of flames. He cocked his arm, hurled his guttering torch toward the sounds of his stalker and gave a loud whoop, letting the Sasquatch know he wasn't fooling anyone. It roared, and the quiet rustling turned into a ground-thudding, branch-cracking charge. Joseph broke into a dead run, heading for the rise.

Sarah blinked the flashlight a few more times as she watched a torchlight sail off into the distant trees. She heard a loud whoop from a human throat followed by sounds of movement. A spine-tingling roar and much louder sounds of pursuit rose from a little farther off.

She ran back to Russ, who was busily igniting several simple torches from his impromptu campfire. "It's coming! It's right behind Joseph."

"OK. Good." Russ sounded nervous but he quickly shook it off. "Here, take the hatchet and a torch." He grabbed another torch and his makeshift spear. He'd made it as sharp as he could and fire-hardened the point. He moved to the pair of trees he wanted to funnel it through and looked back at Sarah. She knew exactly what he was planning and was already planted just beyond the foot trap. He returned his gaze to the woods downslope, looking for Joseph. *There.* A shadow was zigzagging through the trees, headed straight for him.

"Joseph! Up here!"

The figure soon reached the circle of firelight from Russ's torch. "You owe me… a beer… you fucker," he gasped as he reached Russ.

"Name your poison, and it's yours." Russ pulled Joseph toward him through the trees. If the beast was in visual range, he wanted it to see where Joseph went. "Watch your step and join Sarah."

Joseph spotted the snare instantly. "Apache foot trap. Might work. But it's got a long stride, so it might just step over it."

"Yeah, we're gonna need a little luck."

"If it misses, then we'll need to do our best to keep it over the spot until it steps in," Sarah said. "Here." She handed Joseph a burning branch.

He took the torch and drew his large hunting knife from its sheath. "Been a pleasure working with you, Dr. Bishop."

"Back at ya, Mr. Washakie."

"Here it comes!" Russ yelled, waving his torch back and forth.

The thing that had been Silverback was enraged. The human with the black hair had led it all over the forest. The little meat sack was fast; Silverback had crashed into trees and tripped over roots. *I will enjoy eating him*, it thought. It watched its prey run past another human, holding a burning branch. *That human burned my foot. Eat him too!* The Sasquatch loped toward the low hill, and the man waved the flames back and forth. *Taunting me. Kill! Eat!* It bellowed a challenge and charged up the incline. The man backed away between two trees, and Silverback followed, reaching the top. The man was backing toward two other humans, the black-haired jackrabbit and a human female. It felt its stomach rumble. *Kill them all! Eat them all!* Squeezing between the two trees, the ravenous beast rushed at them, venting a mad scream.

Russ kept one eye on the monster's feet at it charged. "C'mon, c'mon, c'mon..." It pushed through the trees; one giant right foot hit the ground... and then the left landed right on the edge of the hole and slid in. The creature howled in surprise as the pointed sticks dug into its lower calf. It immediately jerked its leg to free itself, cinching the snare tight. As the snare tripped it up, it went partway down, catching itself with its hands.

"Now!" Russ yelled. Remembering his trick at the scout camp, he flipped his torch into its face. It didn't catch, most of the facial hair having already burned off, but it dazzled it for an instant.

Joseph darted to the right, coming around behind the monster and ramming his long knife into its lower back, aiming for a kidney, stabbing again and again.

Russ thrust his spear into the spot above its collarbone, aiming for its heart or lungs. He yanked it back out and speared it again.

Sarah moved to the left. The beast still had its palms planted on the ground, and she chopped the hatchet down as she passed, severing two of the fingers on its right hand. She followed with a chop to its forearm as she tried to get around behind it. The Bigfoot briefly stopped struggling with the snare and lifted its bleeding hand, looking at it with annoyance. Sarah chopped at its ribs, the hatchet blade hitting a rib with a dull thud. Almost casually, the monster twisted slightly and swung its wounded arm at Sarah, backhanding her and sending her flying. Had the creature not been so off balance, the blow would have been fatal; even so it was like being hit with a baseball bat. Sarah landed in a heap, out cold. Her torch landed in a patch of pine needles, and a small fire began to spread.

"Sarah!" Russ yelled, jabbing the creature in the neck. It turned to him and started pulling against the snare. Russ saw Joseph crouching low, moving closer to the beast's rear.

The kidney stabs had done nothing. *If I can't kill it, maybe I can hobble it.* Joseph closed in on the back of its trapped leg, planning to hamstring it by cutting the tendons at the back of the thigh. *I dunno… that is one thick thigh*, he thought. He raised his knife in both hands.

"Hokahey!" he shouted and stabbed it into the thigh, twisting and pulling the blade across. The creature roared and twisted, swinging an arm back at him and striking his side with a glancing blow. Joseph felt a couple ribs snap and he tumbled backward, managing to hold on to his knife. Wincing, he tried to stand.

Russ crouched by Sarah. She was unconscious but breathing. *Have to get her away from here!* He dropped his spear and tried to pick her up, but she was limp as a ragdoll. *No way I can outrun that thing if it gets free.* "Wake up, Sarah!" He shook her by the shoulders, glancing over at the slowly spreading flames from Sarah's fallen torch. The ground was soaked, but it had landed at the base of a thick tree where the needles were relatively dry. *Oh, yes, please, let's have a forest fire too.* With growing urgency, he tried again to revive her.

The gigantic alpha braced itself and pulled; the sharp stakes tore at its leg and the paracord went taut and dug into its flesh, threatening to sever the foot. Suddenly the beast paused, looking down at the rope. A low growl gurgled in its throat as it took the paracord in both hands and yanked. The rope strained against its knots, the tree creaking as the creature pulled with a savage strength. Finally, the cord snapped near the tree, and the monster tore its mangled leg free from the hole and began limping toward Russ and Sarah.

Russ grabbed at the hatchet beside him and hurled it end over end. It thumped handle-first into the creature's head and bounced up into the air. *Shit. That always looks easy in the movies*, he thought, grabbing for his spear. Death closed in on him; he could smell the thing's fetid breath as saliva ran in rivulets from its jaws. *Should've grabbed my GoCam... my graphic demise would have made for some riveting footage.*

Joseph scooped up the fallen hatchet, planted his feet, and let loose a full-throated Bigfoot vocalization. The hollered challenge hurt his shattered ribs, but he stood firm, ax in one hand, hunting knife in the other. The beast froze, its attention torn between juicy flesh and a challenge that some deeply buried instinct remembered. Its new nature won out; ignoring Joseph's call, it began moving forward again. Joseph cocked his arm and hurled the hatchet. His broken ribs threw off his aim only slightly, and it buried itself in the creature's back, inches from its spine. Joseph bellowed the challenge again, and this time the shaggy nightmare whirled and howled a response, instinctively pounding its chest. Then it charged. Between the hamstringing and the snare, it was not moving quickly. He waited until it was almost upon him, then dived in a shoulder roll past its left flank. Pain flared in his side, but he rolled to his feet and leapt onto the monster's back, grabbing hold of its long hair and stabbing the hunting knife into his throat, going for the carotid. He buried the knife to the hilt but didn't get a chance to twist or slash the blade. The creature's long limbs reached back over its shoulders with ease, grabbing the Shoshone and hurling him overhead across the little clearing. Joseph crashed into a low-hanging tree branch with enough force to snap the branch from the trunk. He landed hard, the breath knocked from his lungs, ears ringing.

Silverback roared in victory, pounding its chest again. The celebration was interrupted by a poke from behind. The human with the stick again. It grabbed the spear, effortlessly pulling it from the human's grip and whacking the shaft into the side of the puny figure's head. Stunned, the human dropped and the beast tossed the spear aside. *Time to feast!*

Vision blurred from the blow to his head, Russ prepared for the inevitable. The monstrous figure loomed above him, eyes shining with a ravenous hunger. It reached for him… and then was yanked forcefully backward, falling forward and smashing facedown to the ground. Behind the beast, illuminated by the flames, was Brighteyes! The Bigfoot was holding the torn end of the paracord snare that was still attached to the alpha's left leg. The monster roared in frustration, its hunger piqued. It clawed at the ground, scrabbling toward Russ. Brighteyes grabbed the rope tightly and jerked as hard as he could; the snare, already buried in the flesh of the lower calf, tore through, ripping Silverback's foot completely off. Russ felt his vision start to gray out.

The alpha howled and managed to rise up on one knee, grabbing at Brighteyes. The younger male stayed out of reach, scooping up Russ's spear. He'd watched the human using the spear and heard the other human using a mating season challenge; he couldn't let the alpha bite him, and he had a plan. Holding the spear in both hands, he thundered a rival male's call. Silverback, whipped into a frenzy, responded in kind, opening his mouth wide to roar a response. Brighteyes rammed the sharpened shaft straight into the alpha's mouth and charged forward, bulling into the creature and forcing him back against a tree. With a final thrust, Brighteyes pinned the howling monster to the trunk with the spear. A couple more powerful thrusts and the shaft was buried in the tree. Silverback went insane with rage, growling around the spear, blood and drool streaming from his open mouth, his mad eyes locked on his attacker. Brighteyes flicked his eyes to the side, looking for something to crush his former troop leader's skull; in that instant, one of the mammoth alpha's hands shot out, clamping onto Brighteyes' throat like an unbreakable vise.

Brighteyes couldn't believe the monster's strength! Silverback had always been stronger than him—probably twice as strong. But the grip he now felt was unearthly. *Other.* He grabbed at the alpha's fingers, trying fruitlessly to break the creature's hold. The mad howling quieted, and Brighteyes looked up to see a gleam of glee in Silverback's eyes. A hissing gurgle issued from his throat, the foul odor of decay wafting out in a putrid cloud. Slowly, the creature moved forward, dragging itself along the blood-soaked shaft. Brighteyes felt his vision start to dim, and he flailed helplessly at this undead monstrosity as it reached the end of the spear, pulling free with a wet squelching sound. Leaning its weight into its iron grip, the huge alpha bore Brighteyes down to the ground, landing on top of him. Eyes shining with hunger, it opened its jaws wide and began to push its head downward. Brighteyes felt himself losing consciousness but continued to struggle, both hands grabbing and pushing at the slavering horror, trying to keep those snapping jaws from biting into his face. It was close enough now the odor of rot was overpowering, and he could smell the burnt hair on its face.

It was no use. He couldn't breathe. He feared the last thing he would see was Silverback's terrible face before it tore into him. His vision started to dim.

Suddenly, a loud pair of mechanical sounds came from nearby. Silverback turned his face toward the sound, and through his dimming vision, Brighteyes saw confusion enter the alpha's eyes. It started to roar but was cut short. There was a tremendous *BOOM* and Silverback's face was blasted to fragments. The choking grip immediately loosened, and Brighteyes gasped for breath, looking to the side.

Littlefoot was standing to there, holding a human boom-stick. For years, the little Bigfoot had watched many hunters use them, and his fascination with human devices appeared to have paid off. Recovering from the recoil, he pumped the underside of the gun, making a loud clack-clack. Silverback emitted a weird rasping burble, its fingers blindly clutching at the air. Littlefoot put the end of the boom-stick against the alpha's ruined face and pulled the trigger. Brain matter and chunks of skull fanned out in a cone of gore, and the huge beast went still, flopping back to the forest floor.

Sarah regained consciousness, sitting up with a moan. Her brain had trouble processing what she was seeing. A small fire was burning to her left; a dazed Russ was slumped on her right; ahead, a blood-soaked headless Sasquatch lay on its back with Brighteyes lying alongside. But the capper was the baby Bigfoot, standing nearby holding a shotgun and looking very pleased with himself.

"Did we win?" Russ groaned.

"I'm not sure yet," Sarah said quietly, warily eyeing the shotgun-wielding youngster.

Brighteyes crawled out from under the zombie Bigfoot, rolling the corpse aside. He panted and signed to Littlefoot, 'You brave. You help me… help friends.'

The little primate held the shotgun over his head and shook it several times, hooting happily.

Brighteyes held out his hand. 'Give.'

Looking like a human child being asked to hand over some adult treasure he'd been playing with, the youngster lowered the weapon and held it out to Brighteyes, who carefully took it.

Holding it gingerly, Brighteyes brought the shotgun over to Russ and Sarah and placed it on the ground. 'You hurt?' he signed to the two humans.

'We are good,' she replied with a couple gestures.

Brighteyes looked over at the fire from Sarah's fallen torch burning at the base of a pine. It wasn't spreading much due to the wet ground, but it was big enough. He grabbed hold of the alpha's feet and dragged it over to the fire; the fringes of its pelt caught quickly.

Sarah got unsteadily to her feet and offered Russ a hand up. The young Bigfoot approached them, and Sarah signed to him, 'Thank you.'

Littlefoot thumped his chest in a proud manner. 'I brave.'

Sarah laughed and nodded, signing back. 'Yes. Brave.'

"Saved by a baby Bigfoot with a shotgun," chuckled Russ. "Well, now we know they can use tools."

"You still alive, Survivor Guy?" came a voice, pinched with pain.

"Joseph!" Russ went to the Shoshone, who was hobbling toward them from the other side of the clearing. "I thought you were a goner."

"That makes two of us," Joseph replied, wincing as Russ put an arm under his shoulder. "Agh... watch the ribs, Kemosabe."

"Aw, quit your whining, ya big baby," Russ teased.

"Boys," Sarah interrupted. "Need I remind you the female's still out there?" She picked up the shotgun. "Let's get back to camp." She signed their intention to Brighteyes, and the battered group headed east. Behind them, Silverback's body burned brightly.

Dawn was just breaking as they neared the northern edge of camp; there were still several fires burning and a few people milling about. *Everyone is going to be on edge*, Sarah thought. *Probably best to keep our furry friends out of sight.* As they approached, a pair of figures ran toward them. Sarah held out a hand to Brighteyes and Littlefoot and signed, 'Wait.'

She exited the tree line with Russ and Joseph. "Liz! Dhir!"

"Sarah!" Liz called out. "You're alive!" She looked at the bruised and battered trio. "You guys look like hell."

"I've had better days," Joseph grumbled. "I blame Russ."

"Hey, now," Russ protested, "if it weren't for my trap—"

"My *father's* trap, you mean," interrupted Sarah.

"We managed to lock on to where you were with the Ear," Dhir said. "It sounded like a huge fight. Did you kill it?"

"It's dead," Sarah said. "But we had a little help." She gestured towards the trees. Brighteyes and Littlefoot stepped into view.

"Hello there, little fella," said Liz, waving to the Bigfoot child. "I remember you."

The little primate lit up with excitement. He tugged his ear and pointed at Liz, then held his arms out and spun in a circle.

"Yes! You heard me on the drone!"

Littlefoot pointed at Dhir and launched into sign language. He turned and looked at Brighteyes, miming surprise, squealing, and flopping down on his butt.

"Looks like he remembers you too, Dhir." Liz laughed.

"Hey, I hate to rain on the reunion, but there's another creature out there," Russ reminded.

"No, there isn't," said Dhir, grinning. When everyone looked at him, he nudged Liz. "Tell them," he coaxed.

"I… kinda chopped its head off," she said with equal parts shyness and pride.

"Yes, TED the drone gave her life for the cause. That monster was attacking Bud, and Liz rammed one of the rotor blades right into its head. She's an amazing pilot!" he gushed.

"I had a pretty good teacher," she replied, blushing.

"Is Bud OK?" Sarah asked, concerned.

A low rumble came from the tree line to the north, and an ATV motored into view, two riders atop it. Bill Singleton drove up to the group and came to a stop, a man clinging tightly to him. The passenger waved. "Howdy, folks. What'd I miss?"

"Bud!" Sarah ran to him. "Are you all right?"

"Leg's not too happy, but otherwise, I'm good. Thanks to Liz."

Littlefoot ran up to the ATV and waved to Bud before giving the vehicle a close examination. "What happened out there?" Singleton asked, dismounting. "When Liz sent me to get Bud, she said they heard quite a battle."

Russ and Sarah quickly recounted their confrontation with the Bigfoot zombie, making sure to include the contribution of their two Sasquatch friends.

"Where's Carson?" Sarah asked when they finished.

Singleton's face fell. "Cameron Carson is deceased. The young adult must have attacked him when that huge monster charged into the camp. By the time I realized what had happened, he was dead."

Joseph placed a hand on the man's shoulder. "I am sorry for your loss. And please, don't blame the Bigfoot. Whatever afflicted the others infected it too." Suddenly, Joseph tilted his head, listening.

Soon the air vibrated with a rhythmic thumping sound. Littlefoot hopped up and down and began his little spinning pantomime again. The noise grew, coming from the southwest.

"Helicopters," Russ said.

"I managed to contact the National Guard in Boise," Singleton said. "Once the weather cleared, they promised to send Guardsmen and medical personnel."

"The last thing we need is some trigger-happy soldier shooting our new friends," Sarah said quickly. She turned to Brighteyes and pointed up into the sky in the direction of the approaching helicopters. 'More humans,' she signed. She held up the shotgun. 'With these. Not safe. I am sorry. You must go.'

The Bigfoot expelled a sigh and nodded sadly before signing back, 'Yes. Danger. I understand.' He huffed a short pant, calling Littlefoot to him. 'You are good humans. You are friends.' He seemed frustrated as he sought sign language to say what he wanted to say, but the vocabulary Sarah's father had developed with him was limited. Finally he signed, 'I want you see me more.'

Sarah nodded vigorously. "Of course I'll come back and visit," she said aloud, then signed, 'Yes. I see you more.'

Brighteyes gave a short frustrated grunt and gestured in a wide circle around them, signing animatedly. 'Many humans now. We go far.' He pointed north and signed again. 'You look. You find us far there.'

Sarah nodded. "I'll find you."

Littlefoot had been following the gestured conversation and darted forward, hugging Sarah around the waist. Sarah hugged him back, stroking the top of his furry head.

Joseph approached Brighteyes and held out a hand. Brighteyes shook it briefly before Joseph shifted his grip and clasped forearms with the big primate, his fingers tiny on the massive arm. He held the Sasquatch's gaze and nodded once before releasing the grip and stepping back.

Russ stepped forward and simply signed, 'Thank you.'

Brighteyes stuck out his hand and Russ took it. As they shook hands, the sound of the helicopters built to a roar and several large Blackhawks swooped into view over the tree-tops to the south of camp. The Bigfoot turned to look at the choppers and uttered a throaty grunt, urgently gesturing for Littlefoot to come. They headed back into the tree line, the sunrise throwing dappled light on their pelts. They turned and looked back at their human friends.

"Goodbye, Brighteyes," Sarah said, raising her hand in a gesture of farewell.

Brighteyes and Littlefoot raised their hands in reply. As the helicopters descended into the base camp, the pair of Sasquatch turned and loped into the forest, disappearing into the trees.

EPILOGUE

By the time everyone returned to the camp, the National Guard had fanned out and formed a perimeter. Carson's original group of helicopters landed as well. At Joseph's urging, the remaining zombified Bigfoot corpses were burned. He claimed that was the only way to purge the evil spirit of the Wendigo but told Russ and Sarah in private he just wanted the diseased bodies destroyed before any overeager scientist types decided to take tissue samples.

By midmorning, additional helicopters arrived bringing agents from the Centers for Disease Control. The CDC Regional Office in Seattle had sent a rapid reaction team after Joseph and Russ had spoken with the National Guard commander and explained what they'd found in the geologists' camp and at the site of the attack on the Spook Stalkers. Soldiers went into the woods to secure those locations as well as the other known attack sites. It wasn't long before a request went out for additional body bags.

Dhir and Liz returned to the tech tent to lend their help to the forest search. Dhir manned the Ear, and Liz piloted the little quadcopter drone—she'd named it TED Jr.—and they scanned the woods for survivors or victims. Word came that the Cub Scouts had safely reached the tiny community of Orogrande and would be flown out of its nearby airstrip.

In the center of camp, a number of body bags were laid out, ready to be loaded onto helicopters. Bill Singleton sat on the ground beside one of them, staring into space. Joseph joined him and the two sat in silence.

Russ followed Sarah into her tent and stood quietly as she went to the table in the center, laying her fingers reverently on the cover of her father's journal.

"We found Brighteyes," she said quietly before turning to face Russ. "Why couldn't that have been the end of it? We found Brighteyes, we found his troop… he passed down my father's sign language to the others. Why did all the rest have to happen?" She started to tear up. "Goddammit, we made one of the greatest discoveries in history, and then… monsters? People dying, Sasquatch dying." She bit her lip and shook her head.

Russ stepped closer. He didn't try to hold her… he was fairly sure she'd kick his ass if he went all "protective male" on her. He just held her eyes and spoke quietly. "Hey, you *did* make a monumental discovery and exonerated your dad ten times over. The rest of it was… something else. Hopefully we'll find out exactly *what* at some point. And once the dust settles, you can come back here and find your new friends again."

Sarah looked at him for a long time before she spoke. "I wouldn't mind you being there when I do," she said softly. "If Brighteyes moves the troop, I might not be able to find them. I may need your tracking skills."

"I think Joseph would be a better bet for that. That guy runs rings around me."

"Well… maybe I'd want you with me for another reason…"

"My fire-making skills and keen instincts for camera angles? My deft touch with a rubber foot stamp? Oh, I know… it's my rakish smile and winning personality."

Sarah suddenly reached up and grabbed him by the back of the neck. "Shut up, Cloud," she purred and pulled his head close, pressing her lips to his. After a long span of time, she withdrew a few inches. "So. You in?"

Russ smiled. "Count on it, Dr. Bishop."

They held each other's eyes, but then the moment was brutally interrupted by a terrible commotion outside. Shouts, screams… and snarling.

Russ and Sarah burst from the tent and took in the scene: Joseph, Singleton, a couple surviving Carson employees, and several Guardsmen were standing in a circle around a body bag. Carson's body bag. And the bag was snarling and thrashing.

Singleton grabbed a camp medic. "You told me he was dead!"

The man was white as a sheet. "He *was*, sir! The side of his throat was torn out. He had bled out by the time we found him, I swear!"

Joseph drew his hunting knife and started forward. William Singleton, the fussy little assistant, suddenly spoke with steel in his voice. "Stop! You, Guardsmen… restrain that man," he commanded. The soldiers, most of them quite young, did as he asked; they held Joseph by the arms and disarmed him. "This isn't some rabid beast like those things that attacked us. This is Cameron Carson! This is a human being!"

"Mr. Singleton," Joseph said calmly and firmly, "what is in that bag is no longer human."

"Yes, yes… I heard what you said to the lieutenant colonel. Glowing rocks and zombies in the woods with a dollop of Indian mysticism. Utter nonsense. Whatever is happening to him, it is a pathogen! It can be *treated*. My employer is clearly alive and with his considerable resources he will remain that way." He grabbed one of Carson's camp staff. "Quinn, ready the Sasquatch cage."

While Quinn ran to the cage, Singleton instructed several Guardsmen to surround the writhing body bag. The young soldiers were a little unnerved by the horrifying sounds that emanated from the bag.

"Singleton. You must kill it," Joseph said. "The dead should stay dead."

"Listen to him, Bill," Russ said. "I saw those other dead men in the forest…"

"Cameron *wasn't dead*!" Singleton barked, rounding on them. "Don't you see? He was badly wounded, that much is clear… but he must have simply been unconscious."

The cage was rolled alongside the body bag on its pressurized casters. Quinn opened the heavy-duty door while Singleton directed the Guardsmen to load the body bag into the cage. Carefully grabbing the four corners, the Guardsmen quickly lifted the bag and placed it just inside the cage before closing and locking the gate.

"You're making a mistake," Joseph said sadly.

"So you've said."

"If you truly believe Carson is alive… and still human… then I suppose you should unzip the bag. It must be quite claustrophobic in there."

Singleton turned to the Shoshone, who looked calmly back at him. "All right," he said somewhat nervously. He extended his arms through the bars, reaching for the zipper. The body bag bounced and thrashed, feral sounds continuing to issue from within. Taking a deep breath Singleton grabbed the zipper and pulled it down a foot before quickly retracting his arm.

A nightmare face emerged, bloodshot eyes staring wildly, lips drawn back from its teeth, slavering jaws snapping hungrily. In moments the thing tore its way out of the bag and threw itself against the cage, thrusting an arm through the bars and reaching for Singleton with gnarled fingers. The side of its neck was a ragged mess where Scratch had torn into the flesh.

"Alive-Dead," Sarah whispered, recalling Brighteyes' sign language.

Singleton was clearly shaken, but he remained determined to help his longtime employer. "Mr. Carson… Cameron… it's me. Bill."

To everyone's surprise, the raging creature went still. It glared at Singleton for a moment, eyes still shining with madness. Suddenly, it closed its eyes tightly and vigorously shook its head before slowly rising to its feet. Appearing at war with itself, the thing began to speak.

"Mr. Singleton," it rasped. "I seem to be… ill." It started to growl in its ruined throat but violently shook its head again, as if to clear its thoughts. "Would you… would you be so kind as to get me home?"

"Yes, Mr. Carson," Singleton replied in a hushed voice.

"And Bill… call ahead… tell my chef I'll be wanting several Wagyu rib eye steaks."

"Of course, sir," said Singleton.

Carson flashed his famous megawatt smile. "Extra rare," said the Zombie Billionaire.

EPI-EPILOGUE

Sharkey and Farley approached the campsite that their commanding officer had sent them to secure. Apparently it had belonged to a pair of geologists. The commander had been mum about the specifics of what had happened to the occupants, but he'd been absolutely clear on one point: they were not to enter the camp. Once they had located it, they were to simply watch over it until some government eggheads arrived.

"That's it," said Farley. Born and bred in Idaho, he'd done a lot of hunting in his youth and knew his way around the woods. "Green tent. Right where that Indian said it'd be."

"Whattawe do now?" asked Sharkey, a burly Montanan.

"Hurry up and wait," said Farley, slinging his rifle over a shoulder and leaning his hip against a tree.

Sharkey wrinkled his nose. "What's that stink?"

Farley sniffed. "Something died. The campers, I'd bet. Not our problem," He yawned and fished a pair of earbuds out of a pocket before scrolling through his music library.

Sharkey looked around at the sodden ground, still soaked from the previous night's rain. "Ah, fuck this," he grumbled, "if we're gonna have to sit here, I'm gonna go get them camp chairs."

"The lieutenant colonel said to stay out of the camp."

"The lieutenant colonel ain't about to spend the next few hours sitting in the soggy woods. I'll be quick."

"Whatever," said Farley, tucking the buds in his ear and firing up some Kenny Chesney.

Sharkey set his carbine against a tree and jogged to the campsite. Grabbing hold of the two camp chairs that were sitting next to the remains of a campfire, he turned to go back but stopped in his tracks. He heard something. It was… a tone? Very faint. Almost like a sustained note. He looked back at Farley, who was bobbing his head to whatever country music he was listening to. No, it wasn't coming from those earbuds. *It's coming from in there.* Sharkey set the chairs down and made his way to the tent.

His commander had been adamant about staying on the perimeter, not touching anything. But Sharkey really *needed* to find that sound; it seemed to be calling to him. He stepped over a sleeping bag that was hanging out of the tent and went inside. Immediately, he felt drawn to a little bag at the back of the tent interior. Inside was a spherical rock, greenish in hue. It gave off a soft, soothing glow. *There you are*, he thought, reaching down and picking up the rock. It was surprisingly light. The sound was a chord now. *So beautiful… like it's full of tiny angels.* He stumbled back out of the tent, holding the rock in his hands. He stared at it, bathing in that rich chorus of sound. *So beautiful…*

Suddenly the rock was yanked out of his hands. Farley, still pumping Chesney into his ears, grabbed the rock and yelled at Sharkey, "What the fuck are you doing, Sharkey? They told us not to touch anything!" He cocked his arm and pitched the object into the air toward the south, where the terrain dropped off precipitously. It arced down, striking an incline… and began to roll.

The meteorite—for that was what it was—bounced and rolled its way downhill before plunking into the West Fork Crooked River. It bobbed to the surface, its lattice-like structure and mineral makeup making it quite buoyant. The heavy rains had produced prodigious amounts of runoff and the creek ran fast. In a few hours, the meteorite reached Lake Creek and followed the flow south, passing into the body of water with the inspired appellation of Fish Lake. Had the current taken it off to the west and down Whistling Pig Creek, its journey might have come to a dead end; but no, the intrepid meteorite floated straight across the lake and continued along the southern branch of Lake Creek, where flooding allowed it to bump along amidst some runoff debris into the east fork of Sheep Creek, glowing gently in the moonlight after the sun went down.

The following day, the meteorite left the creek for the Salmon River. Picking up speed, it floated west. Occasionally, a salmon would hear its siren song and move in to investigate, but the flow of the river kept it out of reach. By midday, the strange sphere hit the south bank and bumped along it into the mouth of French Creek… then Jackson Creek as the sun went down… then the north fork of the Payette River by midnight. Early in the morning, it floated along Upper Payette Lake before resuming its journey in the river. By noon the following day, it floated into some debris in the many twists and turns of the river and was lodged for a few hours before another powerful storm sent a fresh deluge down into the waterways. The debris pulled free of the river's banks and the whole mass flowed south into Lake Payette, a large alpine lake with an impressive three-hundred-foot depth. The detritus broke apart and the sphere continued on its merry way, reaching the middle of the lake by two in the morning as the storm blew off to the east and the moon resumed her perch in the sky. At this rate, the meteorite would reach the lakeside town of McCall by daybreak.

Three hundred feet down, buried in the sediment of the lake bottom, a huge shape stirred. It was an ancient organism, inhabiting this lake for centuries. To compensate for fluctuations in food sources and occasional harsh winters, the lake's inhabitant had become quite adept at entering a deep state of hibernation—sometimes for a year, sometimes for decades. She could even be frozen solid, all her metabolic processes entering a lengthy stasis, much like the arctic wood frog. Hundreds of years ago, the Nez Perce and Shoshone of the area had occasionally encountered her. They considered the creature an evil spirit that haunted the lake. François Payette, a French trapper for whom the lake was named, had put a musket ball into her shoulder before she'd disappeared beneath the surface. Nearly fifty years ago, Lake Payette had been well stocked with fish, and she remained active for several years. She had been spotted many times in that span and at last she had a name: "Sharlie." She had also been called "Slimy Slim" and "The Twilight Dragon of Lake Payette," but Sharlie was what most of the residents of the lake called her.

It had been nearly fifteen years since her last awakening, and she was still deep in sleep, but something was calling to her. Something was singing. Deep in her semiconscious mind, she could hear the beautiful note; the water amplified the sound and it filled the lake around her. She was fairly certain it had absolutely nothing to do with food, but Sharlie didn't care. She needed to go to this sound and hear what it had to say.

One eye slowly opened. She could make out the dappled moonlight on the surface of the lake far above. Slowly, she stretched her muscles, flexing and twisting to awaken her flesh. The sound continued and she could delay no more. With a burst of energy, she pulled free from the accumulated sediment and headed for the surface. Her serpentine body undulated, propelling her through the water like a giant moray eel. Her legs, sporting razor-sharp claws, tucked against her sides. She felt the pressure change as she neared the surface and swung her long head to and fro, homing in on the tone. It was far stronger now. Her slitted eyes focused on a small object bobbing on the water above. She whipped her tail, surging upward.

Sharlie's snout breached the surface and continued upward into the night air, her head balancing on a long, graceful neck. From this vantage point, fifteen feet above the water, she looked for the object that had called her. The moon shone down, shimmering on the wet surface of her scaly skin. She swam slowly toward the tiny singing sphere as it floated in front of her, gently glowing like a second moon. The tone grew and grew, high in pitch but by no means shrill. No, it was… soothing. Its song became the most important thing in her long, long life. Sharlie wanted to listen to it *forever*, wanted to become *one* with it. A course of action blossomed in her primitive brain: the massive lake monster plunged her head downward, jaws gaping as she neared the meteorite.

She swallowed it.

DID YOU ENJOY *ZOMBIE BIGFOOT?*

If you enjoyed this book please take a moment to visit Amazon and provide a short review; every reader's voice is extremely important for the life of a book or series. And on that note, if you'd like advance notice on the next book's release head on over to

ZOMBIEBIGFOOT.COM

where you can sign up for my email list. If you're like me you hate spam, so rest assured I'll only email every other month or so, or when the new release is imminent. You can also follow me on twitter: @NickTheSullivan.

ACKNOWLEDGMENTS

Writing can be a very solitary experience, but I'm blessed to have many good friends who were good enough to let me bounce ideas off of their patient and tolerant minds.

Angela, Sondra, Kevin, James, Karl, Debbie, Anne, Greg, Bill—my thanks to all for their suggestions and support.

Tom Alan Robbins and John Brady—their suggestions were insightful, and though the rewrites were brutal, those guys were right on the nose.

Thanks to Charl Kroeger for his assistance with Afrikaner lingo and to Todd Thurston and John McElroy for the savvy business advice.

Kristie Dale Sanders did yeoman's work going over my manuscript and lending an ear whenever I needed it. She lent her pen to paper... or 'stylus' to 'pad'... and generated a wonderful cover. And she's a dang good writer, too. Hey, Kristie, let's write something together. Oh, wait...

Chris Sorenson was an early inspiration, and without him I doubt I ever would have started this process. Thank you for your splendid notes on the first draft. I may have to get you a second Bigfoot garden statue to show my appreciation.

Ellen Kushner is a fantastic author of fantasy novels and I've had the distinct pleasure to lend my voice to the audio versions of several of them. She provided valuable advice and encouragement.

Wayne Stinnett, a man with a rich background and a flourishing writing career, was pivotal in many of my publishing decisions. I've been honored to record his audiobooks as well. Go out and buy the *Fallen* series! You'll thank me. And much of his publishing advice is laid out in another book I just recorded for him: *Blue Collar to No Collar*. Wayne, your help was incredibly valuable, and I look forward to recording many more of your books. And thanks for pointing me toward your editor and formatter.

Thanks to my editor, Eliza Dee of Clio Editing Services for whipping the manuscript into shape and to my formatter Colleen Sheehan of Write Dream Repeat Book Design for making it look all purty.

And finally, to my parents: thank you. Dad, you always seemed to have a book in your hand. Sometimes it was Proust or Mahfouz or a book on philosophy; sometimes it was Ursula K. Le Guin, Alan Dean Foster, or Patrick Rothfuss. I know *The Name of the Wind* was one of the last books you read and I wish you'd had a chance to read *The Wise Man's Fear*. I know you would have loved it. And Mom, you made sure I got any book I wanted to read, and when you picked me up from school or drove me to a violin lesson, I remember you would always play Dick Estell's *Radio Reader* on NPR. I think I have you to thank for my love of audiobook narration.

ABOUT THE AUTHOR

Born in East Tennessee, Nick Sullivan has spent most of his adult life as an actor in New York City, working in theater, television, film, and audiobooks. After recording hundreds of books over the last twenty years, he decided to write one of his own. This is his first novel. And, yes, there is an audiobook version. Matt Damon wasn't available, so the author recorded it himself.

Visit Nick at
NICKSULLIVAN.NET/

Made in the USA
Middletown, DE
05 March 2018